In the
Shallows

TANYA BYRNE

In the Shallows

GODWINBOOKS

NEW YORK

Henry Holt and Company, *Publishers since 1866*
Henry Holt® is a registered trademark of Macmillan Publishing Group, LLC
120 Broadway, New York, NY 10271 • fiercereads.com

Our books may be purchased in bulk for promotional, educational, or business use.
Please contact your local bookseller or the Macmillan Corporate and Premium
Sales Department at (800) 221-7945 ext. 5442 or by email at
MacmillanSpecialMarkets@macmillan.com.

Library of Congress Cataloging-in-Publication Data is available.

First American edition, 2024
First published in Great Britain in 2024 by Hodder Children's Books

Printed in the United States of America.

ISBN 978-1-250-86559-5 (hardcover)
10 9 8 7 6 5 4 3 2 1

*To all the teachers, librarians, and booksellers
who are fighting the good fight for stories like this and make sure
they get into the hands of those that need them.*

I want to tell you a story.

It's not one for the history books. No one is going to sing songs about us or write poems about us. In fifty years you won't find a statue of us, standing side by side, hand in hand, mottled with moss, the tips of our fingers and noses chewed. Still, it's a story as old as time. Girl meets girl. Girl loses girl. Girl gets girl back.

I know what you're thinking. You've heard that story before, right?

Well, this one isn't as simple.

But when are these things ever simple?

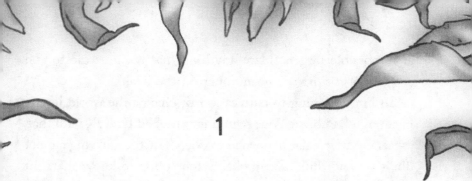

1

Her name is Nico Rudolph and I love her. She loves me as well, and while there have been times when I've questioned that, she does. You should know that now because there will be times that you'll question it as well.

Before I get into all of that, though, I suppose I should tell you who I am. If I'm being honest—and I'm truly trying to be—there isn't much to tell. Until I met Nico, I had a quiet life. My parents are still together, still love each other in that unreachable, uncontainable way that makes me ache sometimes. And, yeah, OK, my quiet life hasn't always been quiet. Being the only desi girl in my class isn't always easy. And the whole *I prefer girls thing* definitely isn't easy, even if saying it out loud finally silenced something in me.

Even so, I've never felt different. Until I met her, I moved through life without leaving a dent, like the stiff red velvet sofa in my grandparents' living room that forgets you as soon as you stand up. I am extraordinary only in my ordinariness. I do well at school, but I'm not destined to go to Oxford or Cambridge, or anything. I can't dance like my mother, or cook like my father, or sing like Nico. I can't draw or paint or speak any other languages apart from a bit of Hindi. And I hate sports. Hate chasing things or kicking things or aiming things at impossible targets. Hate anything that requires me to run or to wear a shirt with a number on the back.

So I'm not going to cure cancer or change the world in any meaningful, Pulitzer Prize–winning way. And I'm OK with that, especially after what happened to Nico. Trust me, having a quiet life is no bad thing. I'm probably too young to know that, but if there's one good thing to come out of all of this, it's that.

I'm lucky. I have a great group of friends who, like my parents, love me with a ferocity—and a constancy—that, now I think about it, kind of ruined me because I thought that's how everyone would love me. I guess that's another thing I'm probably too young to know: not everyone can love you in the way that you need to be loved.

Still, I've had it pretty easy. Other than being charged with fancying every girl I speak to or the odd casually cruel comment in the corridor at school, I've never been bullied. I've never had to walk a different way home or complain about period pain so I didn't have to go to school. Never had to endure more than the usual adolescent tragedies. Fights with friends. Fruitless crushes. Failed exams. Things that felt so much bigger and more impassable until I met Nico and I realized that I didn't have a thing to worry about.

Except I do, of course. We all do. We all have those things only we know. You never know the secret things that people cry themselves to sleep over. The things they'll never tell you. The things that make their easy lives not so easy. The things that distract them. Derail them. Stop them from being bold enough to hope that there's more than this. Even if there's nothing wrong with *this*.

That's who I am, isn't it?

Who I *really* am.

Not just the girl in the photographs of birthdays and holidays that line the walls of my house. Not just the star of my parents' stories, the ones they tell at the end of weddings, after the cake's been cut and they've had too much champagne. Or when a song comes on the radio and they turn to one another and smile, then turn to me and smile a little wider. I'm every mistake I've made. Every scar I've earned. I'm in the songs I listen to on repeat, in the clothes I'm not brave enough to wear and the sentences I underline in books.

That's who I am. Not just the me everyone knows—the me who is chronically early for *everything* and hates kidney beans and overwaters succulents—but I'm all the things I'm too scared to say out loud as well. I'm every hope. Every fear. Every wild thought that makes me weak and woozy with the promise of something else, something beyond me, beyond the borders of photographs and my parents' stories and this tiny corner of the universe that I tread. I'm more than what people think they know. More than this endless, exhausting feeling of something shifting, trying to make space, but there isn't enough room.

Mara Malakar. Only child of Vasudeva and Madira. Born in Brighton and still here. Still in the house on Toronto Terrace my parents brought me back to sixteen years ago. Still in the bedroom overlooking the garden, the one my father painted pink before I was born and has been every conceivable color since then.

Mara Malakar, who is bad with numbers and instructions, but always answers her phone. Who reads too many books and loves words. Even if, until now, they've been contained to the corners of my notebooks that aren't too pretty to use. Other people's words knotted with my own. Lyrics and lines from stories that made me lightheaded with relief that a stranger could know something about me before I did. Scruffy ink-and-paper time capsules of whatever I was feeling, which, I told myself, I didn't need to feel once I'd written it down.

But I want to feel it this time.

Even though this is all still so very tender and every time I put any weight on those tender parts, I'm reluctant to do it again. And I'm even more reluctant to write it down in case I dilute it somehow because I can't find the right words to articulate the misery and magic of it all. But I must because I'm terrified that if I don't, I'll forget. Memory is fickle, isn't it? It can fail you when you need it most. It lies to you, convinces you that something happened when it didn't. It will erase the things that matter, like hearing someone laugh for the first time and knowing it's a prelude to some great joy to come, and replace it with a tiny, thoughtless comment that returns to you months after you said it, unexpected and uninvited, to make you doubt who you are.

That's why I need to write this down now. Before I forget. So forgive me if it isn't perfect. But that's another thing I've learned: things don't need to be perfect. They just need to be true.

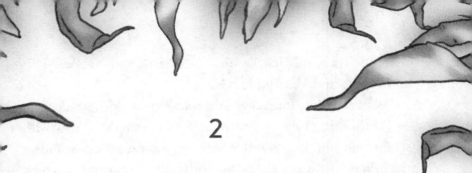

2

I met Nico last June. The day began as every Sunday morning had until then, with me waking up to my friend Michelle snoring gently beside me, swaddled in most of the duvet, and my parents moving around downstairs, laughing and singing along to Joni Mitchell, while my father made pancakes.

It's one of my favorite traditions: waking up on Sunday mornings to Michelle, Joni Mitchell, and pancakes. Given how many we have now, that's saying something. But you just do things, don't you? Then you do them again and again without even realizing it. That's how they become traditions, I suppose. Tiny pebbles of joy that disturb the monotony of running for the bus every morning and homework on Sunday nights. Joni Mitchell and pancakes. My and Michelle's birthday. Diwali at our house. Lunar New Year at Michelle's.

I should say now that Michelle and I are just friends because when you're into girls and you speak about someone the way I do about her, it's often mistaken for something more. For some unbearable, unrequited crush that has left me pining and miserable and settling for being her best friend. Nothing could be further from the truth. Michelle is, in every way other than blood, my sister. Our parents were friends before we were born.

Before Mara and Michelle there was Mads and Nicole. Mads and Nicole and Vas and James.

We were born four days apart and grew up next door to each other, running in and out of each other's houses with scrapes on our knees and whatever treasures we'd found at the beach. Fistfuls of shells. Smooth nuggets of candy-colored sea glass. Spiky mermaid's purses that my father would tell us to check for pearls.

As such, everyone used to refer to us as The Twins, even though we look nothing alike. My parents are Indian and hers are Chinese, so we both have dark hair and eyes, but that's where the resemblance ends. My eyes are a shade or two lighter than hers and Michelle's hair is longer—it's been down to her waist for as long as I can remember—and shampoo-ad smooth, whereas mine is thick and unruly and barely brushes my shoulders.

I don't even notice it most of the time—how different we are—until we take a photo together. Even as kids, it was obvious, but now we're sixteen it's pronounced to the point that the twin thing is almost comical. Everything about Michelle is small. She's small in stature (if not in voice), with a small, sweet face and small, sweet hands and small, sweet fingernails that she paints the sweetest shade of pink. When she smiles—*really* smiles—her eyes disappear and when she laughs—*really* laughs—she snorts. But I'm tall, like my father, and round-hipped and round-faced like my mother. Plus, my skin is much darker than Michelle's. Mine is the same deep brown as my father's, whereas Michelle is nearer to her mother's warm brown that glows in the sunshine.

It's always been me and Michelle. Michelle and me. We're always together, so she was with me that morning. The morning I met Nico. We were walking through Brighton train station and I glanced at the clock to see it was 11:11. 11:11 on June 11th. I told myself to make a wish because that had to mean something, and when we walked out, there Nico was, standing on a bench with her guitar, her chin raised to the sun as she sang.

It was nothing, just a Sunday morning in June.

Then it wasn't nothing.

It was startling.

I hadn't even met her yet and I already knew that I'd never get over her.

Even now, I can remember how my heart ballooned in my chest as I abandoned Michelle mid-anecdote to join the crowd gathered around Nico. And I remember how the sun picked her out like a spotlight, foiling her jaw-length black hair so it almost looked silver as her hips swayed and her fine fingers plucked at the strings of the guitar. I was aware of Michelle next to me, telling me that she kind of looked like Park E Hyun in *Best Mistake*, and I guess she does, but I almost don't want to tell you that because I can't bear the thought of you picturing her as anyone else but her. Just know that she was beautiful. Delicate. All pale skin and inky eyelashes and this air of easy, enviable nonchalance as she sang up at the sky as though none of us were there.

But most of all, I remember holding my breath as I waited for her to open her eyes. When she finally did and they settled on mine, I saw the corners of her mouth twitch—just for a second—and that was it.

I was undone.

With that, something was suddenly, urgently, different. I didn't know what it was, whether it was love or lust or some fleeting, devouring infatuation. I just knew it had changed me so thoroughly that I'd look back on that moment one day—that day being today, apparently—and say, *That was it. That was when everything changed.*

And I was right, wasn't I?

When everything came back into focus and the world began to take shape again—the gulls bobbing and shrieking over our heads, someone's perfume, thick and sweet, the number seven bus spitting out another gaggle of fidgety-looking people eager to get their trains—I expected everything to look different. For the sky to be pink or the air to smell of amusement-park donuts and adventure or for the sun to be low enough to touch. But everything looked exactly the same, even though it didn't feel the same at all.

Six months later and I wouldn't say that Nico and I were together, but we weren't *not* together, either. We were stuck in some maddening purgatory between the two.

We'd kissed, but never held hands. I knew she was fifteen and a Cancer, but I didn't know her birthday. I knew she was an only child, like me, but she never talked about her father so I didn't ask because, I figured, there was a reason she never talked about her father. I knew she lived in Rottingdean, but I didn't know which school she went to. And I'd never met any of her friends, even though she'd met mine. Not *willingly*, in fairness. On the few occasions she'd acquiesced, she was sullen and distracted, which confirmed to my friends that she wasn't right for me and confirmed to me that us hanging out with them wouldn't become a regular occurrence.

So, that Sunday morning I woke up to Michelle, Joni Mitchell, and pancakes, Nico was still as unfathomable—and unreachable—as when I found her singing outside Brighton station.

By then it was New Year's Eve, but instead of feeling a fizz of excitement at the promise of a new year, I did what I'd done every morning since I'd met her.

As soon as I opened my eyes, I checked my phone.

I'd fallen asleep with it in my hand, so it took all of a second to discover that I only had a text from May.

"No word from Nico," Michelle said as she caught me frowning at the screen. She said it with such ease—such certainty—that I refused to give her the satisfaction.

"I'm just reading a text from May."

Then she frowned as she reached for her phone. "There's nothing in the group chat."

"She only texted me."

"Why only you?" The crease between Michelle's eyebrows deepened, and then her eyes widened. "No!"

I shook my head with a theatrical sigh.

"Mara, no! She's not back together with Chesca?"

"They hooked up last night."

"No!" Michelle slapped my arm.

I made a show of rubbing where she'd hit me. "Um. *Ow.*"

"But Chesca is a total fuckgirl!"

"No, she isn't."

"She is!" Michelle shrieked, looking at me like I'd lost it.

"She's not. She just isn't out yet, so she's still processing."

That made Michelle back down.

"Well," she huffed, "that's no excuse to treat May like shit."

That was true.

"If you ghost me," Michelle warned, "you'd better stay dead."

I know I was defending her, but Chesca was *awful* to May. They'd met in the queue for a gig and things were super intense for a few weeks, and then May didn't hear from her again. Not until she met someone else. It was as though Chesca knew because she unblocked her and sent a *Hello, stranger* text.

Then they started things up again and the same thing happened.

Over and over for a year.

Rinse, lather, repeat.

"That explains why she only told you," Michelle said as she scrolled through her phone.

I knew it was a dig about Nico, but I still took the bait. "What's that supposed to mean?"

She ignored me, sitting up and fussing over the duvet so she didn't have to meet my glare.

I shouldn't have, but I pushed it. "Why would she only tell me? Because I'm into girls as well?"

I could tell that Michelle was going to say something else but she thought better of it.

"Because you're a hopeless romantic, Mara. Of course you'd want May to give her another chance."

That stung, but it swiftly solidified into something sharper. Something with purpose.

"Well, I'm sorry that we can't all have the perfect relationship like you and Lewis, Michelle."

As soon as each word snapped off my tongue I regretted it, but at least she looked at me again.

"I don't have the perfect relationship, Mara. I have the relationship I deserve."

It sounded so easy when she said it like that.

"Mara, I'm just saying—"

"What *are* you saying, Michelle?" I interrupted, shooting for sarcastic, but landing on surly.

"I'm *saying* that you'll never get this time back. It sucks that we can't finish high school together, but Stringer doesn't do A-Levels so we have to split up."

"We should have all gone to the same school."

"Mara, we tried, but me, you, and Erin got into BHASVIC, and Louise and May got into Varndean. What can we do?"

I closed my eyes and shook my head. "I know."

"So when we go back on Tuesday, that's it. We only have five months until exams start. This is the last time all of us will be together."

"I know," I said again, more tightly this time because I did know. I was acutely aware that after years of our GCSEs being on our tail, they were suddenly right there, behind us, lights flashing and horn blaring.

It's all we'd talked about.

And all we tried not to talk about.

These are our days, May kept telling us.

I was aware of each one ticking past, but I still didn't feel what I was supposed to be feeling.

"Do you, Mara? Because it'll never be like it is now. We'll keep in touch, but it won't be the same."

"Why are you yelling at me?"

"I'm not yelling," she yelled. She exhaled sharply through her nose, then lowered her voice. "I'm just saying, you'll never get this time back. Don't waste it worrying about her."

I love Michelle, but I wish I was allowed half the patience she expects in return. Wait. I shouldn't have said that. That isn't fair. She was worried about me, wasn't she? So, maybe it wasn't so much *what* she was saying, rather *how* she was saying it. But that's the trouble with being as close as we are.

Michelle would never speak to Erin, Louise, or May the way she spoke to me.

If you didn't know her—or us—you'd be forgiven for dismissing her as having an icy heart. I know better, of course. She's not my sister, but I still hold her in the same regard in that I can say whatever I please about her, but I would fight anyone who says a bad word about her. So, yes, Michelle is frustratingly forthright and immovably logical, but she also listens—really listens—and has the courage and humility to concede when she's wrong. Even if, as she'd say if she were here now, that has never been necessary.

So when Michelle doesn't care about something, she lets it go; but if she doesn't, that's how you know she really cares. And she really cares about me because she wouldn't let it go.

"I mean, you don't even know her, Mara."

That stung as well, but when it passed, it only made me more defiant.

"I do know her, Michelle."

12

It came out sharper than I intended.

Usually I would have softened it with a joke, but I didn't want to soften it.

I wanted her to hear.

To believe me.

But the truth is: Michelle was right.

I didn't know Nico.

Back then I thought I did, but I didn't.

Not really.

Nico had this way of talking that made me stand a little straighter. Smile a little brighter. Try a little harder. She'd talk and talk and talk, but she never said anything. Nothing real, anyway. She talked about the gigs she wanted to go to and the tattoos she wanted to get. She wouldn't let me get a word in, then talk over me if I did, interrupt me, interrupt herself, go in another direction, then back again. But the next day, she'd leave me on read and it was as though she'd said too much, so she wouldn't say anything for weeks.

Then I'd walk out of school to find her waiting for me and I'd be so relieved to see her again, but she'd be brooding and unreachable, the skin under her eyes bruised with some unspoken agony she obviously didn't want to talk about as she sat there, picking at her nail polish.

Her disinterest provoked the opposite response in me, and I'd try to bring her back, telling her story after story. How our parents found out they were pregnant with Michelle and me on the same day. How I was born two days early and Michelle was born two days late, in the car park of Gala Bingo because she couldn't wait. How we got chicken pox at the same time. How I broke my arm jumping off the climbing frame at Queens Park when we were seven because Michelle promised to catch me but didn't. About the shoebox of post-cards and photographs under my bed. All those places we'd been before Michelle's parents had to close their travel agency. India when we were one. Thailand when we were two. Sri Lanka when we were three. Bali when we were four. Morocco when we were five.

It pains me sometimes, how I've seen the world and I don't remember. But I still told Nico the stories as though I did. The blue and white of the Hotel Riad al Madina, where Jimi Hendrix stayed when he was in Essaouira. The blue and yellow of Jardin Majorelle. How the color of the Hawa Mahal changes from pink to red to gold when the sun sets. How the coconuts in Sri Lanka are bright orange.

I sit cross-legged on my bedroom floor sometimes, staring at Michelle and me, standing side by side in matching bathing suits, our little feet touching the earth of some out-of-reach place I'd never know I'd been to if I wasn't holding a photograph.

Nico didn't have any stories, though.

None that she'd told me, anyway.

She only ever spoke about sometime.

Someday.

Always tomorrow.

Tomorrow.

Tomorrow.

Tomorrow.

What she was going to do. What she was going to see. Who she was going to be. How she wanted to go study music at Liverpool Institute for Performing Arts and wanted to see the Northern Lights in Reykjavík and the puffins in St. Kilda. Wanted to sleep under the stars, somewhere wild and open. Wanted to do everything.

All of it.

She spoke of her plans with the same fondness I told my stories, except she was nostalgic for a life she hadn't started living yet.

"I do know her," I told Michelle again.

But she rolled her eyes because despite spending six months lying to her—lying and smiling and making excuses—what little she did know about Nico was enough to convince her that wasn't true at all.

That's the thing with Michelle: she has this horrible habit of only ever seeing things as they actually are.

Whereas I gild them until they become something they never actually were.

It's funny because if you didn't know us, you'd say that me and Michelle were completely incompatible. Me with my onion-skin feelings and her with that knife of a tongue. I'd been thinking about it a lot—long before any of this happened, before Nico—about how everything I'd done and seen and laughed about or mourned over was with Michelle. I don't know if I've ever eaten anything without her trying it first. I don't know if I'm actually scared of spiders, or if I'm only scared of them because she is. Do I even like the music I listen to? Or do I like it because it reminds me of dancing around Michelle's room in sheet masks?

And even when we don't agree, do I really disagree or am

I just being contrary? Did I go one way because she went the other? Did I want to cut my hair, or did I do it because hers is long? When I paint my nails red, is it because she paints hers pink? Or when I read Nora Ephron is it because she loves Taylor Jenkins Reid?

I've always said that our lives overlap, but the truth is, I was beginning to question where Michelle ended and I began. If I'd ever be able to unpick which parts of me are mine, not ours.

When I went back to my phone, pretending to be absorbed by a video of a dog singing along to "I Will Survive," Michelle changed tack. "What would you say to me if Lewis treated me the way Nico treats you?"

I told myself to keep smiling. "I'd say that if he makes you happy—"

She cut me off with a snort because that was bullshit and we both knew it.

But back then, I really thought I was happy.

Or I could be.

It was the *could be* that made all the other stuff worth it.

"I know you've just come out, Mara, but that doesn't mean you have to settle for the first girl you meet."

I finally looked up from my phone. "I'm not settling, Michelle."

"This is Brighton. You can throw a Birkenstock and hit someone else into girls."

I tilted my head at her. "Nice."

"I'm just saying." She shrugged sheepishly.

"Nico isn't Chesca," I told her, but I hated the way my voice sounded all high and shaky.

Michelle ignored that and went back to scrolling, so I said it again.

"She isn't. It's not the same thing."

I remember how hot my cheeks were, how each breath was suddenly sharper. It's funny because I always thought that when I felt that strongly for someone, it would be soft. Delicate. I had no idea it would be so fierce.

So feral.

Like I had no control over it.

"There's no point having this conversation if you're not going to listen, Mara."

"I am listening."

But I wasn't because, looking back on it now, we shouldn't have even needed to have the conversation.

This is what should have happened: I met a girl, and she mucked me around, so I walked away.

But like I said, these things are rarely simple.

All I know is that the first three months were perfect, but then summer was over and by the time we went back to school, something had changed. The space between texts went from minutes to hours to days to nothing at all.

At first, I thought it was me; that I was trying to force it, turn a summer romance into a relationship. But then Nico would demand to see me, and when I arrived, she'd be waiting for me with an aimless, dangerous energy that I didn't know whether to run to or away from. We'd have a dizzying few weeks where we saw each other every day. We'd talk and kiss and make plans I was sure she'd keep this time and I'd go home, my hair warm with sunshine and the smell of grass between my fingers from the daisy chains we'd made and worn like crowns.

But then it would happen again.

If you'd asked me back then why I persisted, I wouldn't have been able to tell you. Looking back on it now, I guess I wasn't holding on to the relationship we had—if you can even call it a relationship—I was holding on to what it *could be*.

The promise of it.

The promise of the next call, the next adventure.

The promise of a promise.

I know now that you can survive on hope alone.

But then, what is love if not the triumph of hope over logic?

Don't get me wrong, I'm not saying that I loved Nico.

Not yet anyway.

It was the *not yet* that kept me going, though.

Kept me trying.

Kept me daydreaming about what it would be like after *not yet*. If it would be like it is in all those books I'd read. Not just bewildering and breathless, but steady. Easy. I wouldn't have to stop myself before I kissed her on the cheek when we greeted one another and I could hold her hand while we walked. We'd swap books and share ice creams and maybe—someday—there would be two toothbrushes in a bathroom somewhere.

"This isn't how it should be, you know? This isn't romantic," Michelle told me.

Just like she did the first time Nico disappeared, then messaged me a week later like nothing happened. I was thrilled—and relieved—to hear from her again, but Michelle didn't berate me. Instead, she told me that I read too many books. I didn't know that was a bad thing, but she said that all those stories had made me think love was hard won. Dramatic. Something to fight for. Something you fail at until you finally succeed. A mystery to be solved with tenacity and intuition. *You think romance is about aching and pining and wandering the moors in search of your lost Heathcliff*, she'd told me when I asked if it was too soon to reply to Nico.

I'd told her it wasn't like that, but thinking about it now, I guess Nico made my quiet life not so quiet. Until I met her, I had no idea how quiet it was. How small. But each time I saw her I felt my world grow a little bigger—a little louder—and I couldn't go back.

I didn't fit there anymore.

So, yeah, I was miserable when she disappeared, but then I'd hear my phone buzz and feel a spark of hope when I reached for it. Nine times out of ten it wouldn't be her, but that tenth time it would be and I'd be so faint with relief it made the waiting worth it because it felt *so good* to know that Nico was still thinking about me.

That I hadn't been forgotten.

Reading that back, it sounds pathetic, but there's nothing worse than being forgotten, is there? I think I'd rather be hated than forgotten because at least hate speaks of the absence—the loss—of affection and betrays *some* emotion, as tender and tired as it may be. But to be forgotten? That implies there's nothing left. Or there was nothing there to begin with.

How terrible to be thought of one moment and not the next.

How cruel to be thinking about someone and know that they never think of you at all.

"Mara, it shouldn't be this hard," Michelle told me, and when my gaze dipped to my phone she snatched it out of my hand. I gasped as she said, "You haven't heard from her for a week. *Again.*"

"It's Christmas," I reminded her. "She's probably been busy with family and stuff."

"Exactly! *It's Christmas* and she couldn't even send you a text?"

"She messaged me on Christmas morning," I lied, then panicked when I remembered that Michelle had my phone in her hand, bracing myself, sure that she'd arch an eyebrow at me and say, *Let's check, shall we?*

And she did arch an eyebrow at me, but she said, "Mara, it shouldn't be this hard."

I felt something in my chest begin to bow then, like a shelf under the weight of too many books, because maybe she was right. Maybe it was time to tuck Nico into the shoebox under my bed with all the postcards and photographs, more out of reach than any of them.

But defeat is a difficult thing to surrender to when you haven't even been given a chance to fight.

"I hear what you're saying, Michelle, but . . ." I started to say, then trailed off when I heard my phone buzz in her hand and she glanced down at it.

"What?" I asked when she groaned and handed it back to me.

I assumed it was another message from May, gushing about how much Chesca had changed.

How it would be different this time.

But it was Nico.

morning sunshine xx
miss you
need to see your face
what you doing today

I tried to be nonchalant, but I'm pretty sure I was swooning with relief.

When I looked up at Michelle again, I probably shouldn't have smirked, but you had to give it to Nico.

Her timing was impeccable.

3

I could hear Nico singing before we got off the bus and I had to stop myself from running down the stairs because it was the song she was singing the morning we'd met. "The Blower's Daughter" by Damien Rice. I didn't know how many times I'd listened to it since then, but I'd spent hours lying on the floor in my room, playing it over and over. So, in a way, I guess it became our song, even if she didn't know it.

Whenever I recall that morning—the morning I met her—all I see is color. The mere thought of it just made me sigh. Even now, I can see it in searing, startling Technicolor. The boisterous blue sky, Nico beneath it with her guitar, its black-and-white checkerboard strap across her chest, her dark hair shining and her mouth a distracting smear of pink as she closed her eyes and sang. I can still remember every tiny detail, a year and a half later. Her chipped neon-green nail polish. Her long black dress sugared with tiny white stars and crescent moons. Her pale skin stretched tight over her collarbones and her face beaming as the sun drenched her in gold.

But on New Year's Eve the scene was very different. It's almost bleached out in comparison. Now when I close my eyes, there's no color. No warmth. The sky was flat and white and Nico was alone, the people going in and out of the station unwilling to linger as the fierce breeze made their scarves flap furiously as they ran for their train or wheeled their suitcases down Queens Road toward the seafront.

The only color was Nico in her baggy red-and-black-striped sweater, the fraying cuffs covering her hands as she played her guitar. She didn't seem to care that no one was listening, her foot tapping steadily on the bench she was standing on as she moved on to something I hadn't heard her sing before.

If you didn't know her, you'd think that she was exactly the same as the morning we met, the shift so slight that I'm probably the only one who would have noticed it. After all, she was still singing sweetly, her hips swaying, but that air of easy, enviable nonchalance was gone, her back straight and her shoulders stiff.

I remember telling myself it was because she was cold, but I knew it was more than that. I could hear the quiver in her voice as she sang, her dark eyes darting around until she found me and her foot stopped tapping. When our gazes met, I found myself—as I so often did—searching for any indication that she was pleased to see me. For the corners of her mouth to twitch or her brow to relax or her cheeks to pinken slightly. But there was nothing. She tipped her chin up at me and when she continued scanning the people milling around outside the station, I knew that was all I was going to get.

There would be no smile.

No wink.

No *This one's for Mara*.

I wonder if it wouldn't have stung as much if Michelle wasn't standing next to me.

I suddenly wished she hadn't come, but Nico and I had been texting all morning and she was in such a good mood that when Michelle said that she was going with me into town because she needed to get something from the drugstore, I didn't object. If anything, I *wanted* her to come. I wanted her to see Nico singing, see her loose and flushed and happy. See the Nico *I* knew. The Nico who grabbed my arm when she laughed and peppered my cheeks with kisses when I got excited about a book I was reading and wanted me to go with her to see the Northern Lights and the puffins and sleep with her under the stars, somewhere wild and open.

When Nico was done, I hesitated as I watched her jump down from the bench and slip the strap of her guitar over her head. Something told me to go, but Michelle was already walking toward her, so I followed.

We reached the bench as Nico was putting her guitar in its case; the back of my neck burned as I asked myself what Michelle made of it all. She was lucky. Lewis always called when he said he would. He was always waiting where he said he would be, always delighted to see her. He'd do this thing, where he'd run up behind her in the corridor at school and pick her up, making her shriek.

It was easy.

The opposite of whatever Nico and I were.

Michelle didn't fall asleep with her phone in her hand. Didn't have to try and predict the precise midpoint between *Too Soon* and *Just Right* when responding to his messages. She didn't have to worry that if she miscalculated, either her eagerness would put him off or she'd leave it too long so they congealed into something that wouldn't survive. Nor did she have to worry that if she said the wrong thing at the wrong time or didn't say the right thing at the right time, he would cut her out of his life without even thinking about it.

I wouldn't wish that on anyone.

I'm ashamed to have committed that to paper. But even if I crossed it out, it'd still be there, beneath the thicket of black ink, and you'd wonder what I didn't want you to know when I promised to be honest, didn't I?

So as uncomfortable—and as unseemly—as it is to have to write that down, the truth is: that's how Nico used to make me feel sometimes. Like she was humoring me until I crossed one of the lines she kept drawing between us without me knowing. She could ask me question after question about my parents—how they met and when I came out to them and how they felt about me leaving home to go to uni—but if I asked about her mother, she'd go quiet, then make an excuse to leave. She could pull me to her in the middle of the street and kiss me, but if I kissed her on the cheek when we greeted one another, she'd tense and step back. She could ask me what I was doing at the weekend, but if I did the same, she'd shrug and say, "I don't know yet."

Then I wouldn't hear from her for a week.

She'd draw line after line after line, and when I got too close to one, she'd draw another.

And judging by her reaction to seeing me at the station, she'd clearly drawn another one.

"Hey," Michelle said tightly as she slipped her hands into the pockets of her coat.

25

"Hey," Nico said back. She cast a bored glance in our direction as she tugged on her coat, then wrapped her black-and-white smiley face scarf around her neck.

"Hey," I added, and I don't know why. I guess I hoped her response to me would be a little warmer. That she'd do what Lewis would do with Michelle: grin, then kiss me and tell me that she'd missed me.

But she just nodded once and said, "Hey."

I waited for her to say something, tell me she'd missed me, like she had earlier, or ask how my Christmas was. But she didn't look at me as she fussed over her scarf and I don't know why she was being like that.

She *knew* I was coming.

She'd *asked* me to come.

Is it because Michelle is with me?

I had no idea, just that there was a beat of silence as the three of us looked at each other. If anyone had been watching, they would have just assumed that Michelle and I were a couple of randoms complimenting Nico on her singing, not that a week ago Nico and I had kissed until I had to stop and catch my breath.

I didn't dare look at Michelle because I was *mortified*. I could feel the anger burning off her as she stood stiffly beside me. And it wasn't even Nico's shameless indifference, it was that it was Michelle. Given my compulsive need to be liked by everyone, I guess I should have envied how Nico didn't feel the need to endear herself to my best friend, but as I watched Nico use the camera on her phone to fuss over her bangs and apply another layer of hot-pink lipstick, I honestly don't know

26

how she didn't recognize how much it would mean to me if she'd make an effort with Michelle.

"I loved that last song," I said brightly, and it reminded me of the tone my mother used when I was a kid and she was encouraging me to take a spoonful of cough medicine. "The one about the short movie. Did you write it?"

As soon as I said it, I cursed myself because that wasn't how it was supposed to go.

I didn't want Michelle to see her like that.

See *us* like that.

Nico cool and monosyllabic and me slightly manic, trying to win her over with stuttering sincerity.

"I wish." Nico snorted. "It's Laura Marling."

Who are you? I almost said.

When we first met, Nico used to talk about music with an adoration so urgent, it would make me wish that she was talking about me. So, me asking about a song would usually prompt a twenty-minute monologue about which albums I had to listen to, in which order, that would have left Nico pink-cheeked and breathless as she demanded I give her my phone so she could make me a playlist.

But *this* Nico?

I didn't even know who she was.

Knowing what I know now, I wish I'd pushed her to tell me what was wrong because I *knew* something wasn't right. It happened slowly at first, then all at once. When we met, everything was great. Everything she said made me laugh. Made me restless. She'd show up to meet me with a bright, dangerous smile full of plans and promises and places she wanted to go. But by the time summer simmered and we'd gone back to school, Nico's smooth swagger had given way to something more manic.

The only way I can think of describing it was that she had the skittish, twitchy energy of someone in witness protection. She was always looking around. Always checking her phone. Always moving. Never still. But whenever I asked her if she was OK, she would just shrug and say she was fine.

So I let it go.

I don't know why.

I guess I was too scared to find out that there was no reason.

No excuse.

It was just Nico.

When she let out a weary sigh, I don't know if the brooding-artist routine was for Michelle's benefit or mine and I wasn't taking the hint, but I almost applauded her. It was quite a performance, even for Nico. Her standing there with her smudged eyeliner and bitten-down black nails. Every bit the Alternative Brighton Teenager—capital A, capital B, capital T—who was too cool to care what my best friend thought of her. She was good, I'll give her that. If her guitar case was still open on the pavement, I would have tossed a one-pound coin in there.

But I saw through it.

Saw through her.

And, yeah, maybe I didn't know her. Not really. And maybe I was trying to turn us into something we were never going to be, but I'd felt her hands shake when she reached for me the last time we were together and I'd heard her say my name in that tender, treasured way only she did.

That was real.

If nothing else was, then that was real, at least.

"OK, then," Michelle said sharply. "We're going to go."

She hooked her arm through mine, and when she began to tug me away, I panicked as I realized that I didn't know when—or if—I was going to see Nico again. So I blurted out, "What are you doing tonight?"

Even thinking about it now makes me want to cringe my skin clean off my bones because I have no earthly idea why I asked her that. After all, Nico had given me no indication whatsoever that she was even pleased to see me, let alone that she wanted to spend New Year's Eve with me.

"I don't know yet." She sniffed, looking around as she reached for her guitar case. "I'll message you, yeah?"

Then she was gone.

4

I know Michelle was *raging*, but she obviously decided to forgo
another *Fuck her. You deserve so much better, Mara* speech and
went straight to: "OK. New plan. We're going to Louise's party
tonight."

"No way," I told her, tucking my hair back behind my ears
as the breeze kicked up again.

"Why not?"

"First of all, it's not a party, is it? It's a '*hang.*' Whatever
that is."

When I emphasized the word with my fingers, she shrugged.
"It's what we do *every* weekend, Mara. Argue over who's in
charge of the music and what takeaway we should get and
which film we should watch. Except tonight we're going to
stop at midnight to sing 'Auld Lang Syne' and drink the bottle
of champagne Erin's sister won at the pub quiz that she can't
drink because she's pregnant."

"Yeah, but it's going to be all couples, Michelle."

"No, it's not," she insisted as she tugged on her gloves.

"Yes, it is. It's you and Lewis, Erin and Dean, and Louise
and Arun. That's all couples, Michelle."

Which was fine when I thought I could persuade Nico to
come.

"May's single," Michelle reminded me.

"May's not coming, is she? *Because it's all couples.*"

"What's May doing tonight, then?"

"She's going to a Brighton College party with Chesca."

Michelle pulled a face. "Christ. I'd rather pull out my toenails with a rusty pair of pliers."

That was one way of putting it.

Still, I'd take a Brighton College party over spending New Year's Eve alone, waiting to hear from Nico.

As I thought it, Michelle said, "Well, you're not spending New Year's Eve alone, waiting to hear from Nico." She clapped her hands. "OK. New plan. Face masks and *When Harry Met Sally.*"

"Michelle, we've watched *When Harry Met Sally* with our parents *every* New Year's Eve for as long as I can remember."

"So?"

"We're *fifteen.* Aren't we supposed to sneak into a club and get off our tits on MDMA, or something?"

"You want to sneak into a club and get off your tits on MDMA?"

"Of course not! Flu medicine makes me loopy, Michelle. Can you imagine me on MDMA?"

She nodded solemnly. "You'd die, for sure."

"I'm just saying. I wanted to do something different tonight. I wanted confetti and balloons."

And for Nico to show up at midnight and give me a big romantic speech in the middle of the dance floor.

Michelle hooked her arm through mine and pulled me to her. "Next year, I promise."

"Promise?"

Michelle stopped walking and held up her little finger. "Promise."

I shook it with mine.

It was then that I realized we were standing outside my parents' café. In my haste to put as much distance between myself and Nico, I hadn't resisted when Michelle tugged me away. But I thought we were just walking—somewhere, anywhere, just *away*—until we were out of sight so I could let my shoulders fall and my heart sag. To be honest, all I wanted to do was go home. To be in the warm embrace of my room with my books and my pillow and my black-and-white poster of the phases of the moon. Where I'd be shielded by the close, safe walls that Michelle and I had painted purple that summer after watching too many episodes of *Friends*.

But it was Michelle, so she knew that, and in an effort to stop me spending the rest of the day lying on the floor listening to "The Blower's Daughter" on repeat, she'd taken me to the one place I was always, truly happy.

My mother was outside, clearing a table. When she looked up and saw us standing there, she grinned and put the tray down, then marched over, hugging us both at once. The smell of her—home and that pomegranate shampoo she uses that always triggers a smoky memory of some far-off place I can't remember—was enough to bring tears to my eyes as I burrowed my face into her neck and held on to her with both arms.

"You OK, baby girl?" she asked, stroking my hair when I finally let go.

"I'm just tired," I lied, but I saw the look that passed between her and Michelle as my mother slung her arms around our shoulders and guided us inside.

Mercifully, I barely had a moment to register the burn of it as my father cheered when he saw us.

"Hey! Hey! Hey!" He beamed from behind the counter, then slung a tea towel over his shoulder and gestured at the stove behind him. "I was hoping you guys would come in. I made Beyoncé bhatura."

"What's Beyoncé bhatura?" the customer standing next to us at the counter asked.

Michelle thumbed at me. "When we were twelve, we tried to run away to London to see Beyoncé, but we only made it as far as the end of the road before Vas lured me back with his chana bhatura."

"Well"—they nodded—"if it's good enough to forsake Beyoncé for, I'll have that."

"See?" I gestured at them as they went back to their table to join their friend. "You did forsake Beyoncé."

Michelle looked utterly unrepentant. "You need to get over it, Mara."

"Never," I told her as we looked for a table.

"Hey, Mara," I heard someone say, and stopped to find Mrs. Preston beaming up at me.

"Hey, Mrs. Preston." I smiled sweetly. "How are you?"

"Marvelous. Look at this." She pointed her knife proudly at the egg naan on the table in front of her. "A double yolk. Your father says it's good luck. That has to bode well for the new year, doesn't it?"

"Not for the poor chicks that are shred *alive* so you can have your lucky double yolk," Max piped up from two tables away, causing everyone in the café to stop eating and look down at their plates.

"Ignore him," my mother said, striding over to stand next to me. She smiled down at poor Mrs. Preston, who looked about ready to faint. "We get our eggs from a local, small-scale organic farmer."

My father pointed a wooden spoon at us from behind the counter. "They're organic *and* biodynamic."

"We've visited the farm, Mrs. Preston," my mother assured her. "Trust me, the chickens live better than we do. This egg was laid yesterday by a brash little Lohmann Brown called Babs."

"She has her own TikTok," I told Mrs. Preston with a nod.

She looked genuinely impressed. "I must tell my granddaughter."

"There are no tables." Michelle huffed as she glared around the café while everyone refused to make eye contact with her. "There should be a VIP section for family."

"It's OK," my mother told her, tipping her chin up at Max. "You're leaving, aren't you?"

He looked horrified. "You kicking me out, Mads?"

"Of course not. But you've been sitting there for *two hours* and all you've ordered is a peppermint tea."

"I was about to order another one."

"Great!" She smiled tightly. "That'll keep the lights on."

Someone at a table in the corner stood up. "We were just leaving, actually."

"Thank you!" Michelle clapped happily and rushed over to claim it.

Before I joined her, I glanced at Max to find he was still put out about being asked to give up his table; I wandered over as he took a bag of tobacco from the pocket of his duffle coat and began rolling a cigarette.

"I watched that video on the Greenpeace website."

"And?" he asked with an eager smile, his gray eyebrows rising.

I drew a cross over my chest with my index finger. "I'll never drink bottled water again."

He nodded, his smile a little wider. "The earth thanks you, Mara Malakar."

5

After we'd devoured my father's chana bhatura, Michelle went behind the counter to return our plates and grab a notebook and pen. She returned with such purpose that I was immediately suspicious because when she's *that* excited about something, it rarely ends well for me. (That's how I signed up for the Brighton half marathon the year before. Mercifully, I sprained my ankle training for it, so Erin did it with her instead.)

"Right!" she said, slamming the notebook down. "It's New Year's Eve. You know what that means."

I groaned. "Not our intentions."

The only thing I intended to do was eat three of my father's chai donuts, then go home for a nap.

"Come on!" Michelle clapped her hands and shimmied in her chair. "It'll be good for you."

I was almost certain it wouldn't, but it was another of our traditions: spending New Year's Eve thinking about what we wanted for the upcoming year. They weren't really resolutions, partly because our parents didn't believe in giving things up, but mostly because none of us had a good track record of honoring them.

So, we preferred to refer to them as intentions instead.

Be more present.

Make more time for myself.

Let go of what I can't control.

The sort of thing that would make my grandmother roll her eyes and mutter something in Hindi.

As such, because they didn't involve anything intolerable like giving up chocolate or promising to go to the gym, that was the first year I'd resisted. Usually, doing them made me excited about what the new year held, but I already knew what—or should I say *who*—my intentions would involve, so I was understandably reluctant.

"Let's do them later," I said, waving my hand as I reached for my can of Cherry Coke.

"No, let's do them now!" Michelle clapped her hands more forcefully this time. "It'll be fun!"

I'd rather eat glass, I thought as she opened the notebook and found a fresh page.

"I've done mine," my mother told us when she wandered over to clear the table next to ours. Then she winked lasciviously. "One of them involves Keanu Reeves, but don't tell your father."

Michelle winked back, then wrote something I'm sure she wouldn't want me to share about Manny Jacinto. I doubt she'd want me to share her other intentions, either, but I can tell you what I came up with:

1. *Let Nico go. Michelle's right, it shouldn't be this hard.*

2. *Don't stress about your GCSEs. You're not going to get all 9s and that's OK. Fran Lebowitz got Fs and was expelled from two schools for reading during lessons.*

3. *Don't reach for your phone as soon as you wake up.*

4. *When you get out of the shower, get dressed. Don't sit on the edge of your bed, wrapped in a towel, contemplating the futility of your existence for half an hour. You'll be late for school and you'll have to run for the bus and you hate running.*

5. *No running.*

6. *Return your library books on time, otherwise you may as well buy them.*

7. *Take your makeup off properly. <u>Every night</u>.*

8. *Actually go with Mum and Dad to the Brighton Soup Run, instead of promising to, then telling them that you can't because you have too much homework, which you know you're not going to do because you'll be immediately distracted by a book that you shouldn't even be reading.*

9. *Use your notebooks instead of putting them on your bookshelf because they're too pretty.*

10. *It's OK to say no to something if you don't want to do it, but not if you're scared.*

Michelle made me write the thing about her being right, of course.

In fact, she wrote my first intention before handing me the pen.

Watching her write it down was sobering. Even now, I remember how dizzy with panic I was at the thought of having to follow through with it. I already knew that I'd cross it out as soon as I was alone, the collar of my sweater suddenly too tight as I closed the notebook and reached for my phone to check whether Nico had been in touch to apologize for what had just happened.

"Right." Michelle tapped the table with her hand. "You gonna stay and help Vas and Mads close up?"

I nodded, but my eyes were on the notebook again, suddenly convinced that by writing it down, the cracks that had begun to appear in my resolve, the ones that appeared each time Nico left me on read or did what she'd just done at the station, the ones I'd papered over with excuse after excuse—lie after lie, each of which I had to conjure myself because Nico felt no need to offer me one—were about to split open and I wouldn't be able to stop the doubt getting in. And I couldn't let the doubt get in because then the cracks would become crevices and the crevices would become a gulf that would be impassable.

"Hey." Michelle tapped the table again. "You listening?"

"Huh?" I grunted as I made myself look at her, not the notebook.

"I said, I'm gonna run to the pharmacy before it shuts and get the face masks." Michelle jumped up and grabbed her coat from the back of her chair. "Then I'm gonna grab snacks for later."

I won't lie, the mere mention of snacks was enough to recapture my attention.

"Oh, can you get me some—"

"Honey roasted cashew nuts?" She pulled a face. "What am I, Mara? An amateur?"

Then it was just me and the notebook.

If I was quick, Michelle wouldn't notice if I ripped out the page with my intentions and tore it up. Then, at midnight, I could go out into the garden and release the pieces. Let them drift away with the dandelion fluff and cigarette ash and all the other things that disappear into the air and float on forever.

But as soon as I reached for the notebook, the door to the café swung open and I froze, sure that Michelle was going to charge over to the table and snatch it from me.

It wasn't Michelle, though. It was Nico in her black-and-white smiley scarf, her guitar case in her hand, and I held my breath as I waited for her to stop in the doorway and scan the tables for me.

This is it, I remember thinking. *This is it.*

It wasn't quite a dance floor. There was no confetti. No balloons. No Harry Connick Jr. singing "It Had to Be You." No countdown from ten. But there she was. She'd found me and she was going to make her big romantic speech and I was going to tell her that I hated her, even though I didn't, because it had to be her.

But she walked over to the counter.

"Hey! Hey! Hey!" my father sang when he saw her.

"Hey, Vas!"

She grinned—actually *grinned*—in a way I'd never seen. Loose and slightly lopsided, exposing the gap between her front teeth, which I know she hated and was the reason I'd never seen her grin. With that, I suddenly saw her as a child—small and sweet-faced with an air of curiosity she'd learned to repress—and she looked so happy that I caught myself wishing I'd known her then. That we'd grown up, as Michelle and I had, running in and out of each other's houses with scrapes on our knees and pockets full of shells and sea glass.

Before whatever happened to make her ashamed of the gap between her front teeth.

"Nico!" my mother said, emerging from the pantry. "I saved you a mango and chili Danish."

"Mads, you're the best! I haven't eaten a thing today."

Not even Nando's? I remember thinking.

But just as I thought it, my father said, "What, no Nando's?"

It's difficult to put into words how it felt hearing Nico laugh as my mother told her off for not eating and she got into a clearly well-practiced argument with my parents as she tried to pay but they wouldn't let her.

As I watched them, I realized that she must have come to the café without me, which would explain why my parents rarely asked about her during those periods when I didn't hear from her. I thought I'd just done a good job of hiding how sad I was, but they probably weren't concerned because they saw her more than I did.

What if she isn't even looking for me? I asked myself as Nico tried again—and failed again—to give my mother a five-pound note. *What if she's just here for a coffee and a Danish?*

I tensed when my father nodded to where I was sitting and said, "I'll bring them over."

When Nico turned around, my spine felt as tight as a piano string as I waited for her face to fall. But to my surprise—and delight—her eyes lit up. She looked so genuinely thrilled to see me that I almost didn't recognize it, her face soft and her cheeks pink as she walked toward me.

"Oh good. You're here."

She leaned down to kiss me quickly on the mouth and I was so startled that I just sat there as she put her guitar case down, then unwound her smiley face scarf and shrugged off her coat.

When she sat in the chair opposite mine, I wondered if the seat was still warm from Michelle. If it was, she didn't mention it as she reached across the table for my hands and took them in her own.

It was the first time we'd held hands and I couldn't help but notice how perfectly they fit together. I wonder if she felt mine trembling as she brought them to her mouth and pressed a kiss to my knuckles. Not just at the shock of her mouth against my skin, but because I had to savor it. Having just felt the chill of Nico's indifference, I feared that this display of affection might disappear as swiftly as it appeared.

"Sorry about earlier." She kissed my hand again, then held it to her warm cheek. "Shitty day."

It was all I could do not to throw my head back and scream. *Where was this Nico two hours ago?*

Why couldn't she have been like this when I was with Michelle?

When I didn't respond, Nico pressed another kiss to my knuckles. "I'm sorry. I was an asshole."

"What happened?" I asked as she rested our clasped hands on the table between us, my skin warming—along with the rest of me—as her thumbs grazed back and forth over my knuckles.

As soon as I said it, I cursed myself. It was always better with Nico to let her volunteer these things rather than ask her outright. So my spine retightened as I expected her to let go of my hands and sit back.

But to my surprise she said quietly, "I had a massive row with my mum."

"You did," I was careful to say this time.

A prompt, not a question.

Prompts were OK.

Questions were not.

I'm still not sure what the difference is, just that one pissed her off more than the other.

Nico made a show of rolling her eyes. "She read my journal."

"She read your journal?"

If we weren't holding hands, mine would have shot to my mouth, and I don't know whether it was Nico's unexpected—and frankly unprecedented—honesty or the revelation itself, but I was *stunned*.

"I caught her in the living room this morning. Can you believe it, Mara? She was sitting on the armchair with a cup of tea and everything. Like it was the morning paper, or something."

"No way!"

"It's such a violation."

She started to say something, but stopped as my mother approached our table. We looked up at her with matching smiles, thanking her as she put Nico's coffee and Danish down, then gave her shoulder a swift squeeze.

Nico watched my mother go with a sore sigh, and by the time she turned back, the moment was gone.

"I love how appalled you are, Mara." She let go of my hands and sat back. "I mean, Mads would never."

"*Never*," I agreed.

And she wouldn't.

She wouldn't even ask to read my intentions because, she says, that's between me and the universe.

"You're lucky." Nico sniffed as she glanced back over her shoulder at my parents, who were now cackling about something as my mother flicked my father with a tea towel, and it felt faintly like being scolded.

Like Nico was telling me that I didn't appreciate it.

For the record—which I suppose this is—I assure you that I *do* know how lucky I am.

Believe me, I've spent enough time with my grandparents to be grateful that I skipped a generation.

And I know how lucky I am to have Michelle, Louise, Erin, and May. The family I've made for myself. Because what I had in them were friends to weather the slings and arrows of adolescent misfortune with. Friends who knew every possible version of me but didn't remind me that I wanted to marry Timothée Chalamet when I was thirteen and I used to think that Ed Sheeran was a genius. Who knew every tragic haircut and hopeless crush and consoled me through each. Who knew who I was and who I wanted to be and cheered me on as I tried to navigate the gulf between the two.

I hope, one day, they look back and can say the same about me.

I hope I give as much as I take.

"My mother's a psycho," Nico hissed as she reached for her latte. "She went fucking mental about LIPA. She doesn't understand why I want to go all the way to Liverpool when I could go to BIMM."

"Fontaines D.C. went to BIMM," I said, and I don't even know why.

Actually, that isn't true. I hadn't told anyone yet—not even Michelle—but all this talk of GCSEs and not wasting our last five months at school together had made me think of university and how, in a couple of years, we wouldn't just be at different colleges, we'd be scattered across the country. So, I'd been considering applying to the University of Sussex because I couldn't bear the thought of leaving home. I knew Michelle and the others wouldn't understand, but, I reasoned, if everything was changing, then that would be the same at least.

So maybe I did know why I was suddenly Team BIMM.

It was in Brighton.

"BIMM in *Dublin*," she sneered. "Besides, Paul McCartney helped set up LIPA. You know? The Beatle."

The Beatles? Never heard of them, I almost said, my cheeks burning as she raised her voice.

Nico began picking at her black nail polish so my gaze fell to the notebook, which was still on the table between us, and all I could think about was Michelle's neat sloping script hidden inside.

Let Nico go.

But then she leaned forward and grabbed my hands so suddenly, she almost knocked her mug over. I watched it wobble, the coffee inside swirling before it corrected itself and grew still again.

"Mara, I need to see you tonight," she said with an urgency that made my cheeks burn for a different reason. "I have to have dinner with Mum, but she never makes it to midnight." When she squeezed my hands, I could feel that aimless, dangerous energy that always made me nervous as she waited for me to meet her gaze. "I'll sneak out when she falls asleep. I can meet you at Queens Park. On our bench."

Our bench.

I referred to it as *our bench* all the time, but until then, I had no idea that Nico did as well.

It was the bench we'd claimed on our first date. If Michelle was here, she'd say that's a perfect example of how I gild things until they become something they never actually were because it wasn't strictly a date.

It was just a coffee.

Not that it was ever *just* anything with Nico.

When she'd suggested going for a coffee, my first thought was the café, but she was the first girl I'd met since I'd come out, so I was terrified my parents would try too hard in an effort to show me how OK they were. Or worse, that Max would corner Nico with one of his increasingly hysterical conspiracy theories.

So, we'd met at the café by Jubilee Library, and while we were waiting for our coffees, we concluded that it was too warm to sit inside. After all, it was one of those perfect June afternoons that would be foolish to waste. The ones that always make me feel like I should be doing something else. Something better.

Or maybe it was nothing to do with the sun.

Maybe that's how it felt when I was with her.

Whatever it was, we got our coffees to go and went for a walk. That would become our thing, I'd soon learn, those long, purposeless walks that felt anything but. Like that afternoon—on our first not-date—we just walked. I don't think either of us knew—or cared—where we were going, too busy talking as we walked down one road, then when that ended, we'd turn and walk down another. Streets I didn't recognize or even notice until Nico stopped to point out a house with a hot-pink front door or a cat watching us from a window.

It was a glorious day, summer suddenly in full voice even though we had to endure another month of school before we could truly enjoy it. But it was a Sunday and all we had was time, so I'd assumed we'd end up at the pier. Everyone ends up at the pier on days like that because it's the only time you can appreciate it in all its roaring neon glory. The creak of the rides. The roll and splash of coins as the 2p machines light up and spit out tongues of tickets. And the smell. The smell of the pier will always be summer to me. Not strawberries, but that inescapable, maddening mix of sea salt and hot oil. Warm donuts and fish and chips and long golden churros.

But we'd gone the other way, to Queens Park. I'm sure it was just a coincidence but given that Queens Park was pretty much on my doorstep, I remember telling myself that it had to mean something. As we approached it, I told Nico that the park had become my and Michelle's other garden over the years. We knew the smell of the earth and the best tree trunks to store treasure like acorns and silver coins made from chewing gum wrappers. We knew how many steps there were to the top of the slide and had named all the birds in the pond. (Geese and moorhens, Michelle learned when we were six. Not ducks, as we had been referring to them until then.)

It was the stage for so many of our adventures, I told Nico as I showed her our primary school and the climbing frame I fell from when I was seven and broke my arm. The source of grass stains and torn T-shirts and the backdrop to more birthday parties than I will ever remember. And as we drifted toward the pond and found a bench, unaware that it would become *our bench*, she told me that the last time she'd been at Queens Park was to see the light installation Luke Jerram had done for the Brighton Fringe. It was this massive moon suspended over the pond and I remember how my voice shook when I told her that I'd seen it as well. It was just after my and Michelle's birthday, so we went every night it was there because we thought he'd done it for us.

"Do you think maybe we were here at the same time?" Nico had asked, her voice shaking this time.

And it felt like the start of something.

Six months later, her voice shook again as she asked me to meet her at our bench.

"Please, Mara." She brought my hands up again and held them to her cheek before pressing another kiss to my knuckles. "You're the last person I want to see this year and the first person I want to see next year."

I knew what Michelle would say, but Nico's mouth against my skin was like a forest fire, burning everything away until it was just her and me on the scorched earth and I couldn't remember why I had to let her go.

6

When I told Michelle, she was uncharacteristically calm. She didn't raise her eyebrows or roll her eyes. Nor did she lecture me or reprimand me for buckling so easily—and completely—under the weight of Nico's desire to see me. She didn't even tell me that I was *that girl* for breaking one of the ten friend commandments.

Thou shalt not blow off your friends at the last minute to see someone else.

Even though that's exactly what I'd done.

On New Year's Eve, no less.

No, Michelle just flicked her hair and said, "Oh good. Now I can wear my new dress to Louise's."

Then she texted Lewis to tell him that they were back on and that was it.

I felt awful, of course—awful and more than a little embarrassed—because no one wants to be *that girl*, do they? I prided myself on not being *that girl*. I always answered the phone when my friends called and knew the right thing to say when they did because—despite never needing relationship advice before Nico—thanks to all those books I'd read, I'd become adept at giving rousing, empowering speeches to remind them of their worth.

When it was my turn, however, I realized that I was better at dispensing advice than receiving it. All of those lines I'd borrowed from books and recycled again and again, immediately forgotten when I needed them.

Or maybe not forgotten, rather dismissed because they didn't apply to Nico and me, did they?

Because we were different, weren't we?

But the truth is: aside from a series of clumsy, fruitless crushes, Nico was my first . . . well, *anything*. So my loyalties had never been truly tested before then, and when they were, I'm ashamed to say, I failed.

I failed miserably.

Still, Michelle didn't seem to care. She was excited to have a reason to wear her new dress and do the eyeliner look she'd been trying to perfect for the last few weeks as she fluttered around her room, calling on me to deliberate on everything from shoes to nail polish.

My other friends, however, weren't as understanding.

"What do you mean you're not staying until midnight?" Erin asked when I told her about meeting Nico. She turned to frown at Louise, who was standing beside her looking equally bewildered.

"Why even bother coming?" Louise snapped, sharp as a slap, a note of betrayal in her voice.

Erin arched an eyebrow. "Because it's easier to sneak out of here to meet Nico than from her own house."

Then Michelle was at my side. "Leave her alone," she said in a way that made my chest warm. "I know we want to spend New Year's Eve together, but we've *all* done it, haven't we?

Louise, you missed Lunar New Year because Arun got you tickets to see YUNGBLUD. And Erin"—Michelle matched her arched eyebrow, raising it even higher—"you missed May's summer barbecue last year because it was Alfie's birthday, remember?"

Erin shushed her at the mention of Alfie's name, her dark eyes darting to the other side of the living room where Dean was with Lewis and Arun, his head stooped as he scrolled through his phone, trying to find a playlist.

"We agreed—" Michelle stopped and waited while Louise rolled her eyes, then started again. "We agreed that birthdays are sacrosanct, but everything else is negotiable, right?"

"Right," they huffed in unison.

"OK." Michelle nodded. "So we're going to let it go now and leave Mara alone, aren't we?"

They huffed again and said, "Fine."

There was a beat of silence as Erin and Louise's gaze met for long enough to make it clear that it wasn't fine, before Erin exhaled sharply through her nose, then turned to me with a quick smile.

"So, what's the plan, Mara? Where are you guys going? Anywhere nice?" she asked, and I don't know if she was genuinely curious or just doing it for Michelle's benefit to prove that she was letting it go.

"Nico's going to sneak out when her mum falls asleep and meet me at Queens Park."

"What if her mum doesn't fall asleep?"

The thought hadn't occurred to me, so I dread to think what my face was doing at that moment, but I'm almost certain that my reaction did nothing to reassure her that Nico and I had a plan B.

"Michelle," Louise hissed, then marched toward the door. "Come help me in the kitchen."

Then I was left with Erin in the living room. I hadn't seen her since she got back from Lagos, so we should have had loads to talk about, but there I was, crossing, then uncrossing my arms because I suddenly didn't know what to do with them, while she fussed over her braids. There was nothing unusual about that—Erin always plays with her hair, which makes sense given that she was forced to keep it short for so long, so now she doesn't have to have a boy cut she can wear it down to her waist—but that night she wasn't twirling and swishing it proudly, like she usually does. There was something almost agitated about it as she told Dean to pick a playlist.

Any playlist.

He did, and when a SZA track started playing, it was enough to fill the awkward silence, at least, as I continued to fidget and Erin continued to fuss over her braids. My instinct was to do what I always do in awkward social situations: find Michelle. But I realized that Louise had summoned her to the kitchen to talk about me and Nico, and I didn't know which was worse; being forced to endure another furious sermon about how awful Nico was or being stuck with an uneasy, twitchy Erin and the elephant suddenly in the middle of the room.

The one in the *MARA RUINED NEW YEAR'S* T-shirt.

At least I'd shown up.

May was with Chesca.

Who they *hated* as well, by the way.

I wanted to remind them, but I'd never throw May under the bus like that. So I took it on the chin as I crossed my arms again and stewed over why it was such a big deal. It wasn't even eight o'clock. I was spending the majority of the evening with them and only ducking out before midnight to meet Nico. And yeah. OK. Fine. I concede, midnight is a pretty integral part of New Year's Eve—if not *the* most integral part—but I was alone and they weren't, so they'd be too busy kissing to notice if I was there or not.

Whereas I *definitely* would have noticed if I was alone and surrounded by kissing couples.

But that was fine, apparently.

I was *always* third-wheeling it with them, but now I wasn't single, *I* was being selfish?

Plus, May wasn't there, so it wasn't like I was the only one bailing.

Now I think about it, I guess it wasn't that I was bailing, it was *when* I was bailing.

On the verge of a new year.

A year that should have held all the possibility of a fresh notebook but already felt too short.

By the summer, we'd have done our GCSEs and would be getting ready to go to different colleges and Michelle was right, we'd keep in touch, but it wouldn't be the same. It was already proving increasingly impossible for us all to be in the same room at the same time, so I guess me bailing that night was another reminder of what was to come.

I didn't make that connection back then, though. I just thought it was woefully unfair that it was OK for them to ring in the new year with their boyfriends, but I wasn't allowed to do the same with Nico. So, yeah. I admit it. I was pissed off. I was pissed off that they were pissed off. I was pissed off that none of it would have happened if Nico could be relied upon to show up and not be disinterested and detached for the half an hour she was there before she made an excuse to leave. And, most of all, I was pissed off that I was stuck there until I heard from her because unless I wanted to sit on a bench for four hours, what else could I do?

Louise didn't have a dog I could talk to, so I had no choice but to retreat upstairs and lock myself in the bathroom for a while, forced to read the label on a bottle of shampoo that promised bouncy, defined curls as I cursed myself for listening to Michelle when she told me that I couldn't bring a book to the party.

This is why I bring books to parties.

I doubted anyone had noticed I'd gone, but I couldn't stay in the bathroom all night. So, I said a little prayer that the awkwardness had passed and they'd forgiven me, but when I got to the bottom of the stairs, they were talking in the kitchen.

"Calm down. Mara will hear you," I heard Michelle say as I inched toward the open door.

I'd hoped enough time had passed for Louise to get whatever she wanted to say about Nico out of her system and move on to divvying up the bottle of whiskey Lewis had "borrowed" from his parents' sideboard.

She obviously hadn't.

"Calm down?" I heard her say as I peered into the kitchen to find her, Michelle and Erin huddled around the island.

Louise slammed down two shot glasses in front of them. "So you're just fine with this?"

Michelle had her back to me, but I saw her shrug. "Of course not, but what can I do?"

That made Louise gasp, her blue eyes suddenly *wild* and her pale face bright pink. "You can at least admit that it's shitty that Mara is using us to kill time while she waits to hear from Nico."

Wow.

I'll never forget the heat that rushed down my face until I was doused in it, my whole body burning with shame, from my scalp to my toes. I had to take a step back from the doorway because Louise was right.

It was a shitty thing to do.

I held my breath as I waited for Michelle to agree, but to my surprise, she said, "Go easy on her."

"How are you being so calm about this?" Erin asked. "Nico is *the worst*."

Michelle did agree this time. "I know, but what can I do? Mara isn't listening."

"Make her listen, then." Louise turned to take another two shot glasses out of the kitchen cabinet.

"What do you think I've been doing for the last six months?"

"Nico's going to break her heart"—Louise slammed them down as well, then waved her arms, blonde curls *everywhere* as she snatched the bottle of whiskey off the island—"and we're just standing around letting it happen."

"I can't bear it," Erin told her. "You need to do something, Michelle. *Please*. She'll listen to you."

"I've tried."

Louise pointed the bottle of whiskey at her, then began decanting it into the shot glasses. "Try harder."

"She won't listen," Michelle insisted. "All we can do is wait for Nico to get bored and move on."

Louise looked at Erin and pulled a face. "You said that *five months* ago, but she hasn't."

Michelle was adamant, though. "She will."

"What if she doesn't?" Erin sounded so desperate, my heart hiccupped.

Louise pointed the bottle of whiskey at her this time. "Then we have to focus on Mara. Get her out."

Michelle shook her head. "We're *way* past that point. It's too late to reason with her. She's *in*. Like, *this Kool-Aid is delicious* in. Nico has her *fucked up*. She's down the rabbit hole and *nothing* is going to get her out."

I'm glad I couldn't see Michelle's face, because hearing the defeat in her voice was unbearable enough.

Not just because what she'd said hurt to hear.

But because I could tell that it hurt her to say it.

Despite all the books I've read, I still can't find the words to describe how it felt to hear my friends so worried—so scared—that I was going to get my heart broken. I wasn't surprised, though. How could I be? They'd tried, but after Nico became so—how do I put this?—*unreliable*, they'd stopped asking how she was. Stopped asking what we were doing at the weekend or inviting her to things because they knew she wouldn't show up.

So no, I wasn't surprised, but it was equal parts sobering

and humiliating to hear them talking about her—about *us*—with such unfettered, unfiltered honesty. But they didn't know I was listening, so they didn't have to be gentle. To sugarcoat it. So I just had to stand there and take it in one focused, unapologetic punch.

That's what I get for eavesdropping.

Reading that back, it's just occurred to me that I didn't have to stand there and listen, did I?

I don't know why I didn't barge into the kitchen and do what I always did.

Defend Nico.

Defend us.

But as excruciating as it was to hear, I knew they weren't gossiping.

They weren't mocking me or being messy and relishing in the drama of it all.

They weren't even being unreasonable.

They were frightened.

I could see the concern on Erin's brow as she said it again. "Nico's going to break her heart."

"I know that," Michelle said through her teeth. "We *all* know that."

You don't, I thought and I remember burning at the injustice of it.

Michelle was right about everything, but she was wrong about that.

But what was the point of telling her?

If I wasn't listening to her, then she wasn't listening to me, either.

"But Mara doesn't know that," Michelle continued, "so we have to let her find out for herself. You know what she's like. She's so stubborn. Remember when she cut her hair because everyone called us The Twins?"

Louise and Erin groaned at that.

"I know Mara." Michelle jabbed the island with her finger. "She's defended Nico too many times to admit defeat now. She's going to persist, even if she's miserable. So we can't push her or she'll just dig her heels in."

Louise threw her hands up. "So what do we do?"

"We just have to let it play out."

"Play out?" The crease between Erin's eyebrows deepened. "What if this goes on for another six months?"

"It won't," she said, and I knew she meant it because Michelle never said anything she didn't mean. "Trust me. This thing with Nico is about to go horribly, *horribly* wrong. All we can do is be there to pick up the pieces."

My legs almost gave way at that.

At how sure Michelle was.

But I barely had a moment to register the shock when the doorbell rang and I jumped. Then I fell against the wall as Louise barged out of the kitchen to see who it was.

"You OK?" she asked as I knocked her Communion photo sideways with my shoulder.

But she didn't wait for me to answer as she continued down the hallway and opened the front door to May, who swept in, all pink hair and cheers.

"I can't stay," she said, hugging Louise. "I'm just swinging by on my way to meet Chesca."

Luckily for May, her misdemeanor was forgiven far quicker than mine because she'd brought pizza.

That's the thing with my friends.

There's very little they won't forgive when food is involved.

By nine o'clock, May had left to meet Chesca and I could see the looks being batted back and forth between Michelle, Louise, and Erin every time I glanced at my phone. Thankfully, they were distracted when we started arguing over what film to watch. After a heated debate, Arun thought he'd won thanks to his impassioned plea for *The Godfather*.

Sadly, it was nearly three hours long, so we'd miss the countdown.

And with that, the whole ordeal started again.

It's only nine thirty, I reminded myself every time I checked my phone.

It's only nine thirty, I wanted to remind Michelle every time she saw me checking my phone.

Finally, Lewis suggested *John Wick*. I can't remember which one, but I was so desperate for a distraction, I didn't care. And it worked, because as the credits were rolling, my phone *finally* buzzed in my hand.

on the 27
just passed the white horse hotel
see you at our bench in half an hour xx

It was all I could do not to leave as soon as I read Nico's message. Especially when she Snapped me a minute later with a photo of her grinning as she held the moon between her forefinger and thumb through the window of the bus with the words *she's watching over us xx*. But I told myself to be patient, my legs shaking as I ran upstairs and locked myself in Louise's bathroom again. Then every bit of me was shaking as I freshened my lipstick and sprayed enough perfume to prompt a sneezing fit so violent I had to reapply my eyeliner.

By the time I got downstairs, the lights in the living room were on again and Erin had obviously taken control of the music because an Ariana Grande song was playing while Michelle cleared away the pizza boxes.

"I'm heading out," I told them from the doorway. They didn't look up, my farewell greeted with a series of waves and muttered *See ya, Mara*s and *Happy New Year*s as Louise asked what time it was.

"11:11," I told her with a slow smile. "Make a wish."

Now that I'm trying to recall it, I don't remember a thing about the walk to Queens Park.

I'm tempted to gild it, like always.

Tell you everything I should have felt because I was fifteen and about to see the only person I wanted to see on New Year's Eve. Tell you how bright the moon was, the clouds blurring its edges like an unfinished poem. How cold it was, the air sharp but heavy with all those things done and not done—and said and not said—as somewhere an hourglass was about to turn over as the year made way for the next. How I could hear my shoes crunching on the frosted pavement and music playing in the houses that lined Queens Park. How I could smell the earth as I approached—that familiar, faithful smell I knew so well—but it smelled brand new.

But the truth is, I don't remember a thing.

Just trying not to run, then giving in to it when I heard a firework pop in the distance, even though it was barely eleven fifteen.

The only thing I remember is getting to our bench to find that Nico wasn't there and the doubt that kicked at the backs of my knees, before I checked my phone to see that I still had thirteen minutes.

Unlucky for some, I thought as I looked out at the still black pond and waited.

Thirteen minutes.

Then thirty.

Then forty-three.

Then it wasn't dark anymore as everything lit up. Bright bouquets of fireworks—one after another—blooming white and yellow and pink in the black sky as cars beeped and friends cheered and I sat there alone.

I didn't cry.

I remember that much.

I didn't cry.

I just waited and checked my phone.

Waited and checked my phone.

Waited and checked my phone.

Finally, I heard footsteps.

Then the fireworks were inside me.

But it was Michelle.

*　　*　　*

I remember how my heart throbbed and I'm still not sure if it was shame or relief as I watched her glossy black waves, which I'd burned my finger helping her do, fluttered and her heels tap-tap-tapped on the paving stones.

Here's something I never thought I'd admit: I wish I'd seen Michelle before she saw me.

I wish I'd had time to run and hide. Let her think that Nico and I were together, somewhere out of reach.

Because Michelle knew, didn't she?

She knew that Nico wasn't going to show up.

That's why she came.

She'd let it play out and she was right.

Michelle didn't say that, though. She just sat next to me on the bench and slung her arm around my shoulders. She tried to pull me to her, but I wouldn't let her, defiant to the last. Or I was until I turned my cheek to avoid her gaze and saw Lewis walking away. That's what finally broke me. I'd been sitting alone on a park bench for over an hour and he wouldn't even let Michelle walk the few minutes to Queens Park by herself.

"Let's go home," she said, holding me tighter.

But I couldn't move as I stared out at the pond.

"I can't." I forced myself to hold my chin up. "What if I miss her?"

When Michelle didn't say anything, I shook my head.

I remember having to swat a tear away as I did, so maybe I did cry. "I don't get it. Nico texted me to say that she was on the bus and she'd see me in half an hour. Then she Snapped me."

I showed Michelle the message and the photo of Nico and the moon.

She nodded, but she still didn't say anything.

"So I'm gonna keep waiting because what if her bus broke down?" I told her with a sniff. "I checked. Walking from Rottingdean to Queens Park takes an hour and eighteen minutes, so she could be here any minute."

Michelle nodded again, but this time she said, "I'll wait with you."

"No," I said a little too loudly.

So loudly that a bird flew from the tree behind us, making us both jump.

"It's OK," I told her as I waited for my nerves to settle. "I'm OK. Just go back to the party."

"I'd rather stay here. Erin and Dean are fighting."

That was enough to make me finally look at her. "What about?"

"I have no idea but she just threw his phone out the kitchen window."

I pulled a face. "Yikes."

"Exactly. At least it's quiet here. Hey"—she nodded at the pond—"where are the birds?"

I hadn't thought about it. "Gone to bed, I guess."

"Remember when I took Daphne home?"

Only Michelle could make me chuckle at a moment like that.

"Your mum's face when you walked into the kitchen cradling that duck!"

"Moorhen," she corrected. "And Daphne was my fave."

"She wasn't your dad's fave when she screeched and nipped at him all the way back to Queens Park."

"Because she wanted to stay with me."

I chuckled again and it felt nice, all soft and warm in my chest as I checked my phone again.

"I think something happened," I finally said out loud. "She was on the bus."

I didn't say, *It's not like the other times*, but I was suddenly aware of it hanging between us.

Still, I braced myself for Michelle to remind me of each time Nico had done this.

Erin's sixteenth.

Louise's Halloween party.

The Jingle Bell Ball.

But Michelle just said, "Maybe."

That was worse.

I think I would have rather endured the laundry list of Nico's no-shows than Michelle humoring me.

"Wait. So, Nico Snapped you when she was on the bus?" she asked.

"Yeah?" I nodded warily, unsure what she was getting at.

"Have you checked to see where she is?"

I cursed myself as I opened Snapchat.

In the panic, I'd completely forgotten that you could do that.

I opened the map and my heart unclenched.

There she was.

"What's she doing at the marina?" I showed Michelle the map. "She should have got off the twenty-seven at the New Steine and walked. The marina's a mile and a half in the *opposite* direction."

Michelle is always so sure of herself, but in that moment she wasn't, and the panic was dizzying because, for once, she didn't have an answer.

Her brow tightened. "Maybe her bus did break down."

I remember feeling a pang of hope then—loud, bright, useless hope—because maybe it did.

Maybe it broke down at the marina and they weren't letting anyone off.

Or maybe a drunk person had tried to get on but didn't have any money to pay. That had happened to Michelle and me once. They refused to get off, so the driver killed the engine and we sat there for fifteen minutes until someone gave in and paid the fare. My mother says that people used to do it all the time when she was my age; get on the bus with a twenty-pound note knowing the driver wouldn't have change, hoping they'd let you on.

My heart slowed as I considered it, but if that had happened, why hadn't Nico called?

As soon as I thought it, my phone buzzed in my hand and I almost dropped it when I saw Nico's name flash up. I was so relieved that the screen went blurry, so it was a second or two before I could read the message.

Sorry, Mara. Bumped into friends. This has been fun, but it's getting too much. Not looking for anything serious so I don't want to lead you on. New year, new start, and all that.—N

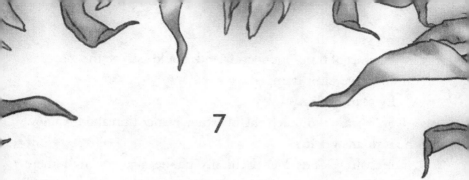

7

There's something about New Year's Day, isn't there? A finality. It feels like a door closing as much as one opening. Suddenly, the Christmas tree and decorations feel inappropriate, like a vase of flowers that are beginning to wilt, and you start thinking about having to go back to school and opening your backpack again to discover the homework you've forgotten among the black bananas and the Christmas cards you'd forgotten to give out.

But I'd never been more aware of it than on that New Year's Day.

It started the same way the last one had.

With Michelle, Joni Mitchell, and pancakes.

Michelle, Joni Mitchell, and pancakes and no word from Nico.

"You OK?" she murmured.

She'd fallen asleep with her makeup on, so one of her lashes was stuck to her cheek.

"Great," I told her with a sore sigh as I reached down to peel it off. "Never better."

"Sorry." She yawned and sat up beside me. "Silly question."

But it wasn't a silly question.

It was a perfectly reasonable, perfectly considerate question.

The sort of thing your best friend should ask you the morning after you've been dumped.

By text, no less.

So it wasn't so much the question, rather that I didn't know how to answer it.

I wasn't OK as I checked my phone again to find there was still no word from Nico. No *I'm sorry, ignore what I said, I was drunk* text. No new posts on her Instagram, her bleary-eyed and beaming with a group of people I didn't recognize. No videos of her twirling and singing along to "Break My Soul."

I don't know what I'd done. I'd been asking myself that all night, Nico's words—*it's getting too much*—turning, over and over, in an endless, maddening loop until at 4 a.m. I'd wanted to shake Michelle awake.

I didn't, though, because I knew what she'd say.

She'd tell me that it was Nico.

That I hadn't done anything wrong.

But I must have.

Even though I was so careful. I was always *so careful*, para-lyzed by the constant, cloying terror that I was going to say something to make Nico decide she'd had enough. So I tried to be uncomplicated—uncomplicated, undemanding, unthreat-ened by it all—as though Nico was a stray cat I was trying not to spook.

But I was still *too much*.

I didn't know how and I was weak with it. Exhausted after lying awake all night, Michelle snoring gently beside me, blissfully unaware of the agony I was in. But she wouldn't have understood because yes, I was miserable, but it was a pain that was unique only to Nico and me.

So, now I think about it, maybe Michelle was right about that as well. Maybe I did think romance was about aching and pining and wandering the moors in search of my lost Heathcliff because there was something almost pleasurable about it.

It felt honest.

Real.

Something that had changed me at some deep molecular level and I'd never get over it.

"Listen," Michelle said, then stopped to smooth her hair with her hands, the waves from the night before now flattened after a sound night's sleep. "I know this is rough, Mara, but it's for the best."

I tried not to sneer as I recalled the conversation I'd overheard in Louise's kitchen the night before and I realized how relieved Michelle must have been that she'd let it play out and she'd been proved right.

"You can't keep doing this, Mara," she told me when I looked away.

"Do what?" I asked, but I didn't want to know what.

I couldn't bear it.

It was over.

I didn't need an autopsy.

"Everything is always on *her* terms." When Michelle stopped to take a breath, I could tell that she was trying to stay calm and it made my hands fist in the duvet. "*Everything*. When you see her or hear from her and when you don't see her or hear from her. Where you go when you do. What you talk about—"

"You don't know what we talk about," I interrupted.

"True," Michelle conceded. "But it's about balance, Mara. Compromise."

That prompted a snort. "Yeah, because you're so good at that, Michelle."

"Um. Excuse you. Didn't I just go and see Brighton play Grimsby with Lewis before Christmas?"

She said Grimsby like it wasn't a real place.

"Don't you want to be someone that you can be yourself with, Mara?"

"I am myself when I'm with Nico."

"No, you're who she wants you to be. Quiet and chill and too unbothered to call her on her shit."

"What shit?"

Michelle looked at me as if to say, *Are we really doing this again?*

"You shrink yourself down when you're with her, Mara. I've seen it. It's like you're worried that you're too loud, that you take up too much space. So you make yourself smaller so she won't notice you're there."

I bristled at that. "I do not."

I did.

After everything that's happened I know now that I did.

Back then, though, I sat a little straighter and told myself that she was wrong.

"*Anyway*," I said before she could say anything else, "who cares? I'm happy."

This time Michelle looked at me as if to say, *Are you?*

"I am," I insisted, but even I could hear the quiver of hesitation in my voice.

"Mara, you're miserable," she told me when I began tapping aimlessly on my phone.

"Today I am. Of course I am. Look what happened last night?"

I could see from the corner of my eye that she was shaking her head at me. "You're not happy, Mara," she said with a delicacy I did not think her capable of, especially when it came to Nico. "I know you, and you're not happy. Maybe when you're with her, but then she ghosts you again."

I felt my jaw click at that. "She doesn't ghost me."

Chesca ghosted May.

Nico just got distracted by her music and school and whatever. It wasn't the same.

"Mara, listen." Michelle waited for me to look at her. "I know how hard it's been for you, watching us all pair off while you weren't sure that's what you wanted. Then you realized why," she said, her eyes suddenly wet, "and you were *so happy*. Happier than I've ever seen you. And I'm worried that in all the *chaos*, you haven't stopped to ask yourself if you even like her because Nico is the first girl to show a passing interest in you."

I blinked at her, slightly stunned. "Of course I like her."

"Mara, she's *insufferable*."

I was fully stunned by that. "She is not!"

"She is! She's a pretentious, self-absorbed fantasist who cares more about picking up whatever obscure album she's pre-ordered from Resident or daydreaming about going to LIPA than getting to know you."

"Michelle!" I gasped.

"Well," she said with a huff as she flicked her hair.

She didn't say *I can say it now she's dumped you* but I still heard it.

She must have known she'd gone too far, though, because she thought about it, then huffed again. "OK. That was way harsh, Tai." She didn't look at me as she crossed her arms. And she definitely didn't apologize. But she did say, "I should give you more credit, Mara. There must be something more to her if you like her this much."

If she didn't apologize, then I certainly didn't thank her because I knew what was coming.

Sure enough, she raised her eyebrows and said, "But—"

I cut her off with a groan.

"Mara, listen."

When Michelle uncrossed her arms and turned to face me, I tipped my head back against the headboard and groaned again because I couldn't keep having this conversation.

I couldn't keep defending myself.

Defending us.

But Michelle persisted. "Listen. I only know one Nico, the one I've met a handful times who, well . . ."

She didn't finish the thought.

But then she didn't need to, did she?

"Listen"—she stopped to hold her hands up—"I don't know what she's like when you're alone. Maybe she's a completely different person. Maybe she's sweet and kind and attentive, but there's obviously something going on with her, isn't there? There's a reason why she comes and goes and blows you off, but if she won't tell you what it is, you can't help her, can you?"

I caught myself nodding.

"So all you can do is give her some time to sort her head out." Michelle shrugged, then flashed me a sad smile. "Mara, you tried. You really, *really* did, but if she wants to go, then you have to let her."

She squeezed my arm and I lifted my head from the headboard.

"It's a shame, but this isn't what you want. I know it isn't, Mara. *You* know it isn't."

I wasn't ready to admit that, so I just rolled my eyes at her.

"It's impossible to take you seriously when you only have one fake eyelash on," I told her as I reached over to tug it off. "Besides, it's not that deep, Michelle."

But it was.

I could feel the ache of it in my bones.

In my marrow.

"It's not like I'm going to marry Nico, am I? We're just hanging out."

Michelle pulled a face at that. "You're not ready for *just hanging out*, Mara."

"What's that supposed to mean?"

"Save *just hanging out* for uni. Now you need a nice, reliable girl—"

"Boring, you mean?" I interrupted with a surly snigger.

She didn't miss a beat, though. "Well, if boring is someone you can text whenever you want and actually shows up when you arrange to meet her"—she tilted her head at me and raised her eyebrows—"then, yeah, *boring*."

We stared at each other for a second too long and I could hear my mother laughing downstairs.

Then Michelle laughed as well.

"You know what you need?" She tugged on the sleeve of my hoodie with a satisfied smile. "A Dean."

"Erin's Dean?"

"No! Dean from *Gilmore Girls*. Nico's a Jess. Your first girlfriend can't be a Jess, Mara." She shook her head solemnly. "You're not ready. You need to work your way up to a Jess. We need to find you a Dean first."

But I didn't want a Dean.

Or a Jess.

I wanted Nico.

And, yeah. OK. I know that despite everything I've said so far, you probably still agree with Michelle, but hear me out: I *know* Nico. You don't. Michelle didn't. And I knew something wasn't right.

Nico didn't mean it.

The thought bumped, grazing the insides of my skull once, then twice, before taking flight.

Nico didn't mean it.

I was suddenly sure of it.

It *was* my fault.

I'd tried so hard to be uncomplicated—uncomplicated, undemanding, unthreatened by it all—that Nico thought I didn't care. Nico always carried herself like someone who'd been hurt and was waiting to be hurt again, so maybe she knew that I was growing weary of her behavior and jumped before she was pushed.

"Listen," I said, suddenly short of breath as Michelle began scrolling through her phone, clearly content that she'd solved the Nico problem. "I've been thinking about her text."

She didn't look away from her phone, the screen like a spotlight, picking out her face in the dim stillness of my room. Her full bottom lip and high cheekbones. The crease between her dark eyebrows. Her long, shampoo-ad hair, as smooth and black as penguin feathers, that somehow looked better for being slept on.

"Don't do this, Mara," she warned.

But I did.

"Nico always ends texts with two kisses."

I pulled them up, scrolling through them to show her.

And Michelle had to clock that when Nico replied, she only used a few words. *on my way xx* or *you up xx*. That sort of thing. So the message she'd sent the night before was pretty much a novel in comparison. And she always used lowercase. Lowercase with no punctuation because she was too cool for punctuation. Michelle peered at the screen, then returned to her own. "She dumped you. Why would she send kisses?"

I stared at her open-mouthed and she was immediately contrite.

"Sorry." She winced. "But still . . ."

"She didn't *dump* me, Michelle!"

That got her to look up from her phone and around the room as if checking that someone else heard that.

Then she glared at me as I responded to Nico's message. "Mara, what are you doing?"

"She said that she doesn't want anything serious, so I'm telling her that I don't, either."

Michelle was too stunned to speak for a second or two. Then she gasped. "You *texted* her!"

But before I could defend myself, she snatched the phone out of my hand and pointed it at me.

"You can have this back when you can be trusted."

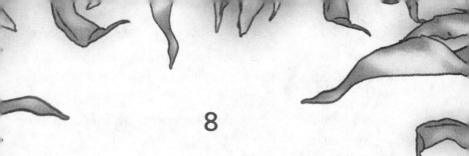

8

Michelle gave our phones to her father, telling him that we were going to have an offline day, which he was thrilled about. He promised to keep them safe and not give them back, no matter how much we begged.

I protested, of course.

"What about Lewis?" I asked as Michelle counted her pancakes to make sure she had the same as me.

"He's at his dad's in Shoreham today, so I'm not seeing him anyway."

"OK." I pivoted. "Well, what about the others? They'll call the police if they don't hear from us."

"I've already told them."

I panicked then, lowering my voice as our parents bustled around the kitchen, laughing about whatever they'd got up to the night before. "You didn't tell them about Nico, did you?"

"Of course not." Michelle reached for a can of whipped cream, then pointed it at me before spraying a generous cloud on top of her stack of pancakes. "But that doesn't mean you can pretend it didn't happen."

I felt that like a punch, my cheeks hot as our parents sat with us at the table.

"Don't worry," my mother said, stroking my back. "Your friends will survive without you for one day."

"Will they?"

Louise couldn't even decide what to wear without consulting the group chat.

"It'll do you girls some good," Nicole told us with a warm smile as she popped a raspberry into her mouth.

I wasn't convinced, but I gave in. Mostly because I had no choice, but mainly because, as excruciating as it was, it was kind of a relief to not have to keep checking my phone. Plus, it allowed me to nurse the growing pearl of hope that when James gave mine back, I'd have a string of messages from Nico.

If it would do me some good, then it would do Nico some good to sweat for a bit.

The thing I love most about Brighton is that whatever time of day or night it is, there's this constant vibration.

This constant feeling that something is about to happen.

I could really feel it that morning, suddenly desperate to do something.

Anything.

Without the weight of my phone in my hand, I felt lighter. Free.

So, I decided to embrace it as I remembered another of our traditions: our New Year's Day walk.

Michelle and I hadn't joined our parents for years, but we used to love it because it gave us a chance to wear the bobble hats and scarves we were given for Christmas, and we'd always get churros from the pier.

Once we entered the apathy of adolescence, though, we preferred to stay on the sofa in our pajamas, fighting over the remaining chocolate and watching *Pretty Little Liars*. But when Nicole said that if she was going to make dumplings for dinner, she needed to clear her head, I told her to wait for me.

Michelle wasn't amused that I was neglecting our new tradition in favor of our old one, but when I reminded her that she could wear her new coat, that was enough to get her off the sofa and into the shower.

We weren't out long, though, before I felt a shift. The clouds began to thicken as we approached the beach and, just like that, a heavy haze settled over everything, so it was like peering through a dirty net curtain. It blurred the pier, a great gray cloud swallowing it so it looked like some sort of magic trick, the end seeming to disappear in a puff of smoke. The air felt heavier, damp with the threat of something that licked at my cheeks. So, I hooked my arm through Michelle's and held on as my father glanced up at the sky and suggested we turn back.

As soon as we were away from the glow of the pier, the light dimmed again. Lampposts creaked and shop signs swung as the wind gathered pace, ushering me on like a hand on the small of my back.

It was dark by the time we got home, and we were followed into Michelle's house by a rumble of thunder and a hiss of wind that slammed the door shut behind us. We ran upstairs and stood at her parents' bedroom window like we always do when there's a storm because they have the best view over

Hanover. The six of us, side by side, still in our coats, as the heavens opened, the rain so hard I was sure the window was going to break.

Then there it was—the first slice of lightning that made the whole room light up—followed by another growl of thunder so loud I felt it in my teeth. Usually, my father cheers and Michelle claps each time a thread of silver splits through the sky, but no one said a word. We just stood there, the rain battering the roofs and knocking over tricycles as our neighbors closed their windows and stood on their doorsteps, calling out for their cats.

The room lit up again—the brightest, whitest white—and when another roll of thunder passed, the rain fell harder. It was like nails spilling on the roofs of the cars parked along our road, the sound of it making the muscles in my shoulders clench. And, under it all, somewhere, streets away, I heard sirens. Sirens and car alarms and someone shrieking with laughter as I imagined them running and holding their coat over their head.

The next bark of thunder was so deep, it made my mother jump and curl her hand around her throat.

"It feels like the end of the world," she said, stepping back from the window.

Then the rest of us stepped back as well, unbuttoning our coats as Nicole offered to put the kettle on while James urged us to reconsider *The Day After Tomorrow* as our first film of the year.

Michelle suggested *Something's Gotta Give* because, as she reminded me with a nudge, we loved it when my mother went off about how unrealistic it was that Diane Keaton would leave Keanu Reeves for Jack Nicholson.

"Impossible," my mother said, muttering to herself as we headed downstairs.

After *Something's Gotta Give* and my mother's well-worn, *deeply* passionate rant about how Julian Mercer was the perfect man, which even made my father nod in agreement, James gave us back our phones.

Michelle shrieked with delight as we sat on the sofa, our legs tangled beneath her mother's favorite red-and-white Christmas blanket, which was about to be retired for another year. When James gave me mine, my heart leaped up into my throat and got stuck there when I saw a string of notifications. But then it plunged back down with such force it made my head spin as I scrolled through to find a flurry of messages from the group chat.

But nothing from Nico.

I checked again, but as I felt the pearl of hope I'd been nursing all day sharpen into something else, Michelle threw her head back and cackled, then showed me her screen and said, "Look what Lewis sent me!"

It was a video of him looking horribly hungover as he pushed his little sister on the swings. Michelle cackled again and she looked so happy—so hopelessly, gleefully *happy*—that I suddenly felt hot all over as I hid my phone under the blanket and went back to my book, the words blurring as I pretended to be engrossed.

"So, what's the first book of the year, Mara?" Nicole asked as she picked at a bowl of cashew nuts.

I closed it to show her the cover.

She nodded and smiled sweetly at me. "*The Year of Magical Thinking*."

"I love Joan Didion," my mother said as she walked into the living room with a bottle of wine.

"That sounds perfect for the new year," Nicole told me with another nod.

Michelle snorted at that. "It's about death."

"Cheery," my father chuckled as he squeezed a wedge of lime into his gin and tonic.

"It's not about death," I insisted. "It is, but it's not. It's quite life affirming, actually."

"Babe, you're fifteen," Michelle reminded me. "You haven't started living yet. What's to affirm?"

"Ignore her, baby girl." Nicole blew me a kiss across the living room. "You enjoy your book."

"Michelle, it's ten o'clock," James said then. "New Year rule, remember?"

"I know. No phone an hour before bed or for an hour after I wake up."

"Ten more minutes," he said with a wink that made her scowl soften.

"I might do that Ottolenghi puy lentil and eggplant stew for dinner tomorrow," my father mused as I went back to my book. "We all liked that, right? It was the black pepper tofu thing the girls hated, wasn't it?"

As I was about to confirm that we did indeed hate it, Michelle kicked me under the blanket.

"What?" I hissed, looking up from my book.

She leaned in and lowered her voice. "Erin dumped Dean."

Given that we'd been phone-free for all of twelve hours, it was remarkable how much we'd missed.

Erin dumped Dean, which wasn't surprising given the phone-out-the-kitchen-window thing.

Louise sprained her ankle dancing to Doja Cat and ended up in accident and emergency.

Where she met May, who was waiting for Chesca while she got her stomach pumped.

Then it was all over the local news that they'd pulled a girl out of the sea that morning.

I shouldn't say this, but I was grateful because it meant Michelle was too distracted to ask about Nico.

"It's in *The Argus*." She stopped to yawn, then read, "Fishermen rescue girl from the sea—"

I pulled a face at that. "Who goes fishing on New Year's Day?"

"I assume you're looking for an answer other than *fishermen*."

"Go on," I conceded with a sigh.

"Shoreham Coastguard teams were called following reports a fishing boat had rescued a teenager from the sea near Black Rock Station just before eight thirty this morning. Sussex Police also attended, as well as the South East Coast Ambulance Service and Brighton and Hove seafront teams. A Maritime and Coastguard Agency spokesman confirmed that she was safely recovered and transferred to an ambulance."

"So, she's OK?"

"No idea. That's all it says."

She turned her phone so I could see the screen. Sure enough, there were a few paragraphs and an ad for a recruitment website, but no picture of the girl, just a stock photo of the pier.

"I doubt she'll be getting drunk again any time soon," Michelle muttered as she resumed typing.

I rolled my eyes because it happens all the time.

People go for a swim—or out on a kayak—then, before they realize it, they're pulled out too far and can't find their way back. Or someone will be mucking around on the pier and decide to jump off to make their mates laugh, but never reemerge.

Still, something nudged at me.

"Yeah, but how do you fall in the sea at Black Rock, Michelle? There's nowhere to fall *from*."

"She was rescued *near* Black Rock. That doesn't mean that's where she fell in."

"I guess she could have fallen off the pier and the tide dragged her that way."

"Or off the sea wall by the marina. That's near Black Rock."

"Yeah, but why would she have been on the sea wall?"

"You're assuming she fell."

I turned to blink at her. "You think she was pushed?"

"No, the other thing."

It took me a second, and when I realized what she was saying, I frowned.

Michelle just shrugged. "Life isn't for everyone, is it, Mara?"

"Shall we see if it's on the news?" James said, reaching for the remote and turning on the television.

"Oh my God!" Michelle shrieked when a shot of Brighton beach appeared on the screen. "Turn it up!"

"We can go to Robert Shelley, who is live for us now outside the Royal Sussex County Hospital," the newsreader said somberly.

Michelle pointed at the screen. "That's where we were born!"

"No, that's where *I* was born," I reminded her. "You were born in the Gala Bingo car park."

She shushed me as it cut to the newscaster in a dark suit and red tie.

My mother's always had a bit of a crush on him, so she shushed me as well.

"Yes, that's right, Amanda," Robert Shelley said with a nod. "Just after ten this morning, Sussex Police confirmed via their Twitter account that a teenage girl was rescued from the sea near Black Rock Station in Brighton and brought here"—he turned to gesture at A&E behind him—"to the Royal Sussex County Hospital, where I can confirm she remains. They have since issued the following appeal for more information."

They then cut to a flurry of flashing lights and a woman with a warm, round face in full police regalia, standing behind a podium. She smiled tightly and introduced herself as Chief Constable Susan Campbell and proceeded to tell us what we already knew. She then confirmed that the girl had not suffered any major injuries but had no recollection of how she ended up in the sea.

"She must have been *wasted*," Michelle sang.

"Nor does she remember who she is," Chief Constable Campbell added. There was a sharp intake of breath around the room and I felt my phone buzz as I heard Michelle's do the same. "She is undergoing treatment. In the meantime, we are appealing to anyone who might know her to get in touch."

A photo flashed up on screen and there was an aching beat of silence as my heart stopped, then started again twice as fast. But when my brain finally registered what I was seeing, Michelle said it before I could.

"Oh my God! It's Nico!"

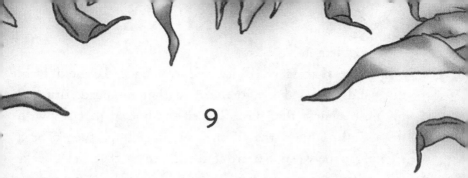

9

I don't remember what happened after that. Actually, that isn't true. I remember it perfectly; I just don't know how to put it into words because maybe, sometimes, things happen that are too big for words. Although, now I'm looking at all the books lined up on the shelf in front of me, that clearly isn't true. So, perhaps it's too soon.

For now, I can only describe how it *felt*, like a bomb had gone off in my chest, shrapnel piercing everything it touched, embedding itself in my heart and lodging in my lungs. It knocked the air clean out of me and I remember sitting there, hands fisted in the blanket, as my vision doubled, adjusted itself, then doubled again. When everything came back into focus, all I could see was her face on the television.

"It *is* Nico!" my mother gasped, turning to stare at me.

Then everything was too loud and too quiet, all at once, as a scratchy white noise filled the room. White noise punctuated with more gasps. Gasps and questions. So many questions. My mother. My father. Michelle, louder than them all as she grabbed my arm and shook me so hard my brain felt like a snow globe. Everything scattered for a moment, then started falling—falling and falling—as I looked at the television again.

It was Nico.

It was definitely Nico.

I knew that face. I'd learned that face. I'd held it in my hands. Pressed my forehead to that forehead. Brushed my nose against that nose. Traced the line of that jaw with my mouth. I knew that if she parted her lips there'd be a slight gap between her front teeth. Knew that her cheeks rose when she smiled and that if I pressed my fingers to them, her skin would flush and become so warm that I could feel it in my bones.

I could hear Michelle saying my name—over and over—calling me back until everything began to take shape again. I was still there, still in her small, warm living room, the wooden shutters hushing the rain outside and the lights on the Christmas tree blinking as everyone stared at me while I stared at Nico's photo, which was now in the corner of the screen as Chief Constable Campbell rattled off the various ways to get in touch.

Of all the things to feel at that moment, all I remember is relief. Sweet, *sweet*, giddy relief as I turned to Michelle, then kicked her under the blanket and said, "I told you something happened to her!"

But Michelle wasn't listening as she tapped something into her phone and thrust it at me. I frowned at her as she gestured at me to take it, then I frowned at the screen for a second before I put it to my ear.

I only heard it ring once before someone said, "Sussex Police."

My instinct was to give the phone back to her, but Michelle waved wildly and mouthed, *TELL THEM.*

"Hello? Sussex Police," the voice said again, and I could tell it was a call center, immediately imagining a stark, aggressively lit office with rows and rows of people talking into headsets.

"Yes. Hi. Hey. Hello," I said, then cursed myself, wishing I'd made Michelle speak to them. I hate talking on the phone at the best of times, but the shock made me sound unhinged.

The call operator was obviously used to unhinged, though, because they softened. "What's your name, darling?"

"Mara. Mara Malakar."

"Can you spell that for me?"

I did, and then they asked if I minded if they called me Mara.

"Of course not," I said as Michelle leaned in to hear.

I tried to shrug her off as they asked, "What are your pronouns, Mara?"

"She/her is fine."

"Mine too. My name is Police Constable Olivia Parsons, but you can call me Olivia."

"OK," I said as I heard her typing through the phone.

"How old are you, Mara?"

"Fifteen."

"And where do you live, Mara?"

"Hanover. Do you need the address?"

She did, so I gave it to her.

And my phone number.

Then she asked, "How can I help?"

My brain felt like a snow globe again as I tried to give Michelle the phone, but she hissed and pointed at me. I don't know what she was threatening to do to me, but it worked.

"I know her," I said, lowering my voice as though I was confessing a secret.

"Know who, Mara?"

All I could say was "The girl."

"Which girl?"

"The girl from the sea."

It was strange—calling Nico that—but that's what they were calling her, wasn't it?

The girl from the sea.

"How do you know her, Mara?" Olivia asked.

I pressed my lips together, unsure how to answer. Nico wouldn't want me to tell her she was my girlfriend. Not that she'd ever know, of course. But she wasn't my girlfriend, was she? And it was the police.

I couldn't lie to the police.

"She's my . . ."

When I didn't finish the sentence, Olivia chuckled softly. "Is it complicated?"

My shoulders fell as I finally let go of a breath. "You have no idea."

"I'll just say that you're friends, then."

"That's probably for the best."

"How long have you known her?"

"Just over six months. I met her on Sunday, June 11th."

"Very precise. I suppose you could tell me the time as well?"

"11:11."

That made Olivia chuckle again. "11:11 on June 11th. Spooky."

Magic, I corrected.

"And what's her name, Mara?"

"Nico. Nico Rudolph."

"How old is she?"

"Fifteen."

"Do you go to the same school?"

"No." I hesitated, then lowered my voice as I admitted, "I'm not sure where she goes. Longhill, I think."

If Olivia was surprised by that after the 11:11 thing, she didn't show it.

Nor did she question why I couldn't answer any of her other questions.

Her address.

Her mother's name.

Her father's name.

Olivia just typed steadily, then asked, "Is there anything else you can tell me, Mara?"

I knew that Nico would laugh so hard sometimes, it made her hiccup. And I knew that she was going to be famous. She had to be, she said. She was called Nico, so she had to be a rock star. And I knew that as well as the guitar, she played the violin and the piano and that when she sang, people would stop and stare.

And I knew that I'd wished for her at 11:11 on June 11th and she'd appeared.

But I don't suppose the police care about any of that stuff.

Michelle nudged me then, and when I looked at her, she mouthed, *PHOTOS*.

"Oh yeah!" I said too loudly. "I have photos of her. Photos of her and me. I can send you some."

"You can?"

"And she has an Instagram."

I gave her Nico's username and she thanked me. When she

stopped typing, she said, "OK, Mara. Leave this with me. We're going to look into this, and if we need to follow up, we'll be in touch, OK?"

Then she was gone.

When she hung up, I remember staring at Michelle's phone for a few seconds as her home screen reappeared, a photo of her and Lewis grinning back at me behind the checkerboard of apps. The sight of them—so happy, so together—made my heart so sore that it was a few more seconds before my breathing settled.

When it did, I looked up to find everyone was staring at me, their lips parted.

"They're going to look into it," I told them with a nod.

They nodded back, and when their shoulders fell, I could hear the rain tapping against the windows again as James pointed the remote at the television and the screen went black.

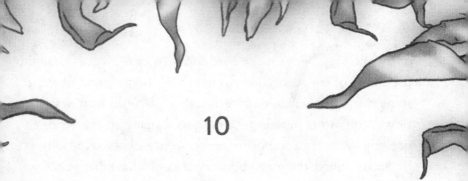

10

I felt each breath tick out of me, quick and steady, then getting quicker and quicker, like a bomb about to explode, my hands shaking as I called Nico . . . but it went straight to voicemail. So I checked her socials, and when there was no trace of her, I kicked off the blanket and sat up.

"I need to go to the hospital."

Michelle did the same, her eyes wide and her mouth open, but before she could say anything, my mother shook her head. "They won't let you near her, Mara. You're not Nico's next of kin."

"Yeah, but—" I stopped to suck in a breath. "If you come with me and we explain—"

Michelle cut me off with a brittle chuckle. "Explain *what*?"

But before she could say it—before she could remind me that Nico wasn't my girlfriend anymore, if she ever was—James said, "You won't even be able to see her, Mara. She's probably having loads of tests and stuff."

"Now isn't a good time," my father agreed. "Her mother's probably worried sick. Give them some space."

"Send Nico a text," Nicole suggested with a gentle smile. "Maybe you can go see her tomorrow?"

So I did, then stared at the screen while Michelle and our parents resumed batting questions back and forth. I was aware of them saying Nico's name over and over, but it was as though the shock of it had swallowed me whole, tugging me down to some deep, unreachable place where all I could hear was the slow throb of my heartbeat in my ears. I made an excuse about needing water to escape the ceaseless assault of questions as they exchanged theories about what could have happened to Nico.

The kitchen was immaculate now, but still smelled of the jiaozi we'd just had for dinner and the smell was so familiar—so comforting—that I closed my eyes and inhaled. Dark, salty soy, sweet Chinese leeks and something else. Something unique to Michelle's house. And I remember wishing that I could go back to a few hours ago, when we were sitting around the kitchen table, folding the wrappers, when all I had to worry about was making sure that mine were better than Michelle's. But when I opened my eyes again, I was still there.

Still in the kitchen.

Still surrounded by questions.

When I headed back to the living room, I heard Nicole lower her voice. "What if it wasn't an accident?"

I was stunned, but James just sighed and said, "Well, Nico always was a restless soul, wasn't she?"

As soon as he said it, I remembered what Michelle had said when she'd read me the article in *The Argus*.

About life not being for everyone.

And the shock of it sent me running out of the house.

Michelle must have heard the front door slam, because then she was there, right behind me as I ran next door to my house and tried to guide my key into the lock. I could hear her talking as I persisted—this breathless babble as she cursed her father and told me to ignore him—but I just wanted to get inside.

Where it was safe.

Where I'd be safe.

When I finally succeeded, Michelle followed me in, still trying to console me as I ran up the stairs. I was aware of her at my heels, and I just needed to get to the bathroom because it was the only room in our house that had a lock. But when I finally got to the door, Michelle reached for my elbow.

"Mara, stop!"

I did, but I didn't look at her.

"Dad shouldn't have said that. He doesn't know what he's talking about."

I could feel the words filling my throat until there was no room for anything else.

"Michelle, do you think she tried to—"

But she wouldn't let me finish the sentence.

"Don't, Mara." When I peered at her from under my eyelashes, she was shaking her head. "*Don't.*"

But it was all I could think about.

What if Nico isn't an asshole, she's just desperately unhappy and I didn't notice?

"Mara, stop," Michelle told me as I tried to retrace my steps.

What did she say the last time I saw her?

She'd had that argument with her mother, hadn't she?

But then, she was *always* arguing with her mother.

Mum's not talking to me again, she'd tell me with a dramatic sigh.

Or she'd roll her eyes when her phone rang. *I'm not getting that. It's probably Mum.*

I felt Michelle's hand on my shoulder then, and with a sharp shake, I was back.

"Mara, *don't*."

But I did.

"Michelle, what if she—"

"She didn't." She smothered the thought with such certainty I believed her.

I really wanted to believe her.

"If Nico wanted to do that, there are *much* easier ways of doing it." She squeezed my shoulder and waited for me to lift my chin again. "She just got wasted and fell off the pier. There's nothing more to it than that, Mara."

But I shook my head. "Nico doesn't drink."

Michelle tilted her head at me. "Are you sure?"

Doubt needled at me then because, no, I wasn't.

Nico only let me know what she wanted me to know and maybe she didn't want me to know that.

But even in the quagmire of my concern, I knew it was the most likely—and comforting—explanation. Nico wasn't the first person to get drunk and fall off the pier and she certainly wouldn't be the last.

"You didn't tell them," Michelle said, tugging me back.

"Tell who what?" I frowned.

"Sussex Police. You didn't tell them that Nico was supposed to meet you last night."

"So?"

"It might help," Michelle said gently, nodding at the bathroom.

We locked the door and sat side by side on the edge of the bath as I called Sussex Police again. When they answered, I told them that I'd just spoken to someone and they didn't hesitate, just asked my name.

"Police Constable Olivia Parsons," a voice said a few seconds later.

"Yes. Hi. Hey. Hello," I blurted out as I sat on the edge of the bath. "This is Mara. Mara Malakar."

She immediately softened. "Hey, Mara. You OK?"

"Yes. Yeah. No. I mean ..."

"Just take a breath, sweetheart," she told me when I stopped to press my hand to my forehead.

I did as I was told and, to my surprise, it actually helped.

"Did you forget to tell me something, Mara?"

"Yes," I admitted, my chin shivering. "I'm sorry. It's just that I was so stunned when I saw Nico's photo on the news and it wasn't even me who called you, it was Michelle—"

"Who's Michelle?"

"My best friend. I was too shocked, so she was the one who dialed your number."

"OK."

"And my parents were there and they know about Nico, but they don't know *everything*, you know?"

"OK."

"Anyway, I'm sorry, but I forgot to tell you that I was supposed to meet Nico last night."

There was a tick or two of silence. Then Olivia said, "You were?"

"Yeah."

I was going to tell her how Nico had said that I was the last person she wanted to see last year and the first person she wanted to see this year, but I didn't know if Nico would want me to tell the police that.

"Where did you arrange to meet her, Mara?"

"At Queens Park."

"At what time?"

"Eleven thirty."

"Do you know how she was getting there?"

"The twenty-seven from the Windmill, then she was supposed to walk from the Old Steine."

"And what happened?"

"She sent me message at ten fifty-eight to say that she was on the bus."

"OK."

"She told me to meet her in Queens Park in half an hour, but she didn't show up."

"Was that the last time you heard from her? That message at ten fifty-eight?"

My face flushed at the memory. "She messaged me again at twelve thirty-nine."

"What did she say?"

I know I shouldn't have lied, but I couldn't say it out loud. "She told me she wasn't coming."

"Is it like her to arrange to meet you and not show up?"

I hesitated and it was suddenly so quiet that I could hear someone else's voice through the phone.

"You still there, Mara?"

I nodded.

"Are you nodding, Mara?"

"Yes," I whispered.

"Which question are you nodding at?"

"Both."

"Is that why things are so complicated?"

"Nico's very"—I stopped to suck in a breath, aware of Michelle watching me—"*complicated*."

"OK. Well, this is very helpful, Mara. Thank you."

I could feel her transitioning back to Police Constable Olivia Parsons, so I stopped her before she could launch into her *We're going to look into this, and if we need to follow up, we'll be in touch* script. "Olivia?"

"Yes, Mara?"

It was a second or two before I could say it. "Is she OK?"

"She's safe, I promise."

And that's all I needed to know.

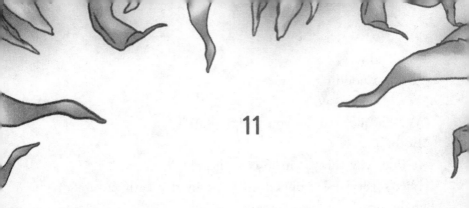

11

"You've been summoned to Zoom," Michelle told me as we were leaving the bathroom.

"Now?" I groaned.

"Well, it's either Zoom or Louise is going to come over right now."

"Can't it wait until tomorrow? We're meeting at the café for lunch anyway."

She tilted her head at me. "Do you really want to do this in front of your parents?"

"Excellent point," I conceded, sure that Louise was already *hysterical*.

Sure enough, we logged on to be confronted by Louise, her blonde hair *everywhere* and her pale face pink with excitement. She was the first one there, of course, and as soon as she saw me, her face got even pinker.

"Where have you been?" she shrieked so loudly Michelle and I had to take our headphones out.

I put mine back in, then told her that I was talking to the police.

Louise shrieked again.

And Michelle and I jumped again.

When we recovered, Michelle glared at her. "Please calm down. Mara is stressed enough as it is."

"Sorry." She winced. "Are you OK?"

I wasn't ready to answer that, though.

So I changed the subject.

"Where are Erin and May?"

Louise rolled her eyes. "They're *always* late."

But, just as she said it, the boxes shuffled and Erin appeared.

When she saw herself on the screen, she recoiled and adjusted her pink satin bonnet. "I want it noted for the record that you are the only ones who are allowed to see me like this," she told us with a pained look.

"What are you talking about?" Michelle pulled a face. "You look amazing."

And she did. Even in the harsh light of her desk lamp her dark skin was *glowing*.

Erin grinned and tapped her fingers across her cheeks. "I just tried that Himalayan charcoal mask."

"Any good?" Michelle asked.

"Hey!" Louise clapped her hands. "Save the skin care talk for later. We have more important things to discuss. Although"— she stopped to point at Erin—"I'll need the name of that mask, OK?"

She reached for her phone. "I'll text you."

Then Louise asked me again, "Mara, are you OK? What did the police say?"

When I hesitated, Michelle must have sensed that I couldn't talk about it yet.

So she changed the subject. "What happened with Dean, Erin?"

Ordinarily, Louise would have been murderous that we were ignoring her, but she frowned.

"Yeah, what did he do? I know you were fighting at mine, but then the Doja Cat Incident happened."

"You OK, by the way?" I asked, and Louise nodded.

"I was sure I broke it, but it's just a sprain."

Michelle raised her finger. "We'll talk about May and A&E in a sec, but back to Dean."

Erin rolled her eyes. "He liked a load of Amy Umar's photos on Instagram."

Michelle and I pulled *Yikes!* faces while Louise yelled something I couldn't make out. I thought she'd thrown her laptop across the room, but then she reappeared, her mouth open and her phone in her hand.

"The ones of her in that white bikini?" she asked, already scrolling.

Erin nodded.

"Why is she wearing a bikini in January?" I asked, which wasn't the point, I know.

"She's in Dubai," Erin sneered as she readjusted her bonnet.

Louise held her phone up to the screen. "*Three* fire emojis?"

Michelle and I leaned forward to look at them, then leaned back and shook our heads.

"He's done," Louise concluded, then took a long gulp from her water bottle.

"Sorry, babe," Michelle said at the same time as I did.

Usually, we wouldn't have been so quick to sentence Dean, but given that's how they met—when he liked one of Erin's selfies with the same three fire emojis, then slid into her DMs to tell her how beautiful she was—we weren't willing to give him the benefit of the doubt.

It was obviously his MO.

Erin didn't even try to defend him. "Oh well. It's Viviana's sixteenth on Saturday."

"Yes!" Louise hissed. "You have to wear that yellow dress!"

"I was thinking of dusting off the pink one, actually."

"The first dress you wore at my fourteenth?"

Erin grinned, then pretended to swoon. "I always feel like a queen in that."

Then the boxes shuffled again and May appeared, a towel around her shoulders. Her room was dark, so it made her pale skin look almost blue in the light from her laptop screen.

"Hey! What's going on? What's so urgent?"

Louise's face flushed again as she snapped, "May! Where have you been?"

"I was dyeing my hair. I have fifteen minutes before I have to wash this off." She pointed at her head. "Otherwise Awkward Peach will become Raging Cheeto. Hey." She frowned at Erin. "What happened with Dean?"

Her jaw tightened. "It's a long story."

Louise shortened it for her. "Dean liked those photos of Amy Umar in that white bikini."

"Oh, well, that's over," May said, reaching for a bottle of nail polish and shaking it.

After ten minutes of thoroughly demolishing Dean and trying to persuade Erin to consider being fixed up with Arun's friend, Louise gasped and clapped at us until we stopped.

"Wait! Wait! Wait! Oh my God. I can't believe I forgot! Mara!"

May looked concerned. "What? What's happening with Mara?"

"You didn't hear?" Louise asked as she tucked a stray curl behind her ear.

"Hear what? I told you; I was dyeing my hair."

"Why are you dyeing your hair at half eleven?" Michelle asked.

"I had to bleach it first and it took ages. Then the toner . . ."

"First skin care tips, now hair care? Come on!" Louise growled, then stopped to take a long drink from her water bottle.

Erin's eyebrows rose as she watched her chug. "Wow. What's in that? Vodka?"

"No, I've got a headache." She groaned miserably. "My little brother had a guitar lesson earlier."

"Are your parents still making him take lessons?" May asked, peering at a strand of hair, then rubbing it between her fingers while Michelle hissed at her to stop before she stained her fingers orange.

"Yes, and he's *terrible*."

Michelle pulled a face. "Why don't your parents let him do gymnastics like he wants to?"

"Because he needs to *man up*, apparently." She stopped to roll her eyes. "And now we're all suffering for it."

"Poor Hunter." Erin exhaled and shook her head. "Remember when my parents thought I was a boy and they made me do karate when I wanted to do pottery with Mara and Michelle?"

"At least you were good at pottery," Michelle scoffed. "Remember those mugs we made for Mother's Day?"

"Mum still drinks out of hers," I said proudly. "She can't overfill it, though, because it's lopsided."

"Hey!" May interrupted, pointing at her head again. "I'm on the verge of Cheeto here!"

"Yes!" Louise took another gulp of water, then pointed the bottle at me. "Mara, come on. Tell us."

"Tell us what?" May asked, completely lost.

"Nico's the girl from the sea," Louise and Erin said in unison.

May's hands fisted in the towel around her shoulders. "Wait. What?"

Then mine fisted in the front pocket of my hoodie as May's eyes widened.

She stared at me through the screen for a moment, then said, "What are you talking about?"

"Nico's the girl they pulled out of the sea this morning," Michelle said gently.

"*Nico* Nico?"

They all nodded.

"*Mara's* Nico?"

They nodded again.

"Is she OK?"

"Yeah," Erin told her. "But she can't remember who she is or how she got there."

The towel fell off May's shoulders as she held her hands up. "My hair is going to be so orange!"

"No one cares about your hair," Louise barked. "Mara, do you know what happened?"

I shook my head.

Michelle reached for my hand and squeezed it. "She didn't have a clue until we saw the news."

Erin looked confused by that. "Weren't you with Nico last night?"

I snuck a look at Michelle, then admitted, "She didn't show up."

Louise, Erin, and May gasped.

"She dumped me," I said sourly.

They gasped again.

"By text."

They gasped again.

Louise looked ready to fall off her bed. "She did *what*?"

I don't know where it was coming from, just that the shock had passed and all I could feel was a spike of anger that got sharper and sharper the more I thought about it until it actually physically *hurt*. Until I was sure that it was about to pierce right through my chest as I realized why I was so angry.

This would never have happened if Nico had been with me.

"She left me sitting in Queens Park for an hour, then texted me to say that she'd bumped into some friends, but it was probably for the best"—I scowled, parroting Nico's text—"because it was getting *too much* for her."

May blinked at that. "What was getting too much for her?"

"Me."

The word snapped off my tongue with such force, it rendered them speechless.

Even Louise.

It took a few minutes, but May was the first to recover.

"Mara, I'm so sorry. Are you OK?" She thought about it, then said, "Of course you're not OK."

"Is there anything we can do?" Erin asked.

"I can come over," Louise offered. "We can watch *Knives Out*. Ana de Armas."

She wagged her eyebrows and I tried to smile. "That's so sweet, but I'm good."

But I wasn't.

I really, *really* wasn't.

"Well, we're here if you need anything," Erin told me as Louise and May nodded.

"Even at, like, four a.m.," May said. "Just text me. I'll probably be up anyway. You know I don't sleep."

"She'll be fine," Michelle said, slinging her arm around me.

She didn't say it, but I still heard, *She's got me.*

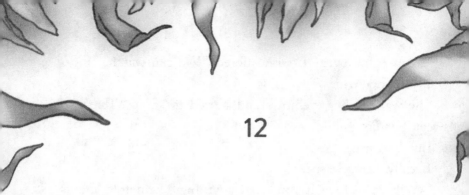

12

I tried to sleep it away, but I couldn't. Every time I closed my eyes, all I could see was Nico in a long white dress, standing on the sea wall at Black Rock against a dark sky, her head crowned in moonlight.

Luckily, Michelle sleeps like the dead, so she didn't notice me checking my phone every few minutes, hoping for some news. But there was nothing. No video of Nico's mother running into the hospital. No camera crews outside, waiting for her to make a weeping, breathless statement. They hadn't even named Nico yet, which only fueled the already spreading speculation. Twelve minutes after they showed her photo on the ten o'clock news someone on Twitter suggested she'd fallen off a dinghy, and that was it. People argued fiercely all night about how we have to close the borders, even though it was quite clear from the photo that Nico's Korean.

I told myself to stop reading it, but I couldn't, guzzling it all up until *finally*, as the moon gave way to the sun and a thread of wintry white light cut through my curtains, there it was.

Nico's face on the BBC News homepage beneath the words, *Girl from the Sea Named.*

By the time Michelle and I met the others at the café, Nico's face was on the front page of *The Argus* as well. At first glance, you'd think no one cared. Even through the steamed-up windows of the café, I could see that the Lanes were back to how they were before Christmas. A ceaseless stream of people passing back and forth, undeterred by the sharp drizzle as they tried to make the most of the precious couple of days before they went back to school and work.

But inside, the café was *buzzing* as people chatted furiously and handed around copies of the paper. "Poor thing," I heard someone at the table next to ours say. "She probably didn't want to be rescued, did she?"

I had to hold on to the seat of my chair with both hands while I turned to stare at them as they nodded at their friend and ate their green chili and cheese omelette like it was nothing.

Like Nico was nothing.

"Ignore them," Michelle whispered.

So I did.

I stabbed at my dosa with my fork and let them carry on, an eye in a storm of Nico.

Nico.

Nico.

Nico.

It was all I could hear—her name—as I glanced at the table in the corner that we'd sat at a couple of days before, when she'd kissed my hand and asked me to meet her at our bench.

When I turned back, I thought everyone at our table would be talking about her as well, but they weren't. I knew that was because of Michelle and my heart stung at the thought of a new group chat that didn't include me. Called something like *Operation Distract Mara*, where they'd decided how they were going to handle it.

I know, because we had one for May and Chesca.

Maybe they'd had one for me and Nico for months.

"Is the orange going to wash out before we go back to school?" Michelle asked May with a frown.

Then that was it.

Operation Distract Mara had been initiated as we passed around bowls of aloo mutter and medu vada and talked about everything from May's hair to Arun's friend who Louise was trying to fix Erin up with.

Everything but Nico.

And that's how it was going to be, I knew.

They were moving on and they were going to drag me along with them.

So I let them think they had. I ate lunch with them, then wandered around the Lanes, smiling and making all the right noises as they picked dresses off the rails and asked me what I thought. Then I went to the cinema with them and watched a Channing Tatum film I don't remember the name of. Ate popcorn and peanut M&M's, and saved the yellow ones for Michelle, like I always do, because she says they taste different.

But all the while, I was thinking about Nico.

While we were outside the cinema, saying our goodbyes, I realized how close we were to the hospital and said a little prayer that Lewis would call Michelle so I could slip away and see her. But he didn't, so Michelle and I went home for dinner and I made myself sing along to Dua Lipa with her while we took our makeup off as though it was just another Tuesday night.

By the time we went to bed, I was so exhausted by the whole performance—me pretending that it was working, that I was fine—that I was sure I'd fall asleep as soon as my cheek touched the pillow.

But I didn't.

As soon as I heard Michelle snoring, I was *awake*, the pain in my chest—which had been a dull, distant ache all day—back and sharper than ever as I reached for my phone, hoping for some word from Nico.

There was nothing, of course. But I kept checking, circling between each place I might hear from her until, by one o'clock, I'd fallen down a rabbit hole of Twitter threads and subreddits in my thirst to find it all.

Everything I could find about Nico.

And I did.

There, among the things I already knew, I discovered tiny, thrilling things I didn't.

Videos I'd never seen that people had taken of her singing outside the station.

Photos of her with people I didn't recognize in the queue for gigs.

Comments from friends she'd never mentioned, asking her to get in touch.

I devoured it all. Everything I could find while I was alone in the dark, safe in that uneasy midpoint between night and day where no one could tell me not to because I was the only one awake.

Me and all the other insomniacs and heartsick misfits.

I learned more about Nico than she had ever told me. Thanks to the article in *The Argus*, I found out that Nico's mother was called Rebecca, and when I googled her, I found her mother's obituary and discovered that Rebecca was born in Brighton, but Nico was born in London and moved here the summer I met her when her grandmother passed away. Then I found an article in the *Guardian* about Nico's father, Henry, who was high up at Samsung, but died in a plane crash. *Henry Rudolph, 33, originally from Jeonju-si, South Korea, is survived by his wife, Rebecca, and their two-year-old daughter.*

By the time the sun came up, I was spent.

But as soon as I closed my eyes, Michelle sat up and clapped her hands.

"Right! Here's the plan," she said with such determination that if I could have, I would have smiled.

Of course she had a plan.

"OK," I muttered, forcing myself to sit up as well.

She clapped her hands again. "We're back at school on Tuesday, right?" She stopped to tug the hairband from around her wrist and swept her hair up into a ponytail. "So, tomorrow, let's do pizza and bowling."

"Bowling?" I looked at her like she'd lost it. "You *hate* bowling, Michelle."

"I don't."

"You do! We haven't been bowling since we were twelve and you forgot to let go of the ball and ended up sliding down the lane on your stomach. You almost scored a strike with your head."

She shrugged it off. "So? That was *years* ago."

"Michelle, you still have nightmares about being chewed up by the thing that sweeps the pins away."

"I know I hate bowling," she said through her teeth. "But you love it, Mara, and I'm trying to be nice."

"I appreciate it"—I waved my hand at her—"but I don't need you getting PTSD on top of everything else."

"Fine. We'll find something else to do. That just leaves today. I *have* to go to my grandparents. It's nǎinai's birthday, so there's *no way* I can get out of it. But you should come with us. It'll be fun. They love you."

"I'm not really in the mood to be around a bunch of people," I admitted with a pained frown.

She'd obviously prepared for that, though. "Why don't you go to the cinema with Louise and Erin, then?"

"And third—actually, *fifth*-wheel it on their double date?"

"I think Erin would appreciate it. You know that dating can be . . ." She stopped to exhale as she tried to find the right word. ". . . *complicated* for her."

"I know." I felt a twinge of guilt at that, but then I remembered. "Louise will be with her, though."

"Yeah, but what if Erin doesn't like Arun's friend?"

"What if she does?" I countered. "Then I'll be in the way."

Michelle tilted her head from side to side, then said, "True."

"I'm fine," I said as brightly as I could. "I don't need a babysitter."

"You're not fine, Mara," she said, her eyes wide. "This is, like, the worst breakup ever."

I couldn't argue with that.

"You can't dwell on it, though," she told me with a firm nod. "I know what happened to Nico is a shock, but it doesn't change anything. New Year's Eve still happened, and while I hope Nico's OK," she added, and I believed her, "she made her feelings clear before she ended up in the sea, didn't she?"

"She did," I was forced to agree with a defeated sigh.

"So, there's nothing you can do." She shook her head before I could say *But* or *Maybe* or *What if* and give her any of the other flimsy, flailing excuses I'd been grasping at all night. "You can't wait around, hoping that falling in the sea made her have some sort of epiphany and she'll want to get back together."

The sudden shot of hope at the thought was dizzying as Michelle stopped to think about it for a second, then said, "I mean, who knows? Nico nearly died. That has to change you. Maybe she'll embrace the fact that she survived and want a fresh start so she can finally live the life she's always talking about. But that doesn't mean it will include you, Mara. A fresh start is just that—a fresh start with no reminders of who she used to be."

The hope burned out as suddenly as it ignited.

I know Michelle was trying to help, to be reasonable and logical and all those other things I needed in that moment, but she has this horrible habit of making me feel hopelessly human.

Weak.

Silly, even.

All those things she wasn't.

But the trouble with being rational—as Michelle always was—is you assume that everyone is trying to be as well, but I just wasn't capable of it.

"You need to keep busy." She clapped her hands again. "So you don't think about her. Don't dwell."

"No dwelling." I nodded as I checked my phone again.

13

I guess I fell asleep after Michelle left because I remember dreaming about Nico in that white dress again, standing on the sea wall at Black Rock. She tried to say something to me this time, but before she could, I was jolted awake by a knock.

I lifted my head off the pillow as my bedroom door opened and May appeared with a cheeky smirk.

"You decent?" she asked, hovering in the doorway.

As soon as I saw her, I swallowed a chuckle because Michelle must have been desperate if she sent May.

Don't get me wrong, I adore May. She's the one person I wanted to see, actually, which is exactly why I know Michelle *didn't* want me to see her. But she was out of options, wasn't she? She obviously didn't trust me to abide by the *No Dwelling* plan (and rightly so, in fairness), so she had to send someone to keep an eye on me.

I'm almost certain that May was her last resort, though. After literally everyone we'd ever met, including Max from the café and the Elvis impersonator who wanders around the Lanes in a white jumpsuit singing "Burning Love." And she was right to be concerned because May was a wild card. I already knew that she'd do one of two things. Either she'd say, "Fuck Nico!" then make us do something reckless that would land one of us—or both of us—in A&E. Or she'd ditch the *No Dwelling* plan and indulge me in wallowing in my growing pit of despair.

I hoped it was the latter, so I knew Michelle was *freaking out* that it would be as well. After all, May and I always had each other's backs when our respective relationships were being dissected over plates of chips in the school canteen. So, if there was anyone who understood what I was going through, it was May.

"I won't ask how you are," she said as I forced myself to sit up and she came to join me, sitting crossed-legged on the bed. She was wearing odd socks—one pink with red hearts and one blue with sushi—and I don't know why I found it so comforting, but given that Michelle had the next two days planned down to the minute, the fact that May had put on different socks and didn't seem to give a shit was a relief.

I answered her with a groan as I crossed my legs as well and raised my chin to look at her.

When I did, she grinned and shook a plastic bag at me. "I brought Pocky and Cherry Coke."

"Bless you!"

I must have had about eight minutes sleep, so it was exactly what I needed.

Sugar.

My mother appeared in the doorway then and I almost spilled the Coke as I twisted the lid off.

"Mum? What are you doing here? Why aren't you at the café with Dad?"

But I already knew.

Michelle had obviously ordered her to stay until May arrived.

My mother played along, though. "I dropped a bag of jeera on the kitchen floor! I've just spent two hours cleaning it up, but we'll still be stepping on it for weeks."

"Yeah?" I said in a way that let her know that I didn't believe her as I sipped my Cherry Coke.

But she pretended not to notice. "It's for the best, though. Your dad's trying out some new recipes this morning, so I'm safer here." She rolled her eyes. "Where's Nico when you need her, eh?" She chuckled, then caught herself and gasped. "Oh God. Sorry, baby girl."

She hurried over to the bed, muttering *Sorry* over and over, then kissed me on the forehead, no doubt panicked that Michelle would find out and berate her for not following The Plan. Then she wisely hurried out to go help my father with the lunch rush before she said anything else.

"What was that about?" May asked as she tore into the box of Pocky.

"Nico's the only one brave enough to try Dad's *experiments*," I told her as she handed me one and I bit into it. "Or *foolish*, I should say. I mean, curried banana ice cream?"

I pretended to heave.

But May looked kind of curious. "I'd try that."

Of course she would.

"Listen," she said, her gaze dipping as she plucked out a stick of Pocky for herself, then put the box on the bed between us. "I'm really sorry about all this, Mara. I really thought you and Nico were endgame."

"Thanks, babe," I said with a sore sigh.

"As for *The Plan*, Michelle filled me in, but if you want to talk about it, you know I get it. I mean, I don't get *this*," she clarified, her green eyes wide, "whatever the hell happened to Nico the other night, but you know I get being in a relationship that everyone is rooting to fail."

Her gaze dipped again when she said it and I felt awful. I'd never seen her like that before, chin down and shoulders slumped. May was usually so fearless. Every day, I'd see her spill over the edges of whoever she'd been the day before and I'd always envied that about her. Envied the ease with which she navigated life, as though every day was a clear road with her favorite song playing on the radio, and it made me wonder if it was really that simple. If I could approach each day without worrying about things that hadn't even happened yet.

So to see the doubt make her light dim like that made my heart hurt even more.

"I know you do, babe. You're the only one who does."

She peered at me from under her eyelashes then, the spark back in her eyes. "Exactly! So don't worry about Michelle and the others. You know what they're like." She waved her hand. "When I broke up with Chesca before Christmas, Michelle took me to Five Guys, bought me a peanut butter milkshake, and told me to get over it."

I blinked at her, horrified.

"So you can talk to me, if you want. I mean, you *need* to process it. Your head must be wrecked." May closed her eyes and shook her head. When she opened them again, she exhaled through her nose. "God, I'd be in a right state if something like this happened to Chesca and I couldn't get hold of her."

"I am in a state," I told her, and the relief of finally being able to say it out loud made the knot in my chest loosen.

"Of course you are," she said, reaching over to clasp my shoulder with her hand. She squeezed it and I made myself look at her. "It doesn't matter if you and Nico broke up, you still care about her."

I did.

I really, *really* did.

I know you probably think I shouldn't have, and you're right, because back then caring for Nico was like throwing a pebble in the sea, hoping that it would throw it back.

But that didn't stop me standing on the beach, waiting for the pebble.

"I just need to know that she's OK," I said at last, because it was May and I could.

Because she wouldn't tell me not to dwell.

To keep busy.

To not think about it.

And I was right because her eyes suddenly lit up with mischief.

"Let's go to the hospital, then!"

It was exactly what I was hoping she'd say, but the shock of it still made me gasp. "We can't!"

"Why not?"

"We *can't*. Can we?" I whispered, as though Michelle could hear me from her grandparents' house.

"Have you heard from Nico?"

"You know I haven't."

"Then how else are you going to know if she's OK?"

When May said it like that, any doubt that it was a terrible idea evaporated.

Still, when Michelle disemboweled me later, I wanted to be able to say that I'd least feigned protest.

"Yeah, but the hospital's *massive*, May. What if we can't find her?"

"We will."

"Yeah, but what if they won't let me see her? I'm not her next of kin."

"Please." She flicked her hair, then thumbed at herself and flashed me a smug smirk. "Who got us into the VIP section at the Arctic Monkeys last summer?"

That's true.

May could talk herself into—or out of—pretty much anything.

I stopped and forced myself to take a breath as a shiver of excitement fizzed through me.

But it didn't help as my cheeks warmed at the thought of seeing Nico.

"This is a terrible idea, isn't it?" I acknowledged, giving her one last chance to talk me out of it.

May just shrugged, though. "Probably, but we're doing it anyway, right?"

"Oh yeah!" I grinned, but as I was about to leap off the bed my phone buzzed in my hand and I almost dropped it, sure that it was Michelle and she knew what we were planning. But it was a Google Alert and I almost dropped my phone again when I saw that it was an article in *The Argus* saying that Nico had been discharged from the hospital. There were only a few scant paragraphs recapping what had happened and that same ad for a recruitment website, but all it said was that she'd returned home safely and her mother was asking for privacy while they recovered from the ordeal.

"Nico's been discharged," I said, turning my phone to show May.

"Oh," she said, mirroring the tone of disappointment in my voice. But she caught herself and said brightly, "That's good! They wouldn't discharge her if she wasn't OK."

That made something in me unravel, the screen blurring as I blinked away tears of relief.

"Thank God," I said with a heave and a sob.

When my eyes refocused, May was sniggering to herself. "Her memory must be back. Mind you, if she's anything like me, she was probably putting it on to get out of sneaking out on New Year's Eve."

She threw her head back and cackled, then reached for the box of Pocky and shook it until one slid out.

"Now you can relax, Mara. I'm sure she'll be in touch when she's ready. She must know that you've been going out of your mind. I know you guys broke up, but *no one* is that much of an asshole to leave you hanging without at least telling you that they're OK."

My shoulders fell then, but my muscles immediately clenched again as I realized what that meant.

"Great." I held up my phone. "I've already texted Nico, like, twenty times, and every time I call her it goes straight to voicemail, so I guess I'll only be putting this down to shower until she calls me back."

May looked confused by that, though. "But Nico won't call you back."

I recoiled, my cheeks hot at the shock of it. And I shouldn't have been so startled—after all, May has the merciless honesty of a toddler sometimes—but I thought she'd at least try and soften the blow given the circumstances. Rather than saying, *Well, she dumped you, so she isn't going to call you, is she?*

"But you *just said* that only an asshole would leave me hanging . . ."

When my chin quivered as I trailed off, May looked mortified.

"No! No!" She waved her hands at me. "No! What I mean is Nico *can't* call."

I swept away a tear with my fingers. "Why not?"

"She doesn't have her phone, does she?"

"How do you know?"

"I don't. But I'm guessing she can't have it."

"Why not?"

"I mean"—May hesitated, picking the box of Pocky and shaking it, clearly uncomfortable that I didn't understand what she was getting at—"she texted you to say that she was on the bus, right?"

I fell back against the pillows with a sigh when I realized what she was saying.

"So Nico probably had her phone with her when she fell in the sea."

"Sorry, Mara. I thought you'd worked that out," I heard her say as I stared up at the ceiling.

"So how's she going to get hold of me if she doesn't have my number?"

As much as I liked Nico, I hadn't memorized hers, so I doubt she'd memorized mine.

I didn't realize I'd said it out loud, though, until May said, "She can go to the café, can't she?"

That made me sit up and look at her again.

When I did, she said, "Plus, she knows you go to Stringer, right?"

She did.

"And you follow each other on Instagram, don't you?"

"And Snapchat."

"There you go." May shook the box of Pocky again. "So she'll be able to find you if she wants to."

I ignored the *if she wants to* as I counted the ways Nico could find me, my heart full-on *thundering* at the thought of walking out of school to find her waiting for me. Or my parents coming home from the café to say that Nico had been in, before handing me a napkin with her new number scribbled across it.

But May tugged me back as she asked, "Have you reached out to her on Insta?"

I sat up again, suddenly breathless. "Should I?"

"Of course! I would. Don't leave a comment, though, Michelle will see. DM her."

"OK," I murmured, my hands shaking as I opened my inbox.

"You've tagged Nico on your Insta, right?" May asked.

"Yeah."

I only had a few photos of us together.

One on the beach, in the peach glow of the sunset. Me smiling and Nico looking away.

One of her in my living room, clutching my mother's *The Velvet Underground & Nico* album.

One of just our feet, in our matching black-and-white checkerboard Vans.

Still, I'd tagged Nico in all of them.

"Good." May slid another stick of Pocky out of the box, then pointed it at me. "So even if she still can't remember anything, at least when she clicks on your profile, she'll see you're not a weirdo and you really do know her."

"What shall I say?" I asked as I stared at the string of messages, the last one from the end of June when we'd swapped numbers a few hours before we met for our first not-date.

"Just keep it light. Something like *Hope you're OK. Message me when you can.* Then give her your number because she probably doesn't have it anymore, does she?"

I wrote exactly that, but as soon as I sent it, my phone buzzed in my hand and I almost screamed.

But it was only Louise posting *The Argus* article about Nico being discharged in the group chat.

"Has she updated?" May asked as I sank back into the pillows again.

"She doesn't have her phone, does she?"

"True. True." May wagged her finger at me. "What about WhatsApp?"

I checked again. "Last seen Saturday at 12:39."

"That's when she texted you, right?"

I nodded, my heart stinging at the memory.

"Did she post anything on her socials on New Year's Eve?"

"What, with the *friends* she bumped into?" I said with a sneer.

"Chesca does that," May told me with a sneer of her own. "She blocks me on WhatsApp but makes sure that I can see her having fun with her mates on Instagram and TikTok."

At least Nico had never blocked me.

"I don't know any of Nico's mates," I muttered as I looked up at the ceiling again.

"You've never met *any* of them?"

I shook my head.

"That's weird."

I sat up and unlocked my phone. "There's, like, *no one* on her Instagram."

I wonder if May heard the *Not even me* as I handed her my phone and she began scrolling through it.

"I mean, she didn't start it until she moved to Brighton, but still. That's weird, isn't it?"

May nodded, her gaze flitting down the wall of selfies and videos.

Nico playing the guitar.

Nico bathed in red light at a gig.

Nico posing in front of a mirror, her bedroom a stew of discarded clothes and books.

Nico.

Nico.

Nico.

"There are a few comments on her latest post," May muttered as she peered at the screen.

But I already knew that.

What do you think I was doing at 4 a.m.?

I'd read them all, sifting through the randoms who'd heard about her on the news and felt compelled to wish her well—or worse, tell her how pretty she was—and the ones who seemed to actually know her.

"There's three interesting ones," I told her, to save her the trouble. "xalydeanx"—I counted off each on my fingers— "lukeyyyb and LaylaE15. They're all private, but they're all from London."

"How do you know they're from London?"

"Well, xalydeanx is a West Ham fan, according to their profile. Their profile photo is of them and lukeyyyb. I'm guessing they're together, so I clicked on lukeyyyb and they've tagged the Newham Athletic Club in their profile, which is in East London. And I think the third one, LaylaE15, is referencing their postcode. So, I looked up E15 and that's Stratford, which, again, is in East London, hence the *they're all in London* theory."

May seemed genuinely impressed. "Nice work, Benoit Blanc."

I saluted her with two fingers. "Thank you."

"But no one in Brighton?"

I shook my head. "Weird, right?"

"What about this one?" May turned the screen to show me a new comment I hadn't seen yet.

"Hey, babe," I read aloud. *"So glad I found you. Hope you're feeling better. DM me. I miss your face xx."*

I miss your face.

That made my heart hiccup.

"An ex?" May said, her eyebrows rising as she clicked on the profile.

I held my breath, bracing myself to be confronted by an onslaught of photos, the pair of them leaning into one another and smiling, as I asked myself if I wasn't the only one waiting to hear from Nico.

But that account was private as well and, apart from her pronouns, her profile was just a string of emojis.

"Nya," I read, then hesitated as I tried to pronounce her surname.

May did it for me. "Kalogeropoulos."

"Kalogeropoulos," I repeated, if less elegantly.

"Blimey," May muttered. "I thought my surname was a mouthful. Petrakis is nothing compared to this."

Still, it sounded like a real name, at least.

So we googled her. Mercifully, there was only one Nya Kalogeropoulos, and while there wasn't much, I was slightly unsettled by how much we managed to deduce about her in a few minutes. We found her Snapchat, but that was private as well. Her TikTok wasn't, though, and while Nico wasn't on it, thanks to Nya's school uniform we found out that she went to Stratford Girls.

"I should probably make my Insta private," I realized as I checked to see if Nico had responded.

My heart slumped when I opened Instagram again and saw that I didn't have any new messages, then it immediately shot up into my throat as I checked Nico's profile. I don't even know why I did it. It had become a habit, I guess. Since I'd met her that morning in June, I did the same thing every time

I opened Instagram—I checked to see if I had any new messages or notifications, and then I went to Nico's profile to see if she'd updated.

"Nico deleted her account!" I gasped, turning my phone to show May the screen.

"When?" She snatched it from me. "You literally *just* messaged her, Mara."

May said that we should check her other accounts as well, so we did and they were gone.

Snapchat.

TikTok.

Spotify.

Even the Bandcamp she'd set up to promote her music.

All of it.

Gone.

"How am I supposed to reach her now?" I asked, my eyes suddenly stinging with tears.

"Why would she do that?" May frowned. But then she thought about it and said, "Maybe she's had enough of the attention? I mean, the comments are wild enough. What do you think her DMs are like?"

"True, but she could have gone private. She didn't have to delete *everything*."

May didn't seem to think that was weird, though. "Maybe someone was being stalkery and she panicked."

Probably, I conceded as I recalled the string of creepy comments beneath each of her selfies.

"Don't worry, Mara. Nico's probably waiting for everything to calm down, then she'll reactivate."

"What do I do until then?" I asked with a miserable shrug.

May shrugged back. "You just have to wait, I guess."

"I hate this." I threw my head back and groaned. "I just want to know if she's OK."

"She is," May said, and she sounded so sure that I dropped my chin to look at her. "They wouldn't have discharged her if she wasn't. And she's obviously well enough to be deleting her socials, so I'm sure she's fine."

That's true.

"Still"—I shook my head, unable ignore the itch of unease any longer—"something's not right, May."

"What do you mean?" she asked as she handed me back my phone.

"Where did she even bump into these friends?"

"What friends? Her London friends?"

"No, the ones she blew me off for on New Year's Eve," I said, waiting for her to catch up as my brain charged on without her.

"On the bus, I guess."

"OK." I pointed my phone at her. "Say she did bump into friends—friends I've never heard of and who aren't on her Instagram, who our age goes out at the marina?"

She tilted her head from side to side, her eyebrows raised as she considered that.

"Especially not on New Year's Eve, May."

Nico was more likely to go out in town, to somewhere like Green Door Store or The Hope and Ruin.

She wouldn't be seen dead at a Wetherspoons.

"Maybe she went to a house party," May suggested.

"No one our age *lives* at the marina. It's all retirement flats and Airbnbs."

"Yeah, but if she was at a house party, that would explain the time difference."

"Exactly." I pointed my phone at her again, because of course I'd thought about the time difference.

I'd thought about everything.

Considered every possibility.

Every scenario.

Every option.

Like I said, what do you think I was doing at 4 a.m.?

"She must have been at a house party because everywhere at the marina would have been shut by two."

"OK." May nodded, but clearly wasn't following what I was trying to say.

So I laid it out for her. "First of all, I've never seen Nico drink. Like, *ever*."

"Doesn't mean she doesn't, though."

"True. It's Nico, so who knows? I never know what she's thinking. Maybe she said *Fuck it* that night, for whatever reason, got drunk, and fell in the sea. But that still doesn't explain how she ended up at Black Rock."

"Why? Black Rock is right next to the marina."

"I know, but even if she was a strong swimmer and it wasn't, you know, *winter*, why would she swim *around* the marina and the sea wall when all she had to do was try to get onto one of the yachts or gangways?"

"She probably fell off the pier and drifted that way."

I pointed my phone at her again. "But why was she even at

the pier? It was eight thirty in the morning. Surely she would have been going home? She lives in Rottingdean, which is five miles in the *other* direction."

"Maybe the night wasn't over yet?"

"OK." That made me falter. "Say that's true. Say her and her mates were up all night and ended up at the pier. They're drunk and mucking around and Nico falls in the sea, right?"

"Right."

"Why didn't her friends call 999?"

May started to say something, then pressed her lips together.

"That's weird, don't you think?" I pushed. "That her friends didn't tell *anyone*."

"Maybe she was on her own. Or maybe her friends got scared and ran off."

"Well, they're not very good friends, are they?"

"People do thoughtless shit when they're drunk," she reminded me.

But I shook my head. "Have you ever been so wasted that you'd leave someone to *drown*, May?"

Given that last summer she went camping and her cousin, Robin, broke her wrist trying to climb a tree after they took a load of shrooms, May was the only one I knew who could answer that with any real honesty.

So when she went quiet, I knew I was right.

"OK," I conceded. "Maybe her mates were more than drunk. Maybe they were off their nut on ket, or whatever, and didn't see her fall off the pier. Or maybe Nico was on her own when it happened."

Or maybe she wanted to be on her own because it wasn't an accident.

The thought arrived unbidden, like someone who shows up halfway through a party, drunk on vodka and aching for a fight. But I pushed it away because I couldn't let it in—let it take root—because if I did, every time I fell asleep with my phone in my hand, cycling through the events of that night, I'd nourish it until it sprouted.

Sprouted and grew into a great unwieldy thing that I wouldn't be able to see past.

But the doubt still gnawed at me. "What about her mum, though?"

May didn't have an answer for that one.

So I carried on. "Nico waited until her mum fell asleep, then snuck out to meet me, right?"

May nodded.

"And Nico definitely succeeded in sneaking out because she Snapped me on the bus, didn't she?"

May nodded again.

"So wouldn't her mum have woken up to find Nico gone and *freaked*?"

She didn't nod this time, but her gaze drifted over my shoulder as she considered that.

"Plus, I told you how strict her mum is, didn't I, May?"

That was always Nico's excuse for leaving.

I'd better go or Mum will kill me.

If I miss dinner again, Mum will ground me until I turn thirty.

Then I remembered what she'd said the last time I saw her. Right before she asked me to meet her at our bench.

She went fucking mental about LIPA.

When May looked at me again, she shrugged. "Maybe she left a note?"

"Come on." I tilted my head at her. "If you sneaked out and left a note, what would your mum do?"

She snorted. "Call me and tell me to get my arse home."

"*Exactly*. And even if her mum didn't because she was used to her doing things like that, and, knowing Nico, she probably was, surely she would have panicked when Nico didn't come home?"

May waited for me to catch my breath, then said,

"You don't know. Maybe her mum reported her missing as soon as she realized that she was gone."

That's true.

She could have.

Something still didn't add up, though.

"OK. Maybe she did. But they'd pulled someone matching Nico's description out of the sea that morning. How did *no one* put two and two together and realize it was her? Besides, if her mum reported her missing, she would have given Sussex Police a photo so they would have seen that it was Nico."

The skin between May's eyebrows creased.

I know she probably had Michelle on her shoulder, telling her not to, but she finally agreed with me.

"You're right, Mara. It's weird."

I threw my hands up. "Thank you!"

"Yeah, but what can you do?"

Nothing, I realized as I fell back against the pillows again.

"I know it's frustrating," she said gently, "but you may never know what happened that night. Especially if she's deleted everything and wants to move on."

As soon as she said it, my heart felt hard, like a piece of gum stuck under a desk as I checked Nico's Instagram again to see that it was definitely gone and asked myself if she saw my message before she deleted it.

"So as much as it pains me to say it, Mara, maybe Michelle is right. Maybe you need to move on as well."

14

I wanted to lie in bed and burn at the injustice of it, but May wouldn't let me. She said it would help to get out of the house, so I wept in the shower, then we walked into town. We said hello to every dog we passed and wandered from shop to shop, trying on clothes and testing lipsticks we had no money to buy. Just wasting time because that's all I had. Minutes and hours I let pass over me in my rush to check the day off so I could add it to the tally.

One day was about to become two, then three, then a week, then a month, then what?

I'd be over it?

That was The Plan, I realized, as we stood in that comic-book shop on Sydney Street, May pulling fiercely colored comics from the shelves and telling me about each one as though she was introducing me to her friends.

By the time we left, May with a bagful of manga and me with a graphic novel of *A Wrinkle in Time*, it was dark. There was something kind of comforting about it and I caught myself letting go of a breath as though I'd survived something, each step a little easier as we headed toward Gloucester Street.

Still, I was achingly aware of the weight of my phone in the pocket of my coat, and with that, the entire afternoon's distraction was undone as I reached for it, desperate to find out if there was any word from Nico.

And yes, I know—*I know*—I was supposed to be moving on, but what can I say?

Old habits die hard.

In my defense, Nico had done that before, hadn't she? So I felt that familiar spark of hope when I saw a string of messages, but they were all from Michelle checking that May and I hadn't Thelma and Louise-ed it.

Why aren't you replying? Do I need bail money? her last message asked.

But as I was replying, someone knocked on the window of the Flour Pot Bakery and I jumped.

May jumped as well, then grinned and pointed as someone I didn't recognize waved at her from inside.

I followed her in, and when May threw her arms around them, I knew *exactly* who it was.

May kissed her on the mouth, then turned to me, her cheeks pink with pride. "Mara, this is Chesca."

"Hey," I said with a tight smile, bracing myself for her to look me up and down, then flick her hair.

But Chesca beamed at me. "So nice to finally meet you, Mara! Thanks for having our backs with the others!"

She held her hand up for a high five and I obliged, if not as enthusiastically, as May cheered.

"You guys off somewhere?" she asked, then gestured at the table she was standing beside. "I'm desperate for a distraction from this book I was supposed to read over Christmas but didn't."

"I love Virginia Woolf." I nodded at the copy of *Mrs. Dalloway* next to her half-drunk coffee.

"Me too," she sighed, "but I'll never finish it before English lit tomorrow."

May sat down first, and when Chesca sat next to her, they smiled at one another and I hesitated, sure I was intruding. Then my heart clenched as I asked myself if May had orchestrated the whole thing—saying hello to the dogs, trying on clothes, Dave's Comics—because she was killing time before she met Chesca. But when Chesca asked me what I wanted, May answered for me and she looked so happy—so hopelessly, shockingly happy, the way I must have looked when Nico walked into the café on New Year's Eve—that I knew seeing Chesca was merely a coincidence.

So, I sat down as May unbuttoned her coat. "I'm so glad you're meeting her first, Mara," she told me as she unwound her lime-green scarf, which should have clashed horribly with her orange hair, but didn't. "If the others were with us, I don't know what I would have done. I probably would have run away."

She looked shaken at the thought as she checked her lipstick using the camera in her phone.

When Chesca returned with a tray, May grinned up at her and it was so shameless that it made the corners of my mouth twitch. I had to corral smiles like that when I was with Nico, but there May was, letting Chesca know exactly how pleased she was to see her without worrying about how she'd react.

That was what won me over.

It's not that I particularly *disliked* Chesca—I didn't know her, after all—but I didn't particularly like her, either. Or I didn't like the way she treated May, I should say. So while I didn't let the others go in on her, it was more out of an unspoken agreement May and I had come to after having to constantly defend our relationships.

You have Nico's back and I'll have Chesca's.

But she wasn't what I expected at all. I thought Chesca would be hard work, that she'd be disdainful and detached and would snigger when May told her to get me a hot chocolate and say that hot chocolate was for kids. But she didn't. Nor did she eye me warily, noting my scuffed boots as she tried to see what I was wearing under my coat or ignore me altogether as she slid closer to May, then leaned in and lowered her voice.

She seemed genuinely sweet, actually.

And that's not because she had two mini blackout cakes on her tray.

"Thank you, Mara." She put one of them down in front of me with a mischievous smirk. "We owe you. Anyone who can go up against Michelle Chen and not back down definitely deserves chocolate cake."

I bristled at the dig at Michelle, but she wasn't lying, in fairness.

When she sat down, Chesca's face softened. "May told me about your girlfriend."

My heart missed a beat at *girlfriend*.

No one ever called Nico my girlfriend.

Only Nico.

Always just Nico.

"I'm so sorry," Chesca said with a soft sigh. "I'd be going out of my mind if that was May."

Chesca pushed her plate toward her so May had first pick of the raspberries on the top of the cake, and when they shared another silly smile, it was so intimate that I felt like I was intruding again.

"But when you're ready," Chesca told me, her smile back to being mischievous as she picked off the remaining raspberry and popped it into her mouth, "I have the perfect girl for you."

May pointed at her. "Charlotte?"

"Yes!" She pointed back at her, then at me. "Her mother's an editor at Penguin."

"You know what that means?" May waggled her eyebrows. "Free books."

I smiled, but I certainly wasn't ready to be fixed up.

I didn't tell Michelle when I got home because I knew she'd tell me that going on a date was just what I needed. (Which is why I didn't tell her, isn't it?) But I did tell her how nice Chesca was while Michelle painted her nails and made me watch a Royal Institution Christmas Lecture about the hidden power of maths.

I didn't understand a word of it, but it didn't matter because I knew that Michelle was trying to distract me. And it worked because within fifteen minutes, I could barely keep my eyes open. Then, the next thing I knew, she was telling me to budge as she slid into the bed next to me and turned out the light.

That helped as well, having her there. The last thing I remember was Michelle wriggling around as she contemplated getting out of bed to put on socks. I don't know if she did, because when I opened my eyes again, I could hear the gulls shrieking outside and my mother downstairs, singing along to Aretha Franklin.

I can't believe I slept, but I guess I was so tired that my brain literally surrendered to it. Still, I remember dreaming about Nico again, and when I checked my phone, I held my breath, but there was no word from her.

Maybe she really has moved on.

When I let out a tender sigh, Michelle sat up and launched into the timetable for that day. Breakfast followed by a visit to Kemptown Books. Then we were meeting the others, and instead of pizza and bowling, we were doing sushi and the Queer the Pier exhibition at the Brighton Museum before we had to go home and perform the usual night-before-school rituals.

I was worn out just thinking about it.

But it worked because I didn't think about Nico *all day*.

Except I did, of course.

When I took a photo of a piece of street art Nico and I had nicknamed Jerry.

When Michelle got a text and smiled in a secretive, pleased way that told me it was Lewis.

When we bickered over what to do at the weekend.

And the one after that.

And the one after that.

Because none of them would include Nico anymore.

Then we went home for dinner and afterward we retreated to my room and lay on the floor, listening to Taylor Swift (because if anyone understood what I was going through, it was Taylor Swift) while I read Michelle the opening to chapter twelve of *The Price of Salt*, Highsmith's description of January making us both shiver. Then, as we were sorting out our backpacks and throwing away the black bananas and Christmas cards we'd forgotten to give out, she made me listen to a podcast about vampire squid, or *Vampyroteuthis infernalis*, which translated to *vampire squid from hell*, confirming that we have no business being in the sea.

That made me think about Nico, of course, but when I dreamed about her that night, she was underwater, gauzy and delicate and surrounded by clouds of jellyfish that bobbed and dipped around her as she smiled serenely. She reached out to me and I woke with a gasp, my phone in my hand, but I barely had a moment to register the blow of not hearing from her as my alarm went off and I was forced, headfirst, back into my routine.

It was such a whir that I showered so quickly I almost forgot to wash the conditioner out. Then we were on the top deck of the bus, the taste of cornflakes still on my tongue as Erin applied liquid eyeliner and May told us that if she was sent home for having orange hair, they'd have to send *everyone* with red hair home.

But if I was hoping that going back to school would provide a welcome distraction from thinking about Nico, I was sorely mistaken. Everyone knew. After four years of passing through the corridors relatively unscathed, suddenly everyone knew who I was. People I'd never spoken to before came up to our table in the canteen at lunch and stopped me as I was heading into class to ask if it was true that I knew her.

The girl from the sea.

It was the same at Viviana's sixteenth. I spent most of it being followed from room to room, flanked by Michelle and the others as they told everyone to get a grip. But as the evening wore on, emboldened by beer and whatever spirits they'd managed to persuade their older siblings to buy for them, it became unbearable.

Mercifully, by the time the party was winding down, they'd forgotten about me—and Nico—because some girl in our year I'd never spoken to shagged some guy in our year I'd never spoken to, and everyone moved on.

Still, that first week was brutal. It was a completely different ache than anything I'd felt before. Different from the way I missed Nico when I hadn't heard from her before. It was just as bewildering, though. Bewildering and exhausting and convincing enough to make me feel like I was unraveling.

Like I was coming apart at the seams.

So, a couple of weeks later, when May mentioned fixing me up with Charlotte again, she was smart enough to do it in front of Michelle, so I had no choice but to acquiesce.

It was a double date—May and Chesca and me and Charlotte—which sounded excruciating. But it was only a coffee at that café on Sydney Street, so it wouldn't be too intimidating, Michelle told me as she helped me get ready and tried to get my hair to bend to her will.

She was right. Charlotte was sweet. Easy. Open. Exactly as I'd pictured. A clear-skinned, shiny-haired Brighton College girl who, much like May, always spoke like she was about to start laughing.

The following Saturday, the four of us went out again. Bowling this time. Charlotte and I won, which she celebrated by throwing her arms around me and holding me so close that I could smell her perfume. A smell that would usually be new and promising, but was so strange—so unfamiliar—it made my heart recoil in my chest.

Then she walked me to the bus stop, and when we saw the number twenty-one coming, she pulled me into a kiss so sudden that it should have swept me off my feet. But I didn't feel a thing, even when she slipped her hands into the back pockets of my jeans. Now I think about it, it felt like the first—and only time—I kissed a boy. Damian Kennedy at Erin's fourteenth birthday party. But it didn't feel right, even though it should have.

I didn't know why with Damian, but I did with Charlotte.

Still, I tried.

I really did.

We went out several times, just the two of us. Drank coffee and talked about books and school. She told me about her family, her two sisters and two brothers—born either side of her, so she was in the middle—and the girl who broke her heart the year before. And every time she kissed me, I kissed her back and waited for a feeling that never came. Even though she'd booked tickets to an adaptation of *Noughts + Crosses* that she knew I wanted to see and talked about spending the summer at her parents' house in the south of France.

Even though it was simple.

Quiet.

Perfect.

Everything I'd ever wanted.

Everything I'd never had with Nico.

But, in the end, it wasn't what I wanted at all.

So, I stopped replying.

And Charlotte stopped trying.

And that was it.

I don't remember much about the period that followed, just telling myself to be patient, because if something shifted the morning they fished Nico out of the sea, then surely it would shift back again. As though all we ever were was a temporary imbalance in the universe that would correct itself eventually.

So, I went back to my routine.

Running for the bus every morning.

Homework on Sunday nights.

Fish and chips on Fridays.

Michelle had even started talking about Lewis again. To be honest, after everything that happened, I hadn't noticed that he hadn't been around. But then it was as though Michelle felt able to say his name again and I could feel something forcing itself back into place. He was by her side at Louise's sixteenth, and then she invited him to Lunar New Year. While it was strange to have this tall, blond-haired cuckoo among us, I was happy.

Happy that Michelle had the relationship she deserved.

By March, we were still waiting for winter to surrender to spring, but it was defiant. All I remember is weeks of stiff fingers and chapped lips and air so sharp it would snatch your breath as soon as you walked outside. The days were dark, the nights darker. And the rain. Not nice rain—rain to dance in or run through and be caught in a breathless Hollywood kiss—but the sort of rain that stripped the paint from bicycles. Storm after storm after storm. So many that we stopped watching them from James and Nicole's bedroom window.

But by the end of March, something finally settled and the fragility of winter returned with its sugared pavements and lacy cobwebs. Then everything felt cold and bright and clean. I remember how *new* Brighton looked, and with that last gasp, winter finally surrendered and spring was here, full-throated and glorious.

I can't recall a spring so loud, the sky so clear, the daffodils so yellow, the trees heavy with great clouds of blossom that dusted the pavements with tiny pink petals, as though everything was desperate to live. After months of going straight home from school and spending the weekend under a blanket on the sofa, I wanted to be outside again. I could hear it calling to me. Beckoning. This long green finger uncurling and saying, *Come closer*.

Because I'd done it.

I'd survived.

That's how it felt as I stood in the queue outside Pompoko that first Friday evening in April. It was the first Friday in *weeks* that Michelle and I weren't side by side in bed pointing sticks of Pocky at one another—strawberry for her, chocolate for me—and bickering about how I couldn't spend another weekend wallowing in my room. I wasn't wallowing, I told her, but she wouldn't let it go. So there we were, outside Pompoko, because Michelle knew that if there was anything that was going to get me out of the house, it was sesame tofu donburi.

I'd never admit this to Michelle, but I'm kind of glad because I'd emerged from my cocoon of books and blankets to find that Brighton was alive again and was as loud as it ever was.

Now the weather was finally welcoming enough to be outside for more than a few minutes, it was as though everyone had come out at once. Town was *heaving* and the sound of it—the laughing and teasing and arguing over where to go next—rekindled something in me, and for the first time since it had all happened, my breath was steady.

Easy.

"Excuse me," Michelle said, poking me in the side.

I looked at her as she slipped her phone into the pocket of her denim jacket.

"Come back, please," she told me when I did. "You're in your head again."

"I am?"

"You're missing it."

"Missing what?" I asked, looking around at the building Friday night chaos as a car rolled past, Beyoncé's "Single Ladies" blaring, which made the bachelorette party across the road shriek, *"Not for long!"*

"*Everything*," Michelle said when I looked back at her. "It's the Easter holidays, Mara."

"I know."

"Our GCSEs start *next month*," she carried on as if I hadn't said anything.

"Don't remind me," I told her with an exaggerated huff as I crossed my arms. "I can't believe I have to sit history on my sixteenth birthday. That should be illegal, or something. Or an automatic nine, at least."

Michelle looked equally pained. "I have biology on mine."

"You love biology, though."

"Still, I'd rather not sit an exam on my birthday. It's not fair. Erin and Louise got to have parties and what are we doing? Revising. At least May's is after our GCSEs."

I uncrossed my arms and hooked my right one through hers, pulling her to me. "Yeah, but we're all going camping, aren't we?" I reminded her. "What's Louise calling it? Our Super Sixteen?"

"That's true," she said, but it still wasn't enough to puncture her pout.

"It'll be here before you know it, babe."

Michelle's eyes widened at that. "Exactly! In a couple of months, it'll all be over and it'll be summer."

I was glad she didn't say our *last* summer. Louise and May were going to different colleges, not countries, so I don't know why it felt like they were moving to Australia and we'd never see them again.

"Hey." Michelle tugged on my arm until I looked at her again. "I don't want you messing up your GCSEs because of her."

Her being Nico, of course.

"Listen." Michelle tugged on my arm when I looked away again. "I get it, Mara."

"Do you?" I asked.

She laughed. "Actually, I don't."

At least she was honest about it.

"I don't either." I shrugged. "I mean, I get that Nico survived this horrible, traumatic thing and she's clearly keen to move on if she's deleted all her socials, but she could at least let me know that she's OK."

"Yes, she could," Michelle conceded with a sharp huff. "It's cruel."

At least she admitted it was cruel.

"I don't understand why she hasn't been in touch, Mara. But then, I've never understood Nico."

I thought I did, I remember thinking, my heart sagging.

"But it's been *three months*, Mara. At some point you have to ask yourself what you're mourning: the relationship you wanted or the one you actually had. Because the one you had isn't worth mourning."

She said it coolly, but I felt the burn of each word against my cheeks.

It's taken almost a year to be able to name what I felt in that moment, but I know now that I wasn't mourning the relationship I wanted. I was mourning the injustice of Nico and me not getting an ending.

Perhaps if it had been my decision, if I'd had the courage to say, *I want more than this*, I could have made my peace with it. But I had two choices: I could either continue wading in the shallows, telling myself how unfair it was. Or I could head out for the open sea and be free.

Thinking about it now, maybe *that's* what I was really mourning. That Nico and I never made it out of the shallows.

Michelle tugged my arm again. "You need to try something new to force yourself out of this funk."

"I'm not in a funk."

I'm heartbroken.

"Come see *Murder Cabin 4* tomorrow night," she said with an eagerness that concerned me.

"Absolutely not."

"Why not?"

"Because I'll *hate* it."

Horror films were her thing with Louise. Erin, May, and I *never* went with them. Sometimes we'd go bowling while we waited for them to be done because it was across from the cinema, but most of the time we'd hang out in May's room, helping her dye her hair while Erin made us watch videos of people removing blackheads.

Monster blackheads were my limit, so going to see *Murder Cabin 4* was out of the question.

"Come on, Mara!" Michelle bounced with excitement. "Take a risk. Try something new. It might help."

Mercifully, before she badgered me until I surrendered, May appeared.

"Oh good. I'm not late," she said, out of breath.

As soon as she saw her, Michelle let go of my arm and pulled her phone out of her jacket pocket.

"You're *seventeen* minutes late, actually," she snapped, holding the screen up to May.

But she just gestured at the queue as if to say, *But you haven't even got a table yet*, which made Michelle even more cross as she looked around and asked, "Where are Erin and Louise?"

As if on cue, they ran across the road, already raucous.

"Someone just tried to come on to both of us *at the same time!*" Louise cackled.

Michelle looked appalled. "Where?"

"Outside the Mash Tun," they said in unison.

Then Erin added, "They said that they'd always wanted to try a chocolate-and-vanilla swirl!"

She pretended to gag and I pulled a *Yikes* face at Michelle, who mock shuddered.

"Ew!" She cringed, her mood forgotten as someone appeared in the doorway of the restaurant.

"Michelle?" they called out. "Table of five?"

She stuck her hand up. "That's us!"

Pompoko is already tiny, but it felt impossibly so that night, the five of us giggling and apologizing as we slid between the crowded tables until we reached one in the corner that was barely big enough for four, let alone five. Still, we squeezed around it, our knees touching as I picked up a menu.

"I think I'm going to get the vegetable yakimeshi," I announced after a few minutes.

Everyone looked up from their menus and stared at me.

Erin looked particularly concerned. "But you always get the sesame tofu donburi, Mara."

"Always," May echoed with a frown.

"I know. But it's time to try something new."

Michelle nodded at me with a proud smile, then looked back down at her menu.

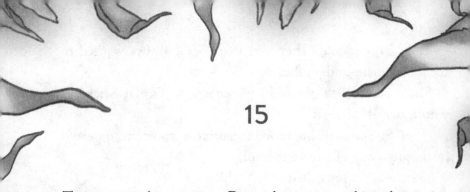

15

Trying something new at Pompoko was one thing, but going to see *Murder Cabin 4* with Michelle and Louise was quite another, but in the spirit of trying new things, I agreed. After all, the vegetable yakimeshi was lush and, that morning, I'd finally honored at least *one* of my new year's intentions by helping my father with the prep for that evening's Brighton Soup Run. So, I felt pretty good as I walked along the beach to meet Michelle and Louise.

It was as though I'd hit a reset button that deleted the last nine months and I'd gone back to before.

Before Nico.

Thinking about it now, it kind of felt like coming home after being away for a few weeks. Everything foreign and familiar, all at once. The sound of the gulls and the smell of the sea and the push and pull of the waves.

Pounce.

Recede.

Pounce.

Recede.

Pounce.

Recede.

Like a metronome my lungs were keeping time with.

I'd missed that. Missed spending the weekend with my friends instead of under the blanket on the sofa with a book that took me far, far away from everything. It was as though I was returning to myself, to that quiet life I used to think was too quiet until all of this happened and it made me ask myself if there was something to be said for quiet. Steady. Real. For friends who were actually *there* and were never more than a text away.

That was the moment, I know now, that something finally realigned and I realized that just because I'd never have the big, loud life I wanted with Nico, I still wanted my old one.

The moment I decided to take it back.

So when Michelle messaged to say that she and Louise were running late, I didn't care because they're always late and I'm always early and that's how it always was. It was almost comforting. Normal.

But it did mean that I had half an hour to kill. Usually, I would have continued on to the marina, grabbed a hot chocolate from the café at the cinema, and finished reading my mother's battered copy of *Just Kids* while I waited. But as I was passing the mini golf course, I remembered that the café had a rooftop terrace.

It was almost six o'clock on a Saturday evening and the day had started to dim, so I have no idea why it was so busy. At least a dozen kids were screaming as they chased one another around the playground next to the mini golf course with the sort of abandon that kids should run back and forth with.

As I waited for my hot chocolate, I could hear their parents trying to gather them up to take them home, but each time they did, they'd run off and refuse to come back, the same way Michelle and I did when we were their age. I don't remember screaming as much—although, I'm sure we did—but I do remember the competitions Michelle and I would have to see how long we could hang upside down from the monkey bars as we waved at everyone on the little burgundy-and-yellow train each time it passed back and forth from Black Rock station.

Mercifully, when I went up to the rooftop, it was much quieter, all the tables empty except for someone in the far corner who was scrolling through their phone as a golden retriever dozed at their feet. So, I headed for one nearest the sea, hoping that my hot chocolate would take the edge off the sharp breeze.

The sea was louder there. Nearer. Soon it would be as still as bathwater, then summer would be here and it would be over. GCSEs. The five us huddled around our table in the library, trying not to laugh too loudly in case Jo, the librarian, told us off as we teased May and rolled our eyes at Louise and all those other things we did every day at school that we didn't even think about but would never do again once summer came.

So I told myself to savor it, the steady sound of the sea and the taste of salt on my tongue. Because in half an hour, I'd be sharing my popcorn with Michelle and shushing Louise as she talked through the film, like it would always be that way, even though I knew we couldn't avoid the inevitability barreling toward us.

But while I was expecting that change, I didn't see the one that was about to knock me off course as I saw a purple leather notebook on the table I was about to sit at. I picked it up and turned it over, but there was nothing to say who it belonged to. So, I opened the cover to the first page, but there was no name, just the words *I WILL BE MYSELF AGAIN* written neatly in the center. Whoever was sitting at the table before me had obviously left it behind, but before I could decide what to do with it, I heard a voice behind me say, "Sorry, that's mine." And it was as though a wave had risen up over the pebbles, crashed over the railing of the café and struck me head-on. I swear I could taste the seawater in my mouth as I turned around and there she was.

Nico.

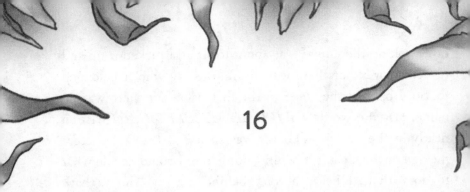

16

I think about that moment all the time, about how impossible it was. My cheeks are warm just thinking about it because if I wasn't early or Michelle and Louise weren't late or if I'd carried on to the marina and not stopped there, at that café at that time, I would have missed her and what happened next might never have happened. How many people live in Brighton? Yet there she was and there I was at the same place at the same time.

That had to mean something.

Not that my brain was able to register any of that as everything went blurry, as though it was restarting, checking that it really was her and that I wasn't seeing her because of all the people I wanted to see, it was her.

Then everything came back in a sudden, dazzling rush. I could hear the gulls wheeling over our heads again, hear the slap of the sea and the horn on the train as it rattled past on its way to the pier, which made the kids shriek with delight in the playground beneath us.

And I remember feeling lightheaded as her voice rekindled something in my chest that had been dwindling and was now suddenly ablaze again.

Nico.

She looked the same, but she didn't. She was vampirically pale, her hair longer and her cheekbones sharper. And she was wearing a pink coat. The same pink Michelle paints her nails. The same pink as the cashmere scarf wrapped around her neck that looked so soft, I had to tell myself not to reach out and touch it.

Looking back on it now, it wasn't cold enough for a scarf, so I have no idea why she was wearing it. But I didn't think about that at the time. All I remember thinking was that Nico never wore pink. Never. She'd smear on a bold hot-pink lipstick sometimes when she was feeling restless and she had that red-and-black-striped sweater that she was wearing on New Year's Eve, but that was the only color I'd ever seen her in. No, Nico only wore black because rock stars wore black and she was going to be the next Joan Jett, wasn't she?

I'm pretty sure Joan Jett doesn't wear pink.

The budding pressure in my temples bloomed at that, so suddenly that my eyes lost focus as the questions that had been warring in my head since I saw her photo on the news were suddenly back and louder than ever. But when I swatted them away as I tried to catch my breath, I was left with a single, thrilling thought.

You're back.

Then I was weak with relief as I made myself meet her gaze. Her eyes were as dark as I remembered, but they'd lost their sparkle, like the sea that first rainy day of October when winter becomes more than a mere promise. I could feel the weight of her name on my tongue as I searched her face for any indication that she was pleased to see me. For the corners of her mouth to twitch or her brow to relax or her cheeks to pinken slightly.

But like that morning outside the station—when I was with Michelle—there was nothing.

So I just stood there, clutching her notebook to my chest, the urge to close the distance between us as urgent as the warning that followed. The voice in my head I heard every time I was near her that told me to be cool.

Not to spook her.

Nico, it's me, I wanted to yell as I waited for her to gasp and pull me into her arms.

I'd imagined that moment so many times. Usually at night, when it was just me and the rain—that endless, relentless rain—and I could hear the thunder closing in. Because I *knew* it would happen. I knew the universe would steer us back onto the same path eventually.

And it did.

I felt my heart again then, a drum roll of suspense as I waited for her to say something.

To apologize.

To explain.

To tell me that she was going to call.

That she'd missed me.

But she didn't say a word. She just held her hand out to me.

I looked down at it, at her pink, padded palm and her skin stretched tight over the pearls of her knuckles, and my fingers fluttered, as though it knew before I did that she was going to reach for me, like she had in the café on New Year's Eve.

Reach for my hand and kiss it, then hold it to her warm cheek as she told me how sorry she was.

But she just said, "Thank you for finding my journal."

"Oh," I murmured, uncrossing my arms and handing it to her. "Sorry."

When she took the notebook from me, the tips of our fingers grazed—just once, just for a second—but it was enough to make my heart hysterical. My gaze flicked back up to hers, expecting her cheeks to look as hot as mine felt, but her face was perfectly still. And it wasn't that unimpressed, indifferent look she used to get when she'd pick at her nail polish while I was talking, but her face was still in the purest sense of the word.

There was nothing.

Absolutely nothing.

But before I could ask her why she was being like that—why she was pretending that I was just a stranger who'd found her notebook—it hit me like a kick to the back of the legs that almost made me sink to my knees.

She still can't remember.

I took a step toward her, her name filling my mouth, making it impossible to catch my breath, but before I could say it—say, *Nico, it's me*—I heard someone call her name.

She turned to look at the stairs down to the café, and when she turned back, she flashed me the briefest, sweetest smile. "Got to go."

Then she walked away.

And it hurt more than the last time she did it.

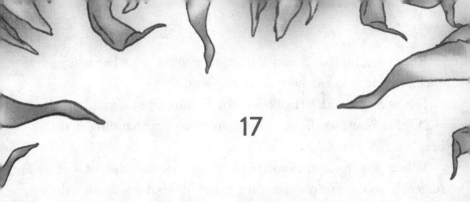

17

By the time I got to the cinema, Michelle was frantic.

"Mara! Where have you been? I've been calling and calling you!" She frowned fiercely when I found her and Louise in the queue for popcorn. She had a bottle of Cherry Coke in each hand and she looked so mad that I took a step back, sure that she was going to hurl them at me. "I've been so worried! You're never late!"

"That's one good thing about you being pathologically punctual," Louise told me as she stepped aside to let the person in front of her past with their nachos. "If you're ever kidnapped, we can say to the police"—she put on a worried face, her voice high with mock panic—"*This isn't like her, officer. She's never late.*"

"Can we stop talking about Mara being kidnapped, please?" Michelle barked as Louise stepped up to the counter to order her popcorn. Then she turned back to me, her face still tight with worry. "What happened?"

I was too stunned to soften the blow, so I just said it. "I saw Nico."

"What?" Louise literally *roared*, turning toward us so suddenly that she showered us with popcorn.

Not that Michelle and I even noticed as we stared at one another.

"You are lying!" Louise told me, shaking the half-empty paper bag at me.

Michelle raised her hands to shush her and I thought she was going to throw the bottles of Cherry Coke at her this time, but she glared at me. "What do you mean *you saw Nico?*"

When I stopped to catch my breath, Louise turned back to the counter. "I'm going to need more popcorn."

The person behind it hesitated, then sighed heavily as they clearly concluded that they didn't earn enough to argue and topped up the bag and handed it back to Louise with a look that said, *Now go away.*

So we stepped out of the queue and headed to the self-service ticket machines.

Michelle stared at me again. "Mara, what the hell happened?"

I didn't know how else to say it, so I said it again. "I saw Nico."

"Where?"

"At the café by the mini golf course."

"The one by the playground we used to go to?"

I nodded.

"Why were you *there?*"

"You were late and I was early, so I decided to get a hot chocolate and—"

"Hey!" Louise interrupted with a mouthful of popcorn. "Does any of this matter? Get to Nico!"

"You're right," Michelle conceded, closing her eyes and shaking her head. When she opened them again, she nodded at me to go on. "So, you were at the café by the mini golf course. Then what happened?"

I tucked my hair behind my ears and sucked in a breath, hoping it would make me feel a bit steadier.

But it didn't.

Michelle must have noticed because she put the bottles of Cherry Coke on top of the ticket machine that we were standing by, then put her hands on my shoulders and squeezed them.

When she nodded, I nodded back.

"OK. So, I went upstairs, and when I went to sit at one of the tables, I found a notebook."

"Nico's notebook?" Louise gasped as she shoved another handful of popcorn into her mouth.

"Let Mara tell us, will you?" Michelle hissed.

I was still too stunned for suspense, though, so I just said, "Yeah. Nico's notebook."

They gasped and looked at one another, then back at me.

"And it was *definitely* Nico?" Michelle asked, her eyes wide.

"Definitely," I insisted, but I didn't sound as sure when I added, "At least, I think so."

"You *think* so?"

"No, it was definitely her"—I shook my head—"but it wasn't."

"What do you mean?"

"I can't describe it. She was wearing pink."

"*Pink?*" Michelle looked slightly unsettled by that and it made me feel better because I was right.

It was strange.

"Yeah, this pink coat and pink scarf. The sort of thing you'd wear to visit your grandparents." Something nudged at me then. "You know who she reminded me of? Remember Francesca Tate?"

Francesca Tate was a shiny-haired Alpha Course Christian who was the love of my life in Year Nine.

"How could I forget?" she groaned, letting go of my shoulders to cross her arms.

"You know how you always say it's all an act with Nico," I reminded Michelle. "Like she's cosplaying an Alternative Brighton Teenager. Well, now she looks like she's cosplaying Francesca Tate."

Michelle shuddered, but Louise asked the one question I didn't want to answer. "What did she say?" Their eyebrows rose as they waited for me to answer, then rose even higher when I shook my head.

"She didn't recognize me."

"She didn't recognize you?" they said at once.

Actually, Michelle said it.

Louise *shrieked*.

But then Michelle tilted her head at me, her gaze narrowing. "Are you sure she wasn't just pretending not to know you because she's embarrassed that she hasn't been in touch?"

"Michelle, there was nothing." I pointed at my face. "Nada. Not even a flicker."

Louise shrugged, then looked between us. "Well, they said on the news that she couldn't remember who she was or how she got in the sea."

I shrugged back. "I figured that was temporary. I mean, they discharged her, what, *the next day*?"

Michelle blinked at me. "Why didn't you tell her who you were, then?"

"I couldn't." I tried—and no doubt failed—not to sound defensive. "It all happened so quickly."

To my surprise, Louise said, "She couldn't, could she?" When we frowned, she added, "What was she supposed to say? *Hi, I'm Mara. You used to put your tongue in my mouth sometimes, but then you dumped me.*"

"Louise!" Michelle snapped, uncrossing her arms to slap her.

But she just shrugged as if to say, *What? It's true.*

Michelle hissed at her again, then turned back to me.

"She's right, though," she admitted with a huff.

"What do you mean?"

"Nico broke up with you, Mara." She said it gently, but it still hurt like hell. "Not remembering who you are doesn't change that. If she hadn't fallen in the sea, then you probably wouldn't have seen each other anyway."

"So what do I do now?" I asked.

And for the first time in her life, Michelle said, "I don't know."

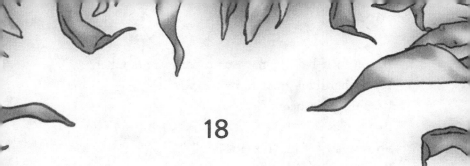

18

"So that's it?" I asked half an hour later, when Louise had summoned everyone, *Murder Cabin 4* forgotten as we sat in the tiny Starbucks inside the cinema and I ignored the hot chocolate Michelle kept telling me to drink.

But they didn't answer. They just looked at one another, then at Michelle, obviously hoping that she'd know what to say, but she didn't. And I remember slumping in my chair because at least before I had *some* hope. I just needed to turn the right corner or get off the right bus at the right time and there Nico would be.

And it happened. The stars aligned, or fate intervened, or maybe it was just pure, unrepeatable luck, but I went to the right café at the right time and there she was. She was there and I was there, in the same place at the same time, and that was supposed to mean something.

Michelle slipped her arm around my shoulders and said, "I'm so sorry, Mara."

But I heard what she didn't say.

What even she couldn't say.

It's over.

I felt something kick in me at that and I almost said, *Maybe if I tell her who I am, she'll remember.*

But even if I did, what was there to remember?

It was hardly a great romance, was it?

It could have been.

But it wasn't.

So instead I said, "It's not fair."

It was over.

Really over.

It wasn't like before, when Nico would disappear, only to return a week later like nothing had happened. So, there was no point waiting for her to sweep into the café one Saturday, my heart hiccupping as she ordered a latte and asked me if I wanted to go for a walk. Or to look for her when I walked out of school, hoping to find her leaning against the wall with a slow smile. No point falling asleep with my phone in my hand, because there wasn't going to be a 2 a.m. text to ask if I was up, which would prompt a slow slide back to whatever we were.

There would be none of that because it had been *months* and she still couldn't remember, so perhaps she never would. Perhaps she fell in the sea that morning and, by the time those fishermen fished her out, everything had been washed clean. Everything we were now at the bottom of the sea with all the other treasure.

We'd always be an unfinished story. A book I'd started, then put down and never picked up again. She'd just be someone I thought about sometimes. At night, when it was raining and the thunder was closing in. Or in thirty years, when I was lying next to someone else, beneath bed linen we'd picked out together.

The injustice of it was *searing*.

All of those books about the misery and magic of love and not one of them ended like that.

With being forgotten.

19

So, I went back to my routine.

Again.

Running for the bus every morning.

Homework on Sunday nights.

Fish and chips on Fridays, followed by Pocky and a K-drama with Michelle.

Easter came and went and then we were back at school. Back to sitting around our table at the library. Much like our table in the canteen, it wasn't actually ours. We'd claimed it our first day of school because it was in the corner by the encyclopedias where no one had cause to go. We sat there every day, each one bookended by meeting there before the first bell and after the last one to trade gossip and commiserate over whatever grisly tragedy had befallen us. Another casually cruel comment in the corridor. Another fruitless crush. Another essay. Another time we'd been caught with our phone in class and had it taken away.

We'd decided everything at that table. What GCSEs we were taking. What colleges we were going to. Which of our classmates' misdemeanors to forgive and which we would brood over for weeks. It was the table we'd sat at with that heavy old atlas in Year Seven, pointing out Tongzhou, where

Michelle's grandparents are from, and Vrindavan, where my grandparents are from, and Lagos, where Erin's grandparents are from.

The table we were going to carve our initials beneath on the last day of school. The table where I read that Nina LaCour novel the librarian, Jo, had added to the pile I'd concluded was enough to see me through spring half term in Year Nine. I was so intrigued by why she wanted me to read it that I started it on the bus home and my whole world immediately felt much, much bigger. The table where Michelle explained osmosis to us and tried to explain string theory and told us about Marie Curie and Mae C. Jemison and Jane Cooke Wright and Einstein's first wife, Mileva Marić, who was never given proper credit for the work they did together.

The rectangular wooden ship we'd navigated the tumultuous seas of adolescence. First love. First loss. The truly *hideous* layers I got in Year Eight that could not be contained by mere bobby pins. That time Jo caught Louise reading out the dirty bits from *Forever* by Judy Blume and we were mortified. The time Erin asked us to call her Erin. The day May's father left and she said that she didn't care, then cried until she couldn't breathe.

"I've been thinking," I told them the Monday we went back to school. When they looked up from their biology notes, I lowered my voice. "About Nico. About why she can't remember."

I felt Michelle stiffen beside me, but I had to say it.

"They said in *The Argus* that she hadn't suffered any major injuries, right?"

They looked around the table at one another, then nodded at me.

Everyone but Michelle, who I could feel watching me, her pen tapping on the page of her notebook.

"So if Nico doesn't remember me, then maybe she has amnesia. I've been researching it."

I felt Michelle flinch and I know what she was thinking. Our GCSEs started in less than a month, but instead of staying up all night mastering the binomial system of naming species or trying to remember who Edward the Confessor had promised the throne to, I was searching for a reason why Nico didn't remember me.

"I don't know how extensive her memory loss is," I persisted, even though I'm pretty sure I could hear Michelle's teeth grinding in her effort not to yell at me in the middle of the library. "But amnesia isn't like it is in the movies. People don't just forget *everything*. They still remember some stuff." I leaned in and everyone else around the table did the same. Even Michelle. "So, maybe Nico has dissociative amnesia."

"What's that?" May whispered.

But before I could tell her, Michelle sat back and said, "It's usually a response to trauma. So, in order to forget whatever happened that led up to her ending up in the sea, Nico is blocking everything else out as well."

"Trauma?" Erin frowned. "So you think it was more than just her getting wasted and falling off the pier?"

Then Michelle said, "Well, falling in the sea and having to be rescued is pretty traumatic, isn't it?"

My jaw tightened because I know Michelle, so I knew what she was doing.

She was trying to control the conversation before I got carried away.

Before I got my hopes up.

Looking back on it now, though, she was trying to protect me, wasn't she? But I was so distracted—so desperate—to find some pearl of hope to keep me going, I couldn't see that. And you know what? I can't blame Michelle for not wanting me to rekindle a relationship with someone who acted like they didn't want to know me even when they could remember me. Plus, our GCSEs were about to start, and there I was, up all night reading articles about profound retrograde amnesia following mild head injuries.

"Will Nico ever remember?" Erin asked, her frown deepening.

"She just needs a trigger," I told her. "Something that will bring her back."

Michelle started to say something, but Louise gasped. "I saw a film about that!" When we turned to look at her, she lowered her voice, her eyes bright, the way they used to when we were kids and she'd tell us about Bloody Mary and Slender Man and all the other creepypasta stories she'd scare us senseless with at sleepovers. "It was about this woman who was in a car accident. She was in a coma for, like, three years, but when she woke up, she couldn't remember *anything*. I mean, she knew how to walk and talk and stuff, but *who* she was had gone."

Like Nico, I remember thinking, even though I knew amnesia wasn't like it was in films.

Still, I leaned in.

We all did as Louise's eyebrows rose. "She couldn't remember her name, how old she was, where she lived, where she worked. *Nothing*. But then, when she was leaving the hospital, they gave her a bag with her personal effects, and when she saw her horseshoe key ring, it all came back to her. Just like that."

Louise snapped her fingers and everyone around the table jumped.

Everyone except me as I sat back in my chair and let go of a breath, suddenly weak with relief.

To my surprise, Michelle turned to me and smiled. "See? Nico just needs to find her horseshoe key ring."

And I smiled back because I *know* she didn't want to say that.

I *know* it went against all reason and logic and all the other things that were telling her not to say it.

But if there's one thing Michelle values more than reason and logic, it's me, and she knew I needed it.

So she threw me a lifeline and I grabbed it with both hands.

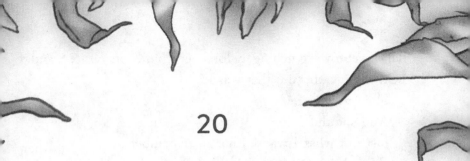

20

It worked.

Later that week, I added something new to my routine.

Studying at Jubilee Library on Saturdays.

The library happened to be next to the café Nico and I got coffee on our first not-date. So each time I went past, I would linger on the pavement outside, hoping to see her.

That's what I was doing that third Saturday in April, two weeks to the day since I'd seen her at the beach. I don't know why it matters that it had been two weeks, but I will say that it felt like much longer. Anyway, I'd just left the library after spending the day trying to decipher my history notes and the café was about to close, so it was empty except for a few stragglers who were finishing their coffees and gathering up their shopping bags.

My heart stung as I watched them and wondered if that's how it would always be. Me, standing on the pavement every time I went past, hoping to see her and burning with the pain and promise that one day I might.

But as I turned away from the window, there she was.

Nico.

In her pink coat and pink scarf.

As soon as she saw me, she stopped, the skin between her

dark eyebrows pinching before her confusion cleared and I held my breath, sure that was it.

She *remembered*.

And she did.

Just not what I wanted her to remember.

"Hey! You're the one who found my notebook."

I nodded and tried to smile back as she tilted her head at me and asked, "You didn't read it, did you?"

"Of course not," I told her with a gasp.

But then my face flushed as I remembered that I hadn't read it, but I had opened it, hadn't I?

I WILL BE MYSELF AGAIN.

She just chuckled, though, and it was a sound I'd never heard before.

Soft.

Light.

The sound her pink scarf would make if it had a voice.

And it was lovely, but it didn't sound like her.

"Well, I'm glad you didn't read it. Those are my plans for world domination," she told me, the corners of her mouth twitching as her eyes lit up, the sparkle suddenly back in full, unavoidable force.

And the shock—and thrill—of it was enough to tug on the corners of my mouth as well as I said, "In that case, I did read it. The monkey thing?" I shook my head and pulled a face. "It'll never work."

She stared at me for a moment, her lips parted, then threw her head back and laughed.

Really *laughed*, this time.

As soon as I heard the sound fly out of her mouth, I recognized it.

It was the way she used to laugh when we first met.

That big, loud, conversation-stopping laugh.

The sort of laugh that made people look over and smile.

"I'm Nico, by the way."

As soon as she said her name, I shivered. But it wasn't like the first time we met that morning in June outside the station when I'd waited for her to finish, then went up to her while she was putting away her guitar. That time she said her name with a slight sneer, all smudged eyeliner and chipped black nail varnish as she handed me a *nicosings* sticker. A sticker I still have and is now stuck to the front page of this notebook I'm writing in.

No, that day in April, it sounded brand new.

Like a door opening.

"I'm Mara," I told her. "Mara Malakar."

I made sure I told her my surname as well, hoping that it would register.

That she would remember that morning in June outside Brighton station.

Remember all of it.

Any of it.

But there was nothing.

She just asked, "How's it going?"

"Good." I shrugged, but given how heavy my shoulders suddenly felt, it was a Herculean effort. "You?"

"I'm great." She stopped to grin at me and it was dazzling. Devastating. "What are you doing?"

I thumbed over my shoulder at the library. "I was just revising."

"Sorry, I mean, what are you doing *now*?"

That threw me. "Now?"

"Yeah."

I panicked.

That was one thing that hadn't changed. Before, when Nico asked me what I was doing, I always had to fight the urge to lie. Tell her that I was meeting friends on the beach to get drunk on Blue Pineapple & Kiwi Dragon Soop before we headed to CHALK to see a band I knew she'd love.

Now I think about it, it's kind of sad because I really wanted to be that person. The sort of person who went to gigs at CHALK. The sort of person who caught her off guard instead of the other way around. Even though Nico would never have said, *That sounds cool. Can I tag along?* Because she wasn't the tag-along type.

She had this energy. Even when she was standing still, she seemed in perpetual motion, like the clouds and the gulls and the sea. Moving. Always moving. Like she had no idea where she was supposed to be, it just wasn't there.

I guess all I ever wanted was for where she was supposed to be, and where I was, to be the same place.

But that day when she asked me what I was doing, I was too stunned to lie and said, "Nothing."

She nodded, and when the corners of her mouth twitched with mischief, I saw her again.

The old Nico.

"OK," she said, her cheeks a little pinker as I felt my own

warm. "You're going to think I'm a complete weirdo, Mara, but that's OK because I am a bit weird and you should probably know that now." She stopped to chuckle, that light, baby-pink chuckle I was still getting used to. "I mean, normal is overrated, right?"

That made my head—and heart—spin because that's what she used to say.

Normal is overrated.

So I was so startled that it didn't register when she asked, "Do you fancy grabbing a coffee?"

I don't know what I said (I'm pretty sure I just grunted) as she nodded at the café—*our* café—and I followed her gaze, looking at it, then back at her as I asked myself if I was actually hearing what I was hearing or if it was just some cruel trick my mind was playing on me. But then I saw the hopeful look on her face and the doubt that pinched at the skin between her eyebrows as I hesitated as though she thought I was going to say no.

As though I could ever say no to her.

"I know we've only met once for, like, two seconds," she said, and I know now that was my chance, wasn't it? My chance to correct her—to tell her the truth—but all I remember thinking is *She sounds nervous.*

Unsure.

If there was one word I would *never* use to describe Nico it was unsure.

It scared as much as startled me because it was her—it was definitely her—but it wasn't. And I don't just mean the pink coat and the pink scarf, but *everything*, from the crease of doubt between her eyebrows to the way her voice faltered. That wasn't Nico. Nico was nothing but bullshit and swagger, to quote Michelle. She was more than that to me, of course, but whatever you thought of her, she certainly knew what she wanted.

I'd always envied that.

But there she was, fidgeting and flustered as she said, "Do you know who I am?"

I nodded warily.

"Well, if you know who I am, then you know what happened to me. So you'll believe me when I say that I haven't seen anyone other than my mum or my therapist for *four and a half months*. I've just come out of group therapy, in fact, so it would be good to talk about something, *anything*, else."

"Sure," I said with a nod that was almost certainly too enthusiastic because I couldn't believe it.

If I'd left the library two minutes later, I would have missed her.

Two tiny minutes and we might never have had that.

A second chance.

So with hindsight, I probably should rewrite that moment so I said something more memorable—more worthy of committing to paper—than *Sure*. But it doesn't matter what I said, just that I said *yes*. Besides, if you haven't already gathered, I'm much better at writing things down than saying them out loud.

"Really?" Nico looked so thrilled that it took me a moment to recover as she reached for the door.

"Sorry, guys. We're closed," Kyle said from behind the

counter as we walked in and I felt Nico's energy dip as my heart did the same. But then he looked up, and when he saw it was me, he smiled. "Oh hey, Mara!"

"Hey, Kyle."

"I didn't know it was you. Don't worry. We haven't turned the coffee machine off yet."

"Great." I smiled back as Nico reached into the pocket of her pink coat and pulled out her purse.

That was pink as well.

Pink with little red strawberries.

But the Nico I knew didn't have a purse. She'd keep whatever she earned singing outside the station in her pockets. Sometimes she'd have so many coins that the sound of them jingling while she walked made me think of the 2p machines at the pier.

"I'll get these," Nico insisted, holding up her purse. "What do you fancy?"

"What are you getting?"

"A peppermint tea."

I had to stop myself before I laughed because Nico only ever drank lattes.

I could actually hear her saying, *Joan Jett doesn't drink peppermint tea, Mara.*

But it gave me the courage to tell her that I wanted a hot chocolate. I still tensed when I did, though, waiting for her to snigger sourly and tell me that hot chocolate was for kids, but her eyes lit up.

"Does that come with cream?" she asked, turning to Kyle.

He nodded, then raised his eyebrows. "And Maltesers."

"Oh yes!" She bounced up and down. "I'll have one of those as well."

When Kyle turned away, she leaned in and said, "Don't tell my mum that I'm drinking hot chocolate. She's got me on a vegan, gluten-free, sugar-free, caffeine-free diet."

"Sounds fun," I said, forced to raise my voice slightly as Kyle steamed the milk.

The look she gave me confirmed that it was not.

"Mum seems to think it will cure me and I'm too weak from the lack of meat, gluten, and sugar to argue."

My heart tripped on *cure me*, but before I could ask myself from what, Kyle turned back to put two paper cups down on the counter that were so loaded with cream and Maltesers, he gave us two spoons as well.

"I know we're closed, but as it's you, Mara, you're welcome to sit over there and drink these." He gestured to a table in the corner by the window. "As long as you don't mind me cleaning up around you."

But when I looked at Nico to see what she wanted to do, she said, "Do you fancy a walk?"

My heart hitched.

It had been so long since we'd been for a walk.

But I tried to sound nonchalant as I said, "Yeah, that'd be nice. I've been stuck in the library all day."

As soon as we got outside, Nico took a deep breath and said, "OK." She nodded, more at herself than at me, I think. "We should get this out of the way so it's done and we can just be normal."

I don't know how I managed to hold on to my cup because

as soon as she said that, the pavement dissolved into water beneath my feet, devouring me in a great, greedy gulp as I asked myself if she knew.

If she knew who I was.

"So, you know my story, right?"

I nodded and it felt like I was treading water.

"*Everyone* in Brighton knows my story. People know my story better than I do." Nico sighed tenderly and rolled her eyes. Then she took another deep breath, and when she exhaled, she said, "I have amnesia."

I hoped I looked like someone who had no idea what that was, not someone who had stayed up until midnight the night before, listening to a podcast about how the brain stores memories.

"I'm fine," she said, and again, I think it was more for herself than me. "I've had every test under the sun and no one knows why I can't remember, so my therapist thinks it's dissociative amnesia."

"What's that?" I asked, feigning ignorance.

But I really wanted to ask if her memory loss was localized or generalized.

"It can happen after a traumatic event, like, I don't know, almost drowning." She chuckled, but there was no lightness to it this time. "I can't remember *how* I ended up almost drowning, though."

"You don't?" I asked before I could tell myself not to pry.

Not to interrupt.

To just let her talk.

But Nico didn't seem to mind as she shook her head, her curls shivering. "All I remember is being on a boat, then being hauled out of the sea. And I remember the ride in the ambulance to the hospital, but everything after that is a blur of police officers and doctors and tests and Mum fussing. But that's all I remember. My therapist thinks that whatever happened was so traumatic that in an effort to forget it, I've forgotten everything else."

"Everything?"

"*Everything*. I remember everyday stuff, like how to walk and how to use a knife and fork and stuff, but everything else is gone. I didn't even recognize my mum when I first saw her at the hospital."

"God, that's awful, Nico. I'm so sorry."

She tried to smile, but couldn't quite lift the corners of her mouth.

"All of it is just *gone*?" I asked, and I shouldn't have—I shouldn't have pushed—but I couldn't imagine waking up one morning to find I'd forgotten *everything*. It was bad enough that I could only remember seeing the world because of the postcards and photographs in that shoebox under my bed, but for my whole life to go? To not recognize my parents. Or Michelle. Or to walk past Louise, Erin, and May at school like they were no one.

Nico's head must have felt like a house someone had taken a match to and burned to the ground.

"Not forever," she said with a shrug.

And it was so hopelessly Nico to act like it was nothing—like she didn't care—that I almost smiled.

"My memory will come back. I mean, for some people it doesn't . . ."

Six percent of the time, I almost said, but managed to stop myself before I did.

"But for most people it does. That's why I'm in therapy three times a week."

I tried not to sound horrified, but I couldn't help it. "*Three times* a week?"

Nico raised her eyebrows as if to say, *I know.*

"Why do you think I need this?"

She held up the hot chocolate, then sighed as she scooped up a spoonful of cream topped with a Malteser. When she slid the spoon into her mouth, her sigh was almost *obscene* as her eyes rolled back.

"God help me, this is amazing," she muttered, crunching on a Malteser as she scooped another spoonful and made a similar sound when she ate it. "Mum isn't convinced, though." She pointed the wooden spoon at me, before going in for more. "She wants me to give up therapy because she's *lost faith in Western medicine*. That's why she has me on this impossible diet, because she read somewhere that eating clean boosts your brainpower."

"Isn't fish good for that as well?"

"Yes! But she says it's full of mercury. So I'm taking omega-3 fatty acid."

"OK. But doesn't that come from the fish that are full of mercury?"

Nico thought about that for a second, then shook her head. "I don't know. She gives me something and I put it in my mouth." When she sniggered, I waited, and sure enough, she followed it with, "That's what she said."

I never thought I'd be so happy to hear a *That's what she said* joke.

But Nico never let an opportunity to say it pass her by.

"Sorry," she winced as if to say, *Don't judge me.* "I'm watching *The Office.*"

Of all the things to reassure me that the old Nico was still there—somewhere—it was that.

Nico was fond of making grand statements like, *I don't watch television.* So, if you didn't know her, you'd think that all she did was read Kazuo Ishiguro novels and listen to Mr Bongo reissues. But she *loved The Office.* She'd told me one afternoon in late July when we were sitting side by side on the beach, our hips grazing and our toes pointed toward the sea. She'd just said that she couldn't stay long because if she missed dinner again, her mother would kill her. So, as always, I'd feigned insouciance and said that was OK because I had a date with Michael Scott. As soon as I said it, she turned to me, her eyes wide. She asked me what season I was on, and when I told her that I'd just watched the episode with the fire drill, she laughed and laughed.

I think that was the first time she'd really let me see her.

The first time I'd seen her as *normal.*

Until then, all I'd seen was the impossibly cool Nico who sang outside the station and only wore black. So, I couldn't imagine her sitting up in bed in her pajamas with her laptop on her knees, watching *The Office.*

But as this Nico chugged on her hot chocolate, I could imagine it.

"What episode are you on?" I asked with a smirk.

"Michael just burned his foot on the George Foreman Grill."

"A classic." I nodded. "I ask Michelle to butter my foot at least once a week."

"Who's Michelle?" she asked, her voice a note higher than it had been a moment before.

"My best friend."

Again, I was probably overthinking it, but when our eyes met, I swear I saw her pupils swell as she smiled. And it was so pure—so unfiltered—that I couldn't help but smile back.

But then Kyle emerged from the café with a bag of rubbish in each hand and the moment was lost.

"Still here?" he asked when he found us standing on the pavement.

"Sorry!" Nico stepped back. "We were just chatting."

"You're good." He shook his head, then tipped his chin up at me. "Tell your parents hello, yeah?"

"Is that how you know him?" Nico asked when he walked away. "Through your parents?"

"Sort of. My parents have a café in the Lanes and Kyle comes in on his day off for lunch."

"A café? What's it called?"

"Malakar's. Original, I know."

We started walking then. I don't even remember where we went. All I remember is Nico next to me and the way her curls rose and fell as she walked and the smell of her sweet, sweet perfume. Even that smelled pink.

And I remember talking.

Talking and talking and talking.

"How did your parents meet?" she asked as we stopped to let someone pushing a stroller pass.

"At uni."

Nico pretended to swoon as I took a sip of hot chocolate. "Was it love at first sight?"

"Not quite. Dad pursued Mum for quite a while before she agreed to go out with him."

"How come?"

"No reason other than he was a nice Indian boy from a nice Indian family and Mum was going through her boys-with-tattoos phase. When they met, she was seeing the lead singer of a band called the Deborahs."

"How did your dad change her mind?"

"She went to see the Deborahs at the student union one night and Dad's band was opening for them."

"No way!" Nico gasped, then tugged at her scarf. "Hold on. I'm suffocating. I told Mum I didn't need this, but she's terrified I'm going to catch a cold, or something." She pretended to pant, then turned to me with a relieved sigh when she'd freed herself from the scarf. "So, your dad's band was opening for the Deborahs?"

"Yeah, the nice Indian boy from the nice Indian family was in a punk band."

"Plot twist!"

"Exactly! As soon as Mum saw him playing the drums, that was it. She was besotted."

"What happened to the band? Are they still going?"

"Nah, they went their separate ways after uni."

"That's a shame."

"I guess. But Dad says it was probably for the best. They were terrible, apparently."

Nico laughed, then said, "So, he decided to conquer the world of catering instead?"

"I don't know if *conquer* is the right word, but the café's still going after nineteen years."

"Did they open it straight from uni?"

"No, they went traveling for a year. Then, when they came home, they got proper jobs."

"What's a proper job?"

"Mum was a teacher and Dad was a pharmacist. Which makes sense, I guess. He loves the alchemy of food. How if you heat something at a certain temperature or add spice, the taste changes completely."

"Like chemistry?"

"Exactly," I said, then let out a soft sigh. "Plus, his mum died when he was four—"

"Four?" Nico interrupted, her nose wrinkling. "That's horrible."

"I know. He was so young when she died that he only remembers her from photos. But then, when he and Mum were traveling around India after they graduated, he had this bottle gourd curry in Vrindavan that tasted *exactly* like the one his mum used to make and he realized that's how he could remember her. Through food."

I saw her eyes darken then as she nodded and began to walk with less purpose. When she turned her cheek to look ahead of us, I knew she was gone and felt that painfully familiar pinch I used to feel when Nico did that before. When I'd say something and she'd look away and I knew she'd gone some-where without me.

I tried to ignore the memory of it as it scratched at some deep, unreachable place and told myself to focus on now.

Here.

This Nico as she stopped walking and turned to face me when I did the same.

"You know how your dad only remembers his mother from photos?" She lowered her voice as though she was telling me a secret. And I guess she was. "That's the only way I can remember who I am, through photos." She pressed her hand to her chest. "Thank God for my mum. Every evening after dinner we sit in the living room with a different photo album and we go through each one."

Nico finished her hot chocolate, then tossed the cup into a bin. "She's taking it slow. She doesn't want to overwhelm me, you know? So we started at the beginning, with her childhood. Then Dad's. He was born in Korea, but she was born here, in Brighton. Her family is, like, loaded and super conservative, so they didn't approve. When we went to my grandmother's funeral last summer, she hadn't seen them for over twenty years. Her older brother died three years ago and no one told her. How messed up is that?"

"That's awful."

"The funny thing is, Dad's grandparents went through the same thing. No one approved because he was American and she was Korean. They met while he was in Wŏnsan during the Korean War. Mum's got all of these great photos of him in his army uniform. That's where my surname, Rudolph, comes from. From him."

I tried not to stare at her because the old Nico didn't tell me her surname. It was a month before I found out it was Rudolph. And even then she didn't tell me; I overheard her say it when we went to Resident to pick up an album she'd preordered. So, I didn't know what to say. And even if I did, I don't think I *could* have said anything as I hung on to every word. Each one—each thing about herself—being shared with such ease that I felt seven again and hanging from the monkey bars at that playground by the mini golf course, Michelle dangling beside me as we waved at the train as it rattled past. And just like seeing the beach I knew so well from upside down, it was as thrilling—and as dizzying—to see Nico from a completely new angle.

So, in my fevered curiosity to hear more—to hear it all—I didn't dare interrupt.

"Mum says it was this epic love story," she told me as my fingers tightened around the paper cup in my hand. "Something from a film. I'm sure she's exaggerating, but they look *so happy* in the photos. They've passed now, but Mum has promised to take me to Korea to visit the rest of my family when things calm down."

"I've always wanted to go to Korea," I admitted. "Michelle was *obsessed* with BTS a couple of years ago, so she got me into K-dramas. We watch one every Friday night."

"Yeah?" Nico said, her eyes bright and wide again. "Can you give me a list of ones to get started with?"

"Sure. There are *tons*, though, so I should warn you—once you get started, you won't be able to stop."

"That sounds perfect. I'm so bored, stuck at home all day, looking at photo albums."

"Is it helping?" I asked carefully, hoping that it wasn't one question too many and she'd shut down.

But she just shrugged. "I think so. It's like Mum's putting me back together, piece by piece. Photo by photo. Filling the void between then and now. But the trouble is, I don't know if I actually *remember* any of it or if I only *think* I do because Mum's told me the story, you know?" When I nodded, I saw another glimpse of the old Nico as she shrugged again and said, "But that's normal, right? I mean, who remembers their first steps?"

"I don't," I told her as I finished my hot chocolate and threw the empty cup into the bin next to hers.

I know the *story* of my first steps, how Michelle and I took ours together at that campsite in Peacehaven that we go to every August bank holiday. (Although *technically*, Michelle walked first, and I followed because, as always, I wanted to know where she was going.) But I don't actually *remember* doing it.

I wouldn't even know that's how it happened if my parents hadn't told me.

When I turned away from the bin, Nico wrapped her arms around herself and said, "But what happens if I don't remember? If I *never* remember it because I don't want to? Because I don't like the person I used to be."

When she frowned at me, I knew what she wanted me to say.

What I should have said.

That it was OK.

That there was nothing to be afraid of.

That she wasn't a terrible person.

But then I thought about the photographs of birthdays and holidays that line the walls of my house and all of my parents' stories that bridged the gulf between what they could remember and what I could remember and how they could have told me anything if they wanted to and I would have no idea. Maybe Michelle and I didn't take our first steps together. Maybe I got up and walked across the living room one morning and they missed it, so they told us it happened at that campsite in Peacehaven because it made for a better story.

Maybe none of it was true. Maybe I wasn't born to the sound of my mother wailing, my father crying, and Van Morrison singing "Brown Eyed Girl." And maybe Michelle wasn't born in the car park of that Gala Bingo because she couldn't wait and was named after the paramedic with the quickest hands.

But they'd never do that to me.

So I couldn't do that to Nico.

I couldn't lie to her because what if she didn't like the person she used to be?

Maybe she never liked that person, which is why she wanted to be Joan Jett.

And that's another word I would never have used to describe Nico.

Happy.

Yeah, she knew what she wanted, but she also knew that it wasn't what she had.

So, instead, I said, "What if it doesn't matter?"

She blinked at me. "What do you mean?"

I thought about it for a second, then said, "I mean, what if it doesn't matter who you used to be? Who any of us used to be. What if it only matters who we are right now?"

Nico smiled, slow and easy. "I like that."

"Let's make a promise, right here and now, by this bin"—I gestured at it, our empty cups crowning the pile of rubbish like two white teeth—"that we will only ever be exactly who we are. Not who we used to be or who we want to be, but who we are *right now* because there's nothing wrong with who we are right now."

I held up my pinkie finger and she looked at it for a moment.

Then her smile sharpened to a grin as she hooked hers around mine and shook it.

21

"You didn't tell her?" Michelle said when I got home to find her rooting through my room, looking for her favorite lip gloss. She was meeting Lewis and was flustered and late, so I probably shouldn't have told her that I'd seen Nico again. But I had to, otherwise I would have spiraled on my bedroom floor until she got home.

"I know," I groaned.

"You told her about Vas's punk band but you didn't tell her you used to be together?"

I covered my face with my hands and groaned again. "I know."

"I can't believe this," Michelle said, and she sounded so genuinely confounded that I took my hands away from my face to find her shaking her head. "I mean, you haven't seen Nico for *four and a half months*, then you see her twice in two weeks. What are the chances?"

"Right?" I slapped her arm. "That has to mean something, doesn't it?"

She slapped me back. "Don't."

"Don't what?"

"Overthink this. It's just a coincidence, Mara."

I huffed because she was probably right, but sometimes it's fate, right?

Why couldn't it be fate this time?

Perhaps the only difference between coincidence and fate is your desire for it to be one, not the other.

"What are you going to do?" Michelle asked, and I remember that she looked more concerned than thrilled.

Not that I expected her to be thrilled. After all, it was Nico, so Michelle—or I, let's be real—had no reason to believe that things would be any different this time. That Nico had emerged from the sea the perfect girlfriend. But just this once, I wished that she wasn't so meticulously, immovably logical. Especially about those magical, movable things that have no regard for logic. Things like fate and luck and that other four-letter word I didn't dare say out loud.

"What do you mean?" I asked, reaching for one of my pillows and hugging it.

"Are you going to see her again?"

"Why wouldn't I?"

"So you swapped numbers?"

"We're going for coffee again tomorrow."

She arched an eyebrow at me. "And whose idea was that?"

"Hers," I told her with a smug smirk.

But when Michelle's gaze drifted over my shoulder to the window behind me, my heart clenched like a fist. It was the look she gets when she's trying to solve a particularly demanding algebra equation, her forehead suddenly so tight that I wanted to tell her to relax because she'd give herself a headache. But I couldn't because I knew what she was doing. She was trying to find a way to say what she wanted to say, but she didn't know how and that made my chest feel even tighter because Michelle always knew what to say.

Always.

Finally, she nodded to herself, then looked me in the eye.

"Mara, you have to be careful. Nico isn't the same person you knew before."

Usually, I'd have a well-rehearsed defense ready to reassure her that I was fine—that I wasn't going to get hurt—even though we both knew that wasn't true. But I couldn't argue with that, could I? Nico wasn't the same person. And I don't just mean her pretty pink clothes and pretty pink purse and pretty pink perfume, but her *attitude* was different. It still felt like she was in perpetual motion, but the swaggering, slightly sullen Nico I'd found singing outside Brighton station had been replaced by someone lighter. Fragile. Not fragile in a delicate, breakable way, but tender, I guess. Tender in the most warm, welcoming way.

"I guess almost dying will do that to you," I heard myself say.

"It certainly puts things into perspective, doesn't it?" Michelle exhaled sharply.

"So, maybe you're the one overthinking it this time?"

Michelle pulled a face at me and I thought that would be it. But then she said, "The thing is, Mara, Nico is *so vulnerable* right now."

"I know," I said, holding the pillow tighter.

"Everything you tell her becomes a new memory that potentially papers over an old one." She tugged on the sleeve of my denim shirt and waited for me to look at her. "So it's not fair to let her think that you're just some random who found her notebook. Especially if she can't remember *how* she ended up in the sea. She was supposed to meet you on New Year's Eve, wasn't she? So you have to tell her. It might trigger something."

I hadn't even thought about that.

But before I was forced to admit she was right, my phone rang. I glanced down at where it lay on the bed between us, but when I saw that it was a number I didn't recognize, I ignored it.

"You're seeing her tomorrow, right?" Michelle asked when I looked up again.

"Yeah, she wants to see my parents' café."

"Perfect. Tell her tomorrow. As soon as you see her. Don't even say hello, just rip off the Band-Aid. You have to, because the longer you leave it, the worse it will be. Otherwise, when everything comes back to her, she's going to know you lied to her and you'll never be able to come back from that."

I hadn't thought about that, either.

"Rip off the Band-Aid," I repeated with a nod as my phone buzzed.

I glanced down at it again to see it was a text and reached for it.

"Hold on," I murmured.

"Who is it?"

"*Mara, darling.*" I remember how the words wobbled as I read them aloud. "*It's Rebecca. Nico's mum. Sorry to call unannounced, but can you please call me back when you get a moment? Thank you. —R*"

Michelle leaned in to peer at the screen. "How did Nico's mum get your number?"

"No idea."

"So she doesn't have it from before?"

"Why would she have my number?"

"Lewis's mum has mine in case of emergencies."

"Michelle, come on." I tilted my head at her. "Nico isn't Lewis, is she? I couldn't get her to commit to two Saturdays in a row. I can't imagine she went home and told her mum about her *amazing* girlfriend Mara."

"True." She raised her eyebrows and nodded. "Nico must have given it to her when she got home, then."

"Yeah, but why?"

Michelle gestured at my phone. "Call her and find out."

I did, then hissed at her as she leaned in to put it on speaker so she could hear.

"Yes. Hi. Hey. Hello, Mrs. Rudolph?" I said when Nico's mother answered. "This is Mara Malakar."

"What did Nico eat?" she literally *shrieked*.

She didn't even say hello, she just started yelling.

So loudly that both Michelle and I recoiled, then looked up at each other.

"Nico's sick!" she shrieked again.

That made me gasp. "Sick?"

Nico was fine when I saw her an hour ago.

"Yes! She's been vomiting since she got home. What did she eat?"

"Nothing. She didn't eat anything."

"Tell me, Mara! Tell me right now!"

Michelle turned her finger in a circle by her temple and I swatted at her.

"Tell me!" she demanded again. "Nico says she only had a peppermint tea, but I know she's lying!"

I was so startled that I blurted out, "Hot chocolate."

"She had a hot chocolate?"

"Yes, Mrs. Rudolph."

There was a tense beat of silence. Then she said, "So sugar *and* dairy?"

"I'm sorry, Mrs. Rudolph," I babbled, close to tears. "I'm sorry."

"Oh, darling girl," she cooed, her voice suddenly sickly sweet. "It's not your fault. You know what Nico's like. She never listens to anyone, does she?"

There was something about the *does she?* that made me hesitate and look up at Michelle again.

Does she know about before? she mouthed.

She can't, I mouthed back.

But I wasn't so sure this time.

"Don't worry, darling," Nico's mother sang. "She's been eating clean for so long that even a hot chocolate will upset her stomach. She'll be fine." But something about the way she said it didn't reassure me. "Especially now she's seen you. She came home walking on air. She hasn't stopped talking about you!"

"Really?" I said, holding the pillow closer to me as I bit down on a smile.

"Your afternoon together did wonders for her," she said, and it wasn't just what she said that made my shoulders fall, rather *how* she said it. Her voice was beautiful. Soft and soothing and stirringly familiar.

It took me a moment to realize why.

She spoke how Nico sang.

"It was *just* what she needed, Mara."

When I grinned at Michelle, she rolled her eyes and mouthed, *But*.

I scowled at her. Sure enough, though, Rebecca sighed and said, "But"—and I didn't dare look at Michelle—"I'm glad you didn't tell her that you knew her before."

So, she does know, I remember thinking, my heart fluttering.

"She's so helpless," Rebecca said, and I noticed how her voice became thinner, the singsongy lightness gone. "Her therapist and I have spent a great deal of time discussing her situation and together—"

"Together? That's good," I heard myself say, but as soon as I did, the back of my neck *burned*.

It was enough to derail Rebecca, who stopped and snapped, "*What's* good?"

My voice trembled as her tone switched again. "That Nico will still be seeing her therapist."

"Why wouldn't she be seeing her therapist?"

"It's just that Nico said earlier that you wanted her to stop going."

There was another tense silence, then her voice was slow and sweet again. "Oh no, I still want Nico to go to therapy. I just think three times a week is a bit much. Don't you?"

I had no idea, so I just muttered, "I guess."

"But that's the problem, isn't it?" she continued as though I hadn't said anything. "All of this is a bit much for Nico. I know when someone loses their memory in books, they taste a madeleine dipped in tea and have a Proustian rush where it all comes back to them, but that's not how it works in real life, darling."

I know that, I thought.

I don't know why it made the muscles in my shoulders tense again, but something about Rebecca's tone—gentle as it was—was giving more Head Teacher than Concerned Mother.

"I know in films it's more dramatic," she went on with a well-polished laugh. "Very Christopher Nolan. Remembering that way is certainly more satisfying than months, even *years*, of hard slog in therapy, but it's not healthy. Remembering everything all at once could completely overwhelm Nico and we don't want that, do we?"

"No, Mrs. Rudolph," I muttered, and even Michelle sat a little straighter.

"No, it's much better that it happens organically, rather than in a rush, which might set Nico back even further. That's why her therapist and I are working together to help her remember slowly. On her own terms."

Michelle lifted her shoulders, then let them fall again as she mouthed, *That makes sense.*

"So, I'd appreciate it if you didn't tell her about your friendship just yet, darling."

I hesitated as I remembered what Michelle said earlier about ripping off the Band-Aid.

"I don't want to lie to her, though."

Rebecca chuckled.

Nico's new chuckle.

"Sweet girl. What a good heart you have," she sang. "You're not lying to her, though. You're *protecting* her. Nico will understand." I think she knew I was going to object again, because before I could, she added, "We will tell her, I promise. When she's strong enough. You just need to be patient. Trust the process."

I nodded. "Trust the process."

"Although," she said, making the word sound about a minute long, "if this is going to be too much for you and you don't think you can spend time with her without saying something, I completely understand if—"

I didn't let her finish. "No. No. I can do it. I can do it, Mrs. Rudolph."

Even I could hear the desperation in my voice, which was hardly convincing.

Still, she sounded thrilled. "Oh good! I'm so glad we spoke, darling girl."

Then she was gone and I was left staring at my phone.

When I looked up, Michelle shrugged. "I guess that Band-Aid's staying on for now, then."

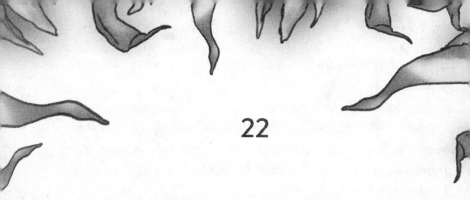

22

I barely slept that night, even with Michelle next to me, fidgeting and murmuring Lewis's name in her sleep.

She'd swept into my room after their date, already in her pajamas, and climbed into bed next to me. She didn't even ask how I was, just started telling me about the film they'd seen. She was obviously trying to distract me and it worked for a while. But then she turned out the light and, as soon as I heard her snoring, it was just me again.

Me and Nico's mother's voice ringing in the dark.

It's for the best, I realized after replaying the conversation several hundred times. I probably shouldn't commit this to paper, but maybe it wasn't such a bad thing that Nico couldn't remember.

After all, there were some things I'd rather she didn't remember.

About before.

About us.

There was a certain appeal to starting again.

Allowing ourselves to be exactly who we were, not who we used to be.

Besides, her mother was right. Perhaps remembering everything all at once wouldn't be good for her.

We had no idea what would happen when she did.

When the wall Nico had put up between herself and what happened that night came down.

Maybe it would take her down with it.

So while it didn't feel right to lie to Nico, to let her think I was just a stranger who'd found her notebook and not someone who knew things about her that she didn't know herself, there was some comfort in knowing there was a plan. That I was doing as I was told. Doing what was best for her. *She'll understand*, I'd decided by 4 a.m., when the night was at its most defiant and it felt like the moon would never surrender to the sun. If I told Nico that I'd lied to her because I *had* to, she might not like it, but she'd understand, wouldn't she?

She'll understand, I told myself again. But as soon as I felt that familiar fizz of excitement at the thought of seeing her that afternoon, it was swiftly followed by a pop of dread. Not because I was afraid that she was going to blow me off like she used to, but because I was afraid that Nico's mother was right about that as well.

I couldn't do it.

I couldn't lie to her.

By the time the sun came up and I could hear my parents shushing one another so they didn't wake us as they got ready to open the café, I was weak with worry, sure that I was going to say something. Something to fracture the wall Nico had put up and it would come tumbling down. Something small— silly—that I'd barely register the weight of until I'd said it out loud. I'd know that she hated broccoli. Or we'd pass Beyond

Retro and I'd laugh and say, "Remember that Camp Crystal Lake T-shirt you bought for Halloween?"

Then that would be it.

Nico would know that I was lying to her.

That wasn't a new feeling. I always felt like I wasn't being honest with Nico. Wasn't being myself. I had to watch what I said. Not say too much. Not push her. Not ask why she hadn't called in case that was the last time she did. But this was a pressure quite like any other because I might not be breaking us beyond repair.

I might be breaking her.

"You're doing it again," Michelle murmured, kicking me under the duvet. "Get out of your head."

"Can I spiral in peace, please?"

"Fine. But can you at least stop hogging the duvet," she hissed, tugging it away from me.

In the end, my spiraling was futile because Nico called to blow off.

If I'm being honest, I should have been relieved. Or at least expected it. After all, I knew she'd been sick the day before, so I shouldn't have been surprised that she wasn't well enough to meet me. But *I'm not feeling great* was her go-to when she blew me off before, so I felt an old wound reopen as I heard her say it.

But I did what I always did when she said that before.

I shook it off and said, "That's OK."

"I feel like shit on toast." I'd heard that melodramatic groan so many times, but that morning it sounded different. Real. Her voice thin and far away as she said, "Don't worry, Mara.

I'll spare you the details, but let's just say that I woke up at one thirty this morning and it was like a scene from *The Exorcist*."

"You poor thing," I said, like I used to when she flaked on me before. But that sounded different as well, because thanks to that phone call with her mother, I knew she was telling the truth this time.

"By 4 a.m. I'd written my will. You're getting my books, by the way."

I shouldn't have laughed, but when she let out an even more melodramatic groan, I couldn't help it.

Michelle stirred, and when I looked over to find her eyes open, she immediately snapped them shut again.

"Was it something you ate?" I asked carefully.

I waited for Nico to groan again and curse the hot chocolate she'd had.

But she said, "I don't think so. Mum made kale soup for dinner."

I didn't know why she was telling me what she had for dinner when she'd started vomiting *before* she'd had dinner, but I went along with it. "Kale soup would be enough to make me vomit as well, to be honest."

"Right?" She stopped to clear her throat. "My kingdom for a Nando's."

I felt a flutter of hope then, because if I subsist on Cherry Coke and regret, then the old Nico was fueled by Nando's and obscure music references. So I wasn't surprised in the slightest that she'd rekindled her love for extra-hot peri-peri chicken. She would have eaten it every day, if she could have.

Now I think about it, that's probably why her mother put her on that awful vegan, gluten-free, sugar-free, caffeine-free diet.

Still, I was unreasonably proud of myself that I hadn't commented on her Nando's addiction. And, yeah, I knew it wasn't the first time I was going to be tested, but I hadn't failed, so maybe I could do it, after all.

"It wasn't the soup," Nico said. "Mum was fine until about ten minutes ago."

"Is she Linda Blair-ing it as well now?"

"She reckons I have a virus that I passed on to her. Are you OK?"

"Yeah. I'm fine. Maybe it's norovirus," I suggested when she groaned again.

"That's what Mum said."

"Norovirus is *super* contagious. Once, my friend Erin was at a wedding and someone must have had it, because by the end of the evening, *everyone* was puking. Even the bride and groom. It was awful."

"Maybe I picked it up on the bus on the way home?" Nico thought about that for a second, then grumbled, "I'd better not tell Mum that, though, otherwise she'll never let me leave the house again."

I waited for her to laugh, but when she didn't, I frowned and asked her if she was OK.

"I'm sad," she admitted, and I remember being taken aback that she answered so honestly.

"How come?" I asked with the sort of care usually reserved for stroking a stray cat.

When she was quiet a beat too long, I waited for her to do

what she always did whenever she said too much—let me see too much—and shrug it off as though it was nothing, then change the subject.

But she said, "Mum just told me that she spoke to Brighton College on Friday."

So you don't go to Longhill? I almost said, but managed to bite my tongue before I did.

I was equal parts surprised and comforted because after the *hours* I'd spent devouring everything I could find about her— her grandmother's obituary, that article in the *Guardian* about her father, those comments from her friends on Instagram— that was the one thing I couldn't find about her: where she went to school.

I almost laughed because I couldn't imagine Nico at Brighton College. I couldn't even imagine her in a school uniform. All I could picture was a scene from *The Craft*: Nico all eyeliner and contempt as she swaggered through the corridors, sneering at everyone with their clean, neat hair and clean, neat nails as they clutched their violin cases and Latin textbooks and told themselves to keep their distance.

She must know Chesca and Charlotte, I realized then, wondering why they hadn't told me.

"I can't go back," Nico said, and when I heard her sniff, I sat up and asked myself if she was crying. "I've missed too much. I can't take my GCSEs now, can I? They start next month."

"I'm sorry, Nico," I said, which, while soothing, was essentially useless. I thought about what Michelle would say if she was trying to console me and asked, "So what's the plan, then?"

"Focus on my recovery," she muttered, but even through the phone I heard her roll her eyes. Clearly her mother's words, not hers. "Then go back and retake the year in September."

"There you go," I said, careful to keep my tone light.

She sighed. "It won't be the same, Mara."

I tried not to sigh back because I'd hate that. Having to start again. Having to force my way into friendship groups that had been forged over years of gymnastics and sleepovers and fallouts over shared crushes.

I couldn't say that to Nico, though.

So I said, "You'll make new friends."

"I don't even have any old ones," she said under her breath, and something in my chest *pinged*.

"You have me."

As soon as I said it, I cursed myself.

Nice one, Mara, I thought.

We'd been talking for all of five minutes and I'd already messed up.

Mercifully, Nico was too distracted to notice.

"You're so sweet, but I must have had *some* friends before but I haven't heard from *anyone*. Not one person. I know I was only at Brighton College for four months before this happened. But what about my friends from London? Why haven't they been in touch?"

I felt awful, because they had.

I wanted to tell her that, but then I remembered what her mother had said about being patient.

About trusting the process.

"They can't get in touch, can they?" I reminded her. "You lost your phone."

I closed my eyes and cursed myself for messing up *again*.

Nico hadn't told me that she'd lost her phone, had she?

I'd worked it out for myself after speaking to May.

But Nico didn't ask me how I knew that, she just perked up and said, "Oh yeah."

"When your memory comes back you can reach out to them. I'm sure they're worried."

"When will that be, though? It's been *months* and I still can't remember a thing." She sighed miserably. "Last night I almost googled myself to see if I had an Instagram, but Mum doesn't want me to. She doesn't want me to read anything before I'm ready. She keeps telling me to be patient. To trust the process."

"No. No. Don't do that. Don't google anything. Your mum's right."

I hoped she didn't notice the hiss of panic in my voice as I remembered falling down that rabbit hole of Twitter threads and subreddits. If she googled herself, she'd find it all. The sullen selfies. The videos people had taken of her singing outside the station. The ones she'd taken of herself, her voice like silver.

A detailed map of exactly who she used to be.

I couldn't imagine what it would do to her to put her name into Google and find everything, all at once.

To find this person she didn't know.

To find me.

Now I think about it, that was what I was actually worried about, wasn't it?

That she might find me.

Then she'd know I'd lied to her.

Thankfully, I must have convinced her, because Nico gasped and said, "Wait. Someone did reach out!"

"They did?"

"Yes! Brighton College sent me flowers when I got home from the hospital," she said. Usually, her voice had the depth and ease of a summer wave, so it was nice to hear her happy. Excited. "Hang on. I put the card in my journal." I heard pages swishing through the phone, then she said, "*Nico. Wishing you a speedy recovery. We hope to see you again soon. With love, Ms. Fisher and all your friends in Year Eleven.*"

"Ms. Fisher? No way! My favorite teacher at Queens Park Primary was called Ms. Fisher."

"I wonder if it's the same one?"

"Let me check," I said, reaching for my laptop from the bedside table and firing it up.

I searched for *Ms. Fisher Brighton College*, and sure enough, her LinkedIn was the first result.

"Nope," I told her when I saw the photo. "Definitely not the same Ms. Fisher."

My Ms. Fisher had a sweet grandmotherly energy that always made me feel better, no matter who stole my favorite pencil or how dramatically I'd fallen over on the playground. The perfect first teacher who had a smile for everyone and always had a Band-Aid in her desk drawer. But according to LinkedIn, the Ms. Fisher at Brighton College was much younger with that immaculate, rosy-cheeked Kate Middleton thing going on.

"That's a shame," Nico said. "It would have been cool if we'd had the same teacher."

"Uh-huh," I muttered, suddenly distracted by another photo of Ms. Fisher.

One of her cheering on the U16 squad at the South East Regional Indoor Hockey Finals.

And there, running across the sports hall in her navy, burgundy, and yellow kit, was Chesca.

I frowned at the photo as I asked myself again why Chesca hadn't told me that Nico was in her year.

Or Charlotte.

Actually, I got why Charlotte didn't want to mention Nico, but that didn't explain why Chesca hadn't.

"Mara!"

Nico said it so loudly, I suspect it wasn't the first time she'd tried to get my attention.

"Huh?" I grunted, making myself look away from the photo of Chesca.

"I'm trying to thank you," she said with that baby-pink chuckle.

Before I could tell her that she didn't need to thank me, she said, "Oh! Before I forget. There's an instore at Resident on Wednesday. If I preorder the album, I get two free tickets. Do you fancy it?"

I felt another flutter of hope then because that was some-thing else she'd obviously rekindled. She used to go to every instore. She liked nothing more than to nod at a poster and say, "I saw them at Resident last year."

But she'd never invited me before.

"It starts at six thirty. I was thinking, we could meet at your parents' café beforehand."

"Sure," I said, like I had the last time.

And like the last time, it was such a tiny word, but it felt much bigger.

Like the start of something.

It was the start of something, wasn't it?

23

An hour later, I was googling *Nico Rudolph Brighton College* to no avail when May finally FaceTimed me.

"Where have you been?" I barked as soon as her face appeared on my laptop screen. Then I snatched my phone from the bed and held it up. "I sent you that SOS message *twenty-two* minutes ago!"

May looked slightly stunned. "I was asleep."

"What if I was dying? Or if I'd been arrested and you were my one phone call?"

"Arrested for what?" She snorted. "Not returning your library books on time?"

"May Elizabeth Petrakis! This isn't funny. I'm having a crisis here!"

"First of all, calm down." She stopped to take a gulp from her Princess Peach mug. "Second of all, it's nine forty-eight on a Sunday morning. How are you having a crisis already? Where's Michelle?"

"She's gone for a run with Erin."

"What?" She looked disgusted. "Why?"

"I don't know." I was equally disgusted. "It's like I don't even know them." I threw my phone on the bed, and when I looked at May again, I saw myself frown. "Why are you on your laptop, by the way?"

"I can't find my phone, so I logged into WhatsApp on here to see if I missed anything. And I did!"

"Your phone's right there," I told her, pointing to it tucked between the folds of her duvet.

"Oh yeah." She chuckled to herself, then held it up to show me the screen.

Two missed calls from me and four texts, the last one concluding with *SOS* and a string of alarm emojis.

It wasn't my finest moment, so I probably shouldn't admit that.

Still, it was proof that I really was spiraling.

"So what happened that requires"—her lips moved as she counted them—"*eight* alarm emojis?"

I filled May in on what she'd missed—seeing Nico, the conversation with her mother the evening before, then the one Nico and I had that morning—although not all of it as I got to what prompted the eight alarm emojis.

"May, I need you to be honest with me," I told her.

She didn't hesitate. "Always."

"Did you know that Nico went to Brighton College?"

Again, she didn't hesitate. "Nico doesn't go to Brighton College."

"She just told me that she does. Or she *did* before all of this happened."

May was adamant, though. "There's no way she goes to Brighton College. Chesca would have told me."

She was so convinced, but I still asked if she was sure.

"Yes! I'll text Chesca now, if it'll put your mind at rest."

"Can't you call her?" I asked when she reached for her phone.

I could hear the squeak of panic in my voice so I'm surprised May didn't tell me to calm down again.

But she just said, "I can't. She's at a study group in the library."

"On a *Sunday?*"

"Right?" May muttered. "Her parents are no joke. If she doesn't get into Oxford or Cambridge, they're going to disown her. They told her that they're not paying thirty-five grand a year for her to go anywhere else."

"*Thirty-five thousand pounds?*"

"Thirty-five thousand just in school fees. So the University of Sussex isn't an option."

What's wrong with the University of Sussex? I asked myself.

But then May's phone buzzed and she held it up to show me Chesca's reply.

No, I don't. I would have told you.

"Is she sure?" I could see myself frowning on the screen again. "Maybe they were in different classes?"

"Mara, come on." May snorted. "Even if they were in different classes, *everyone* would have been talking about it. Remember in the new year when no one would leave you alone when they found out you knew Nico? Don't you think that if she went to Brighton College *everyone* would have been talking about it there?"

That was true.

"Are *you* sure that Nico said that she went to Brighton College?" May asked.

"Definitely. Because I remember thinking, *Why didn't Chesca tell me?*"

"She would have," May said again. "You've met her *loads* of times. We've talked about Nico, so why wouldn't she tell you?"

"I thought maybe Michelle told you not to," I admitted, sheepishly.

May cackled. "When have I ever listened to Michelle Chen?"

That was also true.

"Hang on." May held up her hands. "You're sure Nico said Brighton *College*? Not Brighton *Girls*?"

"No, she definitely said Brighton College."

May pulled a face. "That's so weird."

"It *is* weird, right? They even sent her flowers."

"Who did?"

"One of her teachers. She read me the card over the phone."

"What did it say?"

I couldn't remember exactly, so I paraphrased. "That they hope she feels better soon and they can't wait to have her back." I remembered this part, though. "*With love, Ms. Fisher and all your friends in Year Eleven.*"

May pointed at me. "Oh, like Ms. Fisher at Queens Park Primary!"

"Yes!"

"I wonder if it's the same one."

"I thought the same thing, so I checked and that's when I found this."

I sent May the link to the Brighton College blog about the South East Regional Indoor Hockey Finals.

"There's my girl!" She grinned when she opened it and saw the photo of Chesca.

"*Exactly*. And that person, on the sidelines, cheering her on, is Ms. Fisher."

"Definitely not our Ms. Fisher, then." May shrugged. "Fisher's a pretty common name, though." She thought about it for a second, then said, "Maybe there's a Ms. Fisher at Brighton Girls? I mean, Nico's memory isn't great, is it?"

"True. It's an easy mistake to make, I suppose. Brighton College. Brighton Girls . . ." I searched for *Ms. Fisher Brighton Girls*. But there was nothing. "No Ms. Fisher at Brighton Girls . . . Wait . . . Hang on . . ." I hesitated as I scrolled down further. "There is an *Alan* Fisher who"—I sat back and rolled my eyes when I read his job title—"is the head of the senior school."

May gestured at me as if to say, *There you go*.

"I'm guessing the card Nico got with the flowers was handwritten. So, it's easy to read *Mr. Fisher* as *Ms. Fisher*," I realized with a long sigh of relief as my shoulders fell and I sat back against my pillows.

But then I cursed myself because Michelle was right: I needed to get out of my head.

She was probably back from her run by now and in the shower.

And there I was, recovering from an hour-long panic spiral when there was nothing to panic about.

May clapped her hands and I jumped.

"Well, now that crisis has been averted, can we talk about the dress I want to wear to Chesca's sixteenth?"

"Yes!" I said, desperate for a distraction from feeling like something in my head was fraying.

"I DMed you a link on Insta."

I snatched my phone off the bed, but when I opened my inbox, I didn't just have a message from May.

I had another one as well.

"I knew it was too short," she grumbled when I gasped. "I can't wear that, can I? Her mum will be there."

"No." I blinked at the screen of my phone. "That girl DMed me."

"Which girl?"

"Nico's friend from London. The one we stalked on Insta."

"Nya Kalogeropoulos?"

I stared at her, stunned that she remembered that but couldn't find her phone on her own bed.

"What did she say?" May asked as she took another sip from her Princess Peach mug.

"*Is Nico OK?*" I read aloud.

"That it?"

I nodded.

She sucked in a breath and shook her head. "Definitely an ex."

"You don't know that." I bristled at the thought. "She's probably a school friend, or something."

May didn't look convinced. "How did she find you?"

"I don't know. I've Nico tagged, haven't I? Maybe she did a search for her and found me."

"Yeah, but Nico deleted her Insta, so she, or you, wouldn't show up. *Unless*"—she raised a finger—"Nya searched for Nico *before* she deleted her account, which means that she's known about you since then." She sucked in another breath and shook her head again. "I am telling you, Mara. That is ex energy!"

I looked down at the message, then back at May. "What do I say?"

"Nothing!"

"So I just ignore it?"

"Do you really want to get into it with one of Nico's exes?"

I really didn't.

But if anyone understood what it was like to be desperate to hear from Nico, it was me.

"Ex or not, she must be worried about her, right?"

"Fine. Just keep it simple. I know what you're like, Mara. Don't write an essay."

"I do not write essays!"

"Mara, you're the only person I know who uses semicolons in texts."

"Proper punctuation is sexy."

"Just say something like *She's doing much better*."

I said exactly that, but I barely had time to look up from my phone before Nya replied.

"What did she say?" May asked, and I turned my phone so she could read it.

When you next speak to Nico, can you please give her my number and ask her to get in touch?

"Don't," I warned when May sucked in a breath and shook her head again.

I reread the message, then pressed my hand to my forehead.

"You're right, May. I shouldn't have replied. Now what do I do?"

"Well, you can't give Nico her number," she told me, and my first reaction was relief because what if she—this Nya—was the love of Nico's life and I was about to guide them back together?

Then I felt awful because if Nya was the love of Nico's life, then I shouldn't intervene, right?

But then May made an excellent—and convenient—point. "Her mum told you yesterday not to tell her about before and Nya is *before* before. Before you, even. So, who knows what hearing from her will trigger?" She pretended to shudder. "Besides, assuming this Nya person is an ex, how do you know that Nico *wants* to hear from her? If she's anything like me, she has a scorched-earth policy when it comes to exes."

"That's true," I muttered, slightly concerned that May was just telling me what I wanted to hear.

But then she said, "I mean, we have *no idea* who this Nya is aside from whatever's on her TikTok. She seems normal enough, but what if she's some sort of psycho stalker who Nico blocked so Nya's trying to get to her through you? Nope." May pulled a face and shook her head. "I'd leave well enough alone until Nico remembers."

"OK." That made sense. "So what do I do about this message, then? Ignore it?"

"Just heart it. That way you're acknowledging it, but you're not promising anything, either."

"You're so good at this," I told her as I did what she suggested.

May winked and raised her Princess Peach mug. "Not my first rodeo, babe."

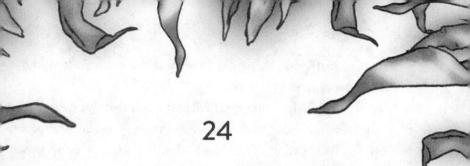

24

"Taste this," my father said, thrusting a teaspoon at me as I walked into the café. "Does it pass your vibe check?"

"Dad!" I gasped, batting his hand away.

"Careful, Vas," my mother warned with a smirk as she walked out of the pantry with a red pepper in each hand. "Mara has her big date with Nico later, so she doesn't want to get kadhi down her."

"Oh yes! The big date." My father grinned, putting the teaspoon into his mouth and sucking it.

"You got a date, Mara?" Max asked, suddenly next to me.

To say I was *mortified* was putting it mildly. I shot a look over my shoulder at the door, then said a little prayer that Max would be gone before Nico got there because worrying about whatever my parents were going to say was enough to contend with. I couldn't cope with Max launching into one of his rants about 5G as well.

Mercifully, he just ordered a green tea to go and ambled out again.

As soon as the door closed behind him, I turned to my parents and scowled.

"It's not a date. We're just going to Resident to see a band. It's no big deal."

But they just stood side by side behind the counter, looking utterly unrepentant.

"No big deal." My father nodded, and I wondered if he knew that I'd spent an hour trying on everything I owned before borrowing May's first-date black denim skirt, which, she insisted, was foolproof.

I don't know about foolproof, but I should have worn tights because it was too short. On her it looked cool, but on me it wasn't much more than a belt. So I already knew that I would be spending the evening tugging it down, which I really didn't need on top of everything else. Seeing Nico and watching every word in case I said something to break her brain was stressful enough without having to worry about showing her my ass as well.

So I just needed my parents to be, you know, *not my parents* for half an hour.

"Mara and Nico sitting in a tree," my father sang, confirming that was impossible.

"Wait. Is that mine?" My mother pointed the knife she was holding at my Run-D.M.C. T-shirt.

"Yeah," I muttered as she went back to chopping the peppers.

I only borrowed it because it went with the red-and-black-striped cardigan I'd bought the day before because it reminded me of Nico's favorite sweater.

Perhaps I shouldn't wear it, I thought. *What if it triggers something?*

But if I didn't wear it, there would be nothing to cover my skirt.

"So what are the rules?" my father asked as he turned to stir the kadhi.

"We have to pretend we've never met her, right?" my mother asked, without looking up from the peppers.

"For the record"—I raised a finger—"coming here was Nico's idea. I would never have agreed if she hadn't insisted."

"Why? We're great liars." She looked up with a theatrical gasp. "The best. Remember when we told you how great your hair looked after you had those awful layers a couple of years ago?"

My father nodded solemnly.

"Plus," she added, "Nico will *love* us."

"Of course she will," he said over his shoulder. "We're cool, right, Mads?"

"The coolest."

"You're really not," I told them as I adjusted my skirt.

My mother pointed the knife at me again. "Well, *I* am, at least. You're wearing my T-shirt."

I ignored her as my father turned to face me again. "Exactly. Plus, we know about YouTik and TokTube."

"Stop it," I said through my teeth, heat rising in my cheeks.

"We're down with the kids, Mara. Your mother has a crush on Harry Styles."

It was her turn to nod solemnly. "He's very beguiling."

This is why I came early, I thought, hoping they'd get it out of their system before Nico got there.

"Beguiling," my mother repeated, in case I hadn't heard her the first time. "He's on my list."

"What list?" I asked, even though, after fifteen years, I really should have known better.

"My list. You know? From *Friends*. The list of five famous people I'm allowed to shag and your father can't get mad." She stopped chopping the peppers and looked up at the ceiling, her right eye closed as she tilted her head from side to side. "Harry Styles, Keanu Reeves, Jason Momoa, Dave Grohl, and Ranveer Singh."

"Your mother is all about the hair." My father grinned, fluffing up his dark curls with his hand.

"Oh my God!" I turned to look at the door again. "*Please* don't say any of this when Nico gets here."

When I turned back, my father shrugged as if to say, *What?* Then carried on stirring the kadhi.

"Listen," I hissed. "Nico is going to be here any second and I need you to not do *this*." I waved my hands at them. "I know it's actually physically impossible, but can you, please, for once, just *be chill*?"

"I'm chill." My father turned to face me again, his arms out. "Right, Mads?"

"The chillest. You'll see." My mother waved the knife at me, then pointed at the door. "When Nico leaves here, she'll be like, *Oh my God, Mara. You're so lucky. Your parents are, like, so chill.*"

"With good hair." My father pulled his Blue Steel face.

"And funny." My mother cackled. "Vas, shall I tell her about the time I—"

"No!" I roared, checking the door again. When I looked back, I lowered my voice in case Nico walked in. "She doesn't want to hear about that time you did acid at Glastonbury and tried to get on stage with Babyshambles. Or that time you gave Amy Winehouse a tampon in the toilets at the Dublin Castle. *Or*"—I raised my voice again before she could interrupt—"that guy you snogged at uni thinking it was Gavin Rossdale."

OK. Fine. I admit it. Nico would have *loved* each of these stories because they're actually pretty cool.

But not when your mother is telling them.

"Ah. Gavin." She sighed dreamily, then turned to my father. "I'm adding him to my list."

He didn't seem bothered, though. "Fine. But someone has to go."

"See ya, Styles," she said, pretending to drag the knife across her throat.

"Extra-hot latte to have in," someone said, making me jump.

"Sure," my father said as my mother went upstairs to look for the order book. "Any particular milk?"

"Normal. But listen." Their sharp blonde bob shivered as they held up their hand. "I want to make sure that you understand what I mean by *extra hot* because no one seems able to get it right."

Because making it extra hot boils the milk so it won't foam properly and tastes like shit, I thought.

But my father was more gracious than me.

"Got it," he said with a tight smile. "*Extra* hot."

"Ten pounds says they send it back because it tastes like shit," I muttered when they went to find a table.

"Ten pounds says it's not hot enough," he countered as he grabbed a cup.

Sure enough, a few minutes later the customer strode back with a face like thunder.

My father winked at me as they slammed the cup down on the counter and we waited to see who'd won.

We were both wrong, though, because they said, "This is too hot!"

I was so stunned, I thought I'd misheard. "Is the milk scalded?"

"How on earth would I know? I can't taste it because it's too hot!"

My father looked at me, then shook his head as he walked toward the pantry chuckling to himself.

"Excuse me! Where are you going? I'm talking to you!" the customer called after him. "Do you mind telling me what's so funny?"

I tried not to laugh because I wished—I *wished*—my mother was there.

They were lucky she was upstairs, though, otherwise no one would be laughing.

"It's not funny. It's just—" I had to press my lips together for a moment to stop myself from giggling and pissing them off even more. "You insisted on an extra-hot latte, but it's too hot. You have to see the irony in that?"

They stared at me, phone in hand as though they were ready to call the police.

"And?" they said, blonde bob full on *swinging* now. "It is too hot!"

I looked down at the cup on the counter between us because I honestly didn't know what to say to that.

"Just let it cool down," I heard someone say.

I looked up and there she was—Nico—staring at the customer as if to say, *Are you serious?*

"Hey," I said with a smile I knew was too loose to be considered remotely cool, my skirt and cardigan and whatever my parents were going to say to embarrass me immediately forgotten.

"Hey," she said back.

Now I think about it, her smile wasn't particularly cool, either. Especially as I could see the gap in her front teeth. But she didn't seem to care, her cheeks pink as she peered at me from under her stiff black eyelashes.

"Um. Excuse me," the customer barked, looking between us.

I'd forgotten they were there and felt something in me deflate.

"I cannot *just let it cool down*." They turned to glare at Nico, a tiny blob of spit settling on their bottom lip. "When I pay for something, I expect it to be right and this isn't right. I want another one."

"Another one?" Nico blinked at them. "You do realize that in the time it took for you to come over here and complain, your coffee probably cooled to the perfect temperature. Whatever that is."

My father emerged from the pantry then, carrying a massive meat thermometer.

"Is there a temperature you prefer?" He held it up. "Fifty-seven point two degrees perhaps?"

The customer gasped, hand on their chest. "Well, if this is how you treat all your customers, I shan't be coming back."

"Be sure to tell your friends about Malakar's! Home of the extra-hot latte!" He saluted with two fingers.

My mother did the same as she emerged from upstairs with

the order book to find the customer marching out of the café. "Don't forget to leave us a review on Tripadvisor!" she called after them.

When I turned to Nico, she looked delighted as I sighed and said, "Yeah, so these are my parents."

"You'd better get out there," my father warned, waving the meat thermometer at the window while I tried to make Nico the best latte she'd ever had.

(For the record, I tried to talk her out of caffeine, but she wasn't having it.)

I turned to see what he was pointing at and found Max by her table, his face red as he frowned earnestly.

"Oh no!" I gasped.

I grabbed her coffee and got outside as Nico tilted her head at Max and said, "So planes are just flying around"—she raised her hands and turned them in a circle—"spraying biological agents all over us?"

"Yeah, man." He nodded, his blue eyes wide. "They've been doing it for years."

"Who's they?"

He ignored her. "It's psychological manipulation, man. They're trying to control us. Keep us in line."

"OK," I said, putting Nico's latte down on the table in front of her. "See you tomorrow, yeah, Max?"

Luckily, he took the hint. Not before he winked lasciviously at me, though, which made me shudder as he wandered off. When I looked down at Nico, I expected to find her slightly shell-shocked, but she looked amused.

"Well," she said as she watched him disappear around the corner. "He's very . . . um . . . *Brighton*."

"Oh yeah. He's easing you in with chemtrails, though. Wait for his theory about Paul McCartney."

"Paul McCartney?"

"He died in a car crash in the sixties, apparently, and the surviving Beatles replaced him with a lookalike."

"Sure." Nico raised her right shoulder, then let it drop again. "Makes sense."

Now the thrill of seeing her again had passed, I could really look at her and saw that something was different. She wasn't wearing her pink coat, I realized. Rather a long, loose black kaftan embroidered with white leaves and flowers. It was the sort of thing the old Nico would have worn and it made me falter for a moment.

"This is nice," I said, hoping I sounded curious rather than startled. "Is it new?"

"Yes! I didn't have anything Resident appropriate, so I just bought it in Beyond Retro. Do you like it?"

She held out her arm to show me the black fringe and I smiled. "Very Stevie Nicks."

"That's so funny! When Mum goes to bed, I've been listening to one of Dad's albums and last night it was *Rumours*. So when I saw this, I thought of Stevie Nicks. I can't believe you thought the same thing!"

Her smile sharpened to a grin and there she was.

The old Nico.

Just for a second.

And it was all I could do not to weep.

* * *

"You're so lucky." Nico grinned as we walked to Resident. "Your parents are *so cool*."

"Please don't tell them that," I pleaded, rolling my eyes.

But she just laughed.

"So, tell me about this band we're going to see. What are they called?"

Her face lit up like the pier. "Cowboy Mouth. Except it's not a band, it's a dude called Franklin Welsh."

"They're a Patti Smith fan, I take it?"

"Patti Smith?"

"*Cowboy Mouth* is a play she wrote with Sam Shepard."

Nico turned to me, clearly impressed, and I had to look away as my face flushed with pride.

"I *love* that you know that!" She stopped and turned in a circle, the fringe on her kaftan rising, then falling. "One day, I want to be cool enough to make casual references to plays Patti Smith wrote."

The funny thing is, the old Nico would have known it was a nod to Patti Smith, so I shook my head as I acknowledged the irony. "I only know that because I just read my mother's copy of *Just Kids*."

"What's that?"

"Patti Smith's memoir. Or part of it, anyway. It's about her relationship with Robert Mapplethorpe and moving to New York. The Chelsea Hotel. Warhol's Factory. All of that."

"I want to live in New York one day," she said with a wistful sigh.

I almost laughed because the old Nico thought that wanting to live in New York was a cliché.

"And I love that your mother has a book like that." When she sighed again, it wasn't as wistful. "Do you know what my mum's reading? *The Body Keeps the Score*, which is about the effects of traumatic stress."

I tried not to pull a face, but I don't think I succeeded.

"I wish she'd read something like *Just Kids*."

"You should read it. I'll lend you Mum's copy. It's great. Full of anecdotes about the people Patti Smith knew back then. One of the first songs she wrote was for Janis Joplin. The last time they saw one another, before Janis died, she asked Patti how she looked and she told Janis that she looked like a pearl. A pearl of a girl."

When I was brave enough to look at her again, she was smiling. "I want to be someone's pearl of a girl."

It's impossible to convey with mere words how quickly—and completely—my life changed with that smile. I could feel my heart in a way I hadn't before. As though until then, it had been tucked in that shoebox under my bed with all those other precious, forgotten things and was now free. I remember telling myself to memorize every delicate detail because one day— today, apparently—I'd want to remember it all. The rise and fall of the fringe on her kaftan. Her cheeks, as pink as cat's paws. That slow, secret smile I'd never seen before. That was just for me.

Just think. All of those tiny moments that had to align for us to see each other again.

If she hadn't left her journal behind.

Or if I hadn't stood outside that café by the library, looking for her, I would have missed her.

It was nothing short of magic.

I didn't know until then that I believed in magic. And I shouldn't have. I had no reason to. Not after everything that happened before. But, looking back on it now, I suppose even hoping things would be different this time—that she would be different, that we would be different—reflected a willingness to be disappointed.

Later, I'd promise Michelle that I wouldn't get carried away. That I'd be careful. But as soon as Nico said it—*I want to be someone's pearl of a girl*—I had already decided that it was worth the risk.

But such is the misery and magic of love.

You'll break your own heart at the mere promise of it.

Nico didn't stop talking as we headed to Resident, each step lighter. She asked about my friends and I did my best to describe them. Louise's energy. Her incurable curiosity and how she was the only one who could corral us when we were going in five different directions. Nico asked if Louise was the ringleader, which she was. But not in a manipulative way, more in a way that made us do things we'd almost certainly say no to.

Which was no bad thing, now I think about it.

When she asked about Erin, I described her as devilishly confrontational, but made sure Nico knew that she was fiercely loyal. A quintessential sister who constantly took the piss out of you but wouldn't let anyone say a bad word about you. And I told her that if Erin was our big sister, then May was the baby.

Unreliable and unpredictable, but also mischievous and mutinous.

"She's *wild* sometimes," I told Nico as we joined the queue outside Resident, "but my mother says that you should always be friends with the wildflowers because they know how to survive."

She looked up at me with another slow smile. "I like that."

"I wish I was more like May. She's so brave and you have to be brave to be fifteen sometimes."

"I never thought about it, but I guess you do."

"I think about it a lot," I confessed as the queue began to move. "How I should give as much as I take."

She thought about that, then nodded and said, "Tell me more about Michelle."

So I did.

I told her all of my stories again. How I was born two days early and Michelle was born two days late, in the car park of Gala Bingo. How we got chickenpox at the same time. How I broke my arm jumping off the climbing frame at Queens Park when we were seven because Michelle promised to catch me but didn't. About the blue and white of the Hotel Riad al Madina and the blue and yellow of Jardin Majorelle and how the Hawa Mahal changes from pink to red to gold when the sun sets.

And I told her how the coconuts in Sri Lanka are bright orange and that Michelle and I didn't want to leave. So we told our parents that we were going to live on the beach and survive on fish we'd caught ourselves.

Then I told her the story about us running away to see Beyoncé.

"I'll never forgive her for forsaking Beyoncé for chana bhatura," I told Nico, shaking my head when we were finally inside Resident and flipping through the records while we waited for Cowboy Mouth to come out.

"Understandable." She nodded, then grinned when I pulled out the *Velvet Underground & Nico* album with the Andy Warhol banana. "But I can't say definitively until I've tasted your dad's chana bhatura."

"Fair enough. I'll get him to make you some and you can make your judgment."

"I wonder if I have a Michelle?" she said then, her eyes a little darker.

I could hear the sadness flowing like water beneath the words as I realized that she probably did.

There must have been a group of friends sitting around a table in the library at Brighton College or messaging one another asking if they'd hear from her again.

I couldn't say that, though.

"Listen. I love Michelle, but it's dangerous. I can never piss her off. She knows all my secrets."

"I don't have any secrets." Nico shrugged. "This is all I've got."

It's enough, I almost said, but someone in a Resident T-shirt suddenly appeared next to us.

"Nico!" they barked. "Where the hell have you been? I thought you were dead!"

I stared, as stunned as Nico looked as they walked behind the counter and began peering at the shelves of records.

"Here it is!" they said, pulling one out and holding it up.

"That Sharon Van Etten album you preordered. It's been here since the new year. And you missed the Ezra Furman instore. What's going on? You love her."

They looked so genuinely confused that I continued to stare across the shop at them as I asked myself how they could possibly not know what had happened to her. But then I felt Nico relax next to me.

"Sorry. I've been super busy," she told them with a shrug. "GCSEs, you know?"

They seemed satisfied with that as they pointed the album at her. "You're into Sufjan Stevens, right?"

She half nodded, half shrugged, then turned to me, her eyes wide as if to say, *I'm into Sufjan Stevens.*

We followed them as they strode back around the counter and headed to the middle of the shop. "Where is it? Where is it?" they muttered as they rooted through a stack, then pulled one out. "Here we go!" They thrust it at her. "Luke Sital-Singh. He went to BIMM, you know? If you don't love it, the next one's on me."

I held my breath when they said BIMM, my heart gasping to a halt as I waited.

Waited for Nico to blink a few times, before something registered and it finally happened.

For the wall to fall and there, in the debris, she'd find herself.

The Nico who wanted to go to BIMM and preordered Sharon Van Etten albums.

But she just said, "Thanks."

Then followed them back to the counter to pay.

They slid the records into a Resident tote, then nodded toward the corner of the shop, by the bookshelf.

"Go claim your favorite spot. Cowboy Mouth is about to come out."

"I have a favorite spot," Nico whispered, her eyes shining.

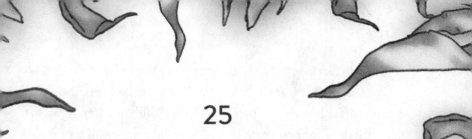

25

I couldn't help but relax after that.

Maybe I didn't need to watch every single word.

Michelle agreed when I got home to find her in my room, painting her nails.

"God, Mara," she said with a sad sigh as she stopped to shake her hands, then blow on her nails, "whatever happened that night must have been *awful* for Nico to lock it up so tight."

That didn't make me feel better, though.

But then, I don't think Michelle was trying to make me feel better.

Rather reminding me—again—to be careful.

So, when my phone rang a few minutes after she'd gone home, I knew it was her, calling to reassure me because she knew that what she'd just said would keep me up all night. I didn't even look at the screen. I just answered with "Oh my God. Have you watched that blackhead video Erin just sent? It's *disgusting*."

There was a long silence, then I heard a laugh that definitely wasn't Michelle's.

I moved my phone away from my ear to check who it was and swallowed a scream.

Nico.

"Sorry!" I cringed. "I thought it was Michelle."

"It's OK. It's my fault. I shouldn't have called unannounced at ten thirty. Is this weird?" Before I could tell her it wasn't, she sighed. "Don't answer that. I just heard myself say it out loud and I know that it is."

I couldn't help but laugh. "No, it's fine."

"Are you sure?"

"Of course," I told her, because I was painfully aware of how treacherous the transition between swapping numbers with someone and being able to casually call them was. Do it too soon and you look desperate with no boundaries but leave it too long and you risk never being able to make the transition.

It was kind of nice not to be the one agonizing about it for a change.

"OK." I heard her let go of a breath. "So how disgusting is this video?"

"Do you want me to send you the link?"

"Immediately."

I did and I heard it playing through the phone as she asked, "Do I need any context?"

"OK." I laid back against the pillows again and restarted the video so we were in the same place. "This person had a blocked pore in their stomach for, like, five years, and it turned into a *monster* blackhead."

"I didn't even know you could get blackheads in your stomach."

"Me either."

"Holy mother of Beyoncé," Nico gasped as the dermatologist showed it to the camera.

Not that they needed to.

It was impossible to miss.

"What is *that*, Mara?"

"I know!"

"Listen. Don't get me wrong." She raised her voice over the dermatologist's commentary. "The human body is a wonder. It can heal itself and grow babies and, much like my own, can somehow survive on nothing but lattes and *The Office*, but when I see stuff like this, I remember that it's a strange and hideous thing."

"Right? How can a blocked pore turn into *that*?"

"I'm definitely taking a shower after this," she said, then yelped. "They're digging!"

"I know!"

"Man, they're really going at it."

"That poor soul."

"Why am I watching this?"

"Why am I watching this *again*?"

We both sucked in a sharp breath as the dermatologist managed to expose a piece of it. Then Nico began muttering a series of *Oh my God*s that got progressively louder and louder until she shrieked, "Oh my God!"

"I know!" I shrieked back.

"Mara, it's *so big*!"

"I know!"

"How is it so big?"

"I don't know!"

"It looks like a mini Mars bar!"

"I know!"

"They have an actual hole in their stomach now! What are they going to do with it?"

"Put a Band-Aid over it and hope for the best, I guess."

"No. No. No. I can't. I can't." I heard Nico's laptop snap shut. "Listen. Let me calm down. I have to stop screaming before my mother thinks I'm being murdered and comes in here. She's already pissed at me."

"Why is she pissed at you?"

"For going to Resident."

"Why?" I asked, then gasped when I realized what she was saying. "You didn't tell her about the instore?"

"Not exactly."

"Nico!"

"I know. I know. But she never would have let me go if I'd told her."

"Where did she think you were?"

Nico let out another sigh, and when I heard her sheets shifting, I pictured her curled up on her side in a cloud of white cotton, her dark hair spilling across the pillow. "Hear me out, OK?"

"OK," I promised.

"So I only have therapy on Wednesdays now, which is great, but also not great, because it's the only time she lets me out of her sight and I can have an hour to myself. Well, myself and my therapist."

"She must let you out of her sight *sometimes*. What about when she's at work?"

"She doesn't work."

I don't know why I was so shocked at that, but I was stunned into silence for a moment.

When I went quiet, Nico said, "She used to. She used to work in PR for Samsung; that's how she met my dad. She took some time off when she had me, but then . . ." She paused and I already knew what she was going to say, grateful that she was telling me on the phone so I didn't have to look surprised. "He died when I was two."

"Oh, Nico. I'm so sorry," I said quietly.

I almost added *I had no idea* but I stopped myself.

Pretending to be surprised was one thing, but I didn't have to full-on lie, did I?

"He used to go back and forth between London and Korea a lot for his job and, one day, his plane went up, and thirteen minutes later, it came back down again."

"I'm so sorry, Nico."

"Mum didn't go into any detail when she told me, but I got the impression that between the payout she got from the airline and his pension from Samsung, she doesn't have to worry about money."

"That's nice."

As soon as I heard myself say it, I cringed.

Nice?

Really, Mara?

Nice.

How nice that her husband was killed in a plane crash leaving her alone with a two-year-old.

Nico didn't falter, though. "Anyway, I only have therapy on Wednesdays now, and tonight the stars aligned because one Wednesday a month Mum has group therapy with other parents who are *managing and learning to cope with trauma*, so

I should have had plenty of time to go to Resident and be home before her."

"Should have?" I asked, sensing where this was going.

"Yes. Well." Nico huffed and I heard the sheets rustle through the phone again. "All that tempeh she eats has obviously awakened some sort of superpower that has allowed her to master the art of time travel because she got home before me. Even though I gave myself half an hour and it only took seventeen minutes—"

"Very precise," I interjected.

"Thank you. But that's the point, Mara. I timed it *to the minute*. And I could because she insists that I get a cab to and from therapy now so I don't catch norovirus on the bus again."

"That is if the cab driver doesn't have norovirus, of course."

"Mara!" she wailed. "Don't tell her that, otherwise she'll lock me in this room and throw away the key."

I shouldn't have teased her, but I'd never heard her like that before.

The old Nico was usually so cool.

So nonchalant.

It made a pleasant change not to be the one spiraling, for once.

"Sorry," I said, trying not to laugh. "So was she mad?"

"Mad?" Nico scoffed. "When she got home and realized I wasn't there, she called me, and when I didn't answer, she freaked out, Mara. She had a full on DEFCON 1 meltdown. She called the police and everything."

I waited for her to take a breath, then said, "You can't blame her. She didn't know where you were."

Usually, I'd *never* side with a parent, but on this occasion, I understood why her mother panicked.

"I know," Nico snapped, and usually it would make me regret what I said, but for once, I didn't assume it was aimed at me. "I know what happened to me is every parent's worst nightmare. But I'm OK, Mara. I'm still here. I survived. And I'm doing everything she tells me. I only leave the house to go to therapy or for our daily walk. I'm not going back to school. I'm eating kale soup and swallowing the fistful of supplements she makes me take every day and I let some random called Serenity who looks like Sinéad O'Connor and has a hamsa hand tattoo do reiki on me. What more does she want? What's the point of surviving if she won't let me live?"

I waited for her to take another breath, but she didn't.

"And I *hate* that she's right, Mara. I hate it."

"Right about what?"

"I've only been home an hour and I already feel like shit. I'm shaking and lightheaded."

"Of course you are. You just had a run-in with your mum. Have a peppermint tea and calm down."

"Mum just made me have one." She went quiet for a moment, then said, "But I still threw up."

"You were sick again? When?"

"Just now."

"Are you OK?" My brain lurched, grasping for an explanation. "Maybe it's the shock of coming home to find your mum freaking out. Erin has really bad anxiety, and whenever she's about to have a panic attack, she has all the same symptoms. Shaking. Dizziness. Nausea. Chest pains. Do you have chest pains?"

"It's not anxiety," Nico murmured.

"Are you sure? Michelle says that loads of people have anxiety, but they don't even know it. They just think they're stressed and ignore it until they have a panic attack and are forced to deal with it."

"It's not anxiety." She sounded so sure that something in me sank.

"Is your mum being sick as well?"

"No, she's just *sick with worry, darling*," she said, putting on her mother's singsongy voice.

I shouldn't have laughed, but Nico did first.

Her laugh swiftly turned into a groan, though. "Why is my mother *always* right?"

"I assume you're looking for an answer other than *because she's a mother?*"

Nico chuckled, then groaned theatrically again.

"It can't be norovirus again. Do you think it was the latte?" I asked when she began muttering to herself. "You haven't had caffeine for so long, Nico. Maybe you're allergic to it now, or something?"

"Or maybe I've been stuck in this house so long, I'm allergic to outside," she said with a petulant huff. I waited as she began muttering to herself again, and after a minute or so, she let out another huff and said, "Maybe it was. Mum says that I'm detoxing, so while my body purges itself from all the toxins and heavy metals—"

"Heavy metals?" I asked with a frown.

"Don't ask. Mum says it's going to be like this for a few weeks. I just need to ride it out."

"So this is normal?"

"Apparently. I'm literally *expelling* the toxins."

"And the heavy metals," I added, desperate to make a Black Sabbath joke, but it wasn't the time.

"It's not fair." Nico whimpered. "I really wanted to see you after school tomorrow and borrow *Just Kids*."

"Hopefully it'll be quick like last time and you'll be better by the weekend."

"I will *definitely* be better by Sunday. I want to go to the Booth Museum."

"Maybe we should skip it until your mum's calmed down," I suggested.

"She's all for it, actually. She says it will do me good to get out and experience some culture."

"That's good!"

"Plus, she loves you. She says that every time I see you, she can see the old me."

I think I prefer the new you, though, I thought as she laughed brightly.

But I bit my tongue.

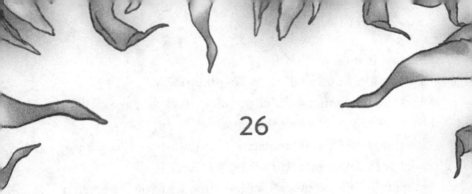

26

"Morning, Malakars!" Nico sang as she swept into the café on Sunday morning. She was obviously feeling better, her eyes clear and her cheeks flushed as she skipped over to the counter in the black embroidered kaftan she'd bought the week before. And she was wearing makeup. Not much, but I noted the sweep of black eyeliner and how much pinker her lips were when she smiled and exposed the slight gap between her front teeth.

"Morning, Nico," my mother said before I could as my father emerged from the pantry.

"Nico!" he cheered, holding up the bag of coffee beans he was carrying. "Do you want a latte?"

"No!" I pointed at him, then turned to do the same to her. "No coffee. You're detoxing, remember?"

"Don't I know it." She stuck her tongue out. "It feels like The Great Purge will never end."

When she crossed her arms, I noticed the sharp lines of her collarbones poking through her kaftan and I remember asking myself how much the loose fabric was hiding. I knew that Nico had lost weight in those months I hadn't seen her, but it had become more pronounced.

Still, she seemed full of energy as she clapped her hands and announced, "I brought you a present!"

My mother didn't even try to be cool about it. "I love presents!"

Nico reached into the pink-and-red Feminist Bookshop tote bag hanging from her shoulder and pulled out a dark wooden picture frame. When Nico handed it to my mother, she squealed.

"Oh my God!"

"My mum made it," Nico said with a clumsy smile.

"I love it!" She turned the frame to show my father and I saw it was a needlepoint of a steaming cup of coffee that said, *MALAKAR'S. HOME OF THE EXTRA HOT LATTE*, which made my father howl.

"I love it!" my mother told her again as she twisted around and took the photo of Michelle and me as three-year-olds, sitting side by side on the counter, off the wall and replaced it with Nico's needlepoint.

"Nice," I said when she tossed the frame on the side by the order book.

"Oh." Nico raised her finger at me, then reached into her tote bag again. "And I got this for you, Mara."

"Me?" I was so thrilled that I let out a small chuckle as she produced a book.

"Oh my God," I said under my breath.

The Price of Salt.

It was as though my heart had tripped on a paving slab and when it started again, twice as fast, I heard Michelle telling me it didn't mean anything.

It was just a book.

But it's a sapphic classic.

"Have you read it?" I heard her ask as I stared at the cover, my hands trembling.

It doesn't mean anything, I heard Michelle tell me again.

"It's my favorite book," she told me when I made myself look up, her pupils suddenly twice the size.

But before I could tell her that it was mine as well, a customer appeared at my side.

"Are your mangoes local?" they asked, peering at the Danishes.

My mother didn't flinch. "Of course. I picked them this morning at East Brighton Park."

I hadn't been to the Booth Museum since we went there on a school trip when we were eight. With Ms. Fisher, funnily enough, who had to tell Louise to stop daring us to touch the yellowing skeletons while Michelle told us what each one was. It was just as bizarre as I remembered. Gloriously Victorian, stacked floor to ceiling with glass cases featuring dioramas of stuffed birds and animals in various unnaturally natural poses.

The butterflies were still my favorite, I discovered. When we were eight, Michelle had refused to go near them even though they were long dead, saying that butterflies couldn't be trusted because they were just moths with better outfits. Nico loved them, though, her kaftan floating as she drifted from case to case, pointing to some that were as pale as the pages of an old book, while others seemed to exist in sheer defiance of them, their wings shimmering with splashes of Brighton blue and egg-yolk yellow and glowing, gaudy lime green.

"Do you need to get back?" she asked, her eyes bright with something as we left the Booth. "I'm not distracting you, am I? I know your GCSEs start soon, so you probably need to study, right?"

"You're not distracting me," I told her, even though she was. Distracting me in the most delightfully corrupting way.

"Are you sure?"

"Absolutely. I was in the library all day yesterday, so my parents made me promise to take today off. Dad's worried my head is going to explode. Which, after trying to perfect quadratic formulas, is entirely possible."

"OK." She shivered with excitement. "What do you want to do?"

"Shall we walk?"

"Let's walk."

So we walked.

Walked with the sort of urgency that only a sunny Sunday when you have nowhere else to be allows. It's funny, because from the moment I walked out of Brighton station and found her, I'd always been achingly aware of the space between us. Not just the days—or weeks—when I hadn't heard from her, but how near I let myself get to her, constantly calculating the difference between *enough* and *too much* to make sure I got it just right.

But the new Nico had no regard for personal space. It wasn't like before when she'd walk stiffly beside me, so quickly that I had to gallop to keep up. Now she was everywhere at once. Skipping and cackling as she asked question after question. Our knuckles would catch and our hips would graze, only for a second, but it would be enough to make me weak. To make my legs unsteady and my heart marvel at the wonder of her.

That afternoon was punctuated by each of those swift, startling collisions, and each time they happened, it reignited something in me that made me want to break my promise to Michelle to be careful. To not get carried away. Because with each step, I watched Nico grow a little stronger. A little brighter. So bright that I told myself not to stand too close to her, like I was soaking up her light, or something.

I could see a new Nico taking shape right in front of me.

A Nico who laughed and twirled and pointed to things as though she was seeing them for the first time.

Thinking about it now, she was, wasn't she?

She was seeing *everything* for the first time.

I couldn't take my eyes off her, and when she spotted a mural ahead and ran over to see it, I stopped and watched her. Her sure, straight back. The rise and fall of her curls. The flutter of her kaftan. But then she noticed that I was no longer by her side and stopped, waiting for me to catch up, then smiled at me when I did, and I remember how it made my heart sing at knowing that she'd registered my absence. She slipped her arm around my shoulders and took a photo of us in front of the mural, her cheek so close to mine that I could feel the heat of her. And I remember telling myself to memorize it as I closed my eyes and inhaled so deeply, I was sure I'd inhaled the sun. This ball of heat in my chest that burned everything away until it felt like we'd finally made it out of the shallows and into the open water, our future rolling from our feet, as far and as deep as the sea they'd pulled her out of five months before.

I wonder if she felt it too?

I think she might have because then she asked what I had planned for the summer. Asked if I wanted to go with her to the Brighton Book Festival and Pride and to see some band

I'd never heard of who were playing the Dome at the end of August. And I didn't know what to say. The old Nico wouldn't commit to two Saturdays in a row, let alone a gig in three months' time. Not that we'd even been to a gig before that instore at Resident. She'd tell me about them the next day or want to meet up beforehand. We'd grab a coffee and kiss for a while until she checked her phone, then say she had to go.

Thinking about it now, I guess I was just someone to waste time with.

Someone to keep her company until it was time for her to do what she actually wanted to do.

But the new Nico *wanted* to be with me. Before, we'd just walk around, her talking and me hurt and burning for her to feel something that never came. But now she talked *to* me, rather than *at* me. She even asked about boring stuff, like school. She wanted to know how my revision was going and when my exams were so she could make a note of them and send positive energy. I teased her about that, of course, and she laughed—wild and bright—saying that the months of kale and reiki had finally rubbed off on her.

Oh, it was perfect. Nico was perfect. So happy. So light. So excited about everything as we sat cross-legged on the grass beneath the shadow of the Pavilion, making daisy chains. Even the afternoon was perfect. The first fine day of the year, the sun high and bright, crowning the tops of our heads.

It's always my favorite day of the year when, from nowhere, you feel spring tip into summer. The year before—before I met Nico, before any of this—Michelle, Louise, Erin, May, and I had sat on the beach, drinking bubble tea, and I remember telling myself to enjoy it because soon the tourists would be there, discovering our secret places. Then everything would be loud and strange and there'd be no room for us as they took up all the tables at the café and their towels claimed our favorite spots on the beach so they became their favorite spots on the beach. Until September when they left with pockets full of pebbles and Brighton was ours again.

That afternoon, I told myself the same thing.

To enjoy it.

I should have known what Nico was planning, though, when we eventually ended up outside Nando's.

"No," I told her sternly, shaking my head. "Look how sick you were last weekend after *one* latte."

But she was already heading inside, and when I followed, she smiled sweetly at me.

"I'll go easy, I promise," she said, pointing at the chili poster. "Lemon and herb."

And I know—*I know*—I should have tried harder to stop her, but she looked so happy as someone led us to a table. A table that I knew from experience was her favorite, because it was by the sauces.

So I let her order her lemon and herb chicken and watched as she devoured it, then waited for her to have a Proustian rush. And she did—sort of—as she swooned and said, "I could eat this every day."

But that was it as we talked and she tried all the sauces. I don't know how she did it, but she got it all out of me. Everything. Things I hadn't even said out loud before. Like how scared I was that everything would change when we'd done our GCSEs. How I wasn't sure if I wanted to go away for uni. How I worried it was weird that I wanted to stay at home when everyone else couldn't wait to leave.

It was as though with each question, she was searching for a loose thread until she found it, then tugged.

Let me lead her through my life until I'd told her everything.

Every fear.

Every hope.

Every secret.

Looking back on it now, I wonder if she kept it all.

Stored it somewhere.

My memories where hers should be.

When I was done, she looked at me with a slow smile and said, "I told my therapist about you."

My heart thundered because no sentence that begins with *I told my therapist about you* ends well.

"My therapist says I'm trying too hard." She twirled her straw in her glass of Fanta. "She says I'm so focused on trying to remember who I used to be that I'm never just *here*, you know? In the present."

I get that, I thought as I recalled how May tells me that I'm always thinking, never just being.

"My therapist says I need to be more present. So I told her what you said."

My heart hiccuped. "What *I* said?"

"Yeah. When we promised to be exactly who we are right now because there's nothing wrong with who we are." Nico stopped to take a deep breath, then exhaled. "So, I need to tell you something, Mara. But it's really hard, so you're going to have to give me a second, OK? Because you're literally my only friend and I'm scared that once I tell you this, things are going to be weird between us and I don't want that because this is the safest I've felt since they hauled me out of the sea. But I need to talk to someone, OK?"

"OK," I said when she stopped to suck in a breath.

And I don't know how, because it felt like a trapdoor had opened beneath me and I was falling.

Falling and falling.

"I don't know how else to say this, Mara, so I'm just going to say it, OK?"

"OK," I said again, but all I could think was *Don't say it.*

Don't tell me that you know.

Don't tell me that you know that I've been lying to you.

But she didn't.

She said, "I realized something when I was reading *The Price of Salt*, which is why I gave it to you."

I was so sure that she knew that it derailed me for a moment and I blinked at her, my lips parted.

"I realized . . ." She trailed off, her cheeks going from pink to red. "You know?"

I just continued to stare at her.

Nico looked confused. "Have you read *The Price of Salt*?"

I nodded.

"So you know what it's about?"

I nodded again.

I watched her eyebrows rise as she waited for me to catch up. "It's about . . ."

She paused so I could finish the sentence.

"You like girls!" I gasped, then covered my mouth with my hand.

I didn't mean to yell it like that.

Not while we were in a packed Nando's on a Sunday afternoon.

I'd forgotten that we were until a dozen heads turned to glance our way.

I took my hand away from my mouth to press it to my forehead. "Shit. Sorry." I cringed, my whole face burning when everyone around us went back to their conversations. "Did I just out you in Nando's?"

I was *mortified*, but Nico just laughed. "Like I care what they think. I care what *you* think, though." She pressed her hand to her chest. "Like I said, I don't want things to be weird between us, Mara. I couldn't bear it."

I had to choose my next words very carefully, I knew, the burden of it pinning me to the chair as the words jostled for space in my mouth, repositioning themselves as I thought about what she really needed to hear.

"Things won't be weird, I promise. Nothing's changed."

I saw her relax then. She looked up at the ceiling as she let go of a long breath, and when I saw her eyelids stuttering in the fluorescent light, I felt my heart flickering on and off in my chest like a light bulb.

On.

Off.

On.

Off.

On.

Off.

Then she looked down at me again with a loose smile. "I'm glad I told you, Mara."

"I'm glad you felt able to tell me. Even if I yelled it out for everyone in Nando's to hear."

The back of my neck stung, but she just laughed again, her dark curls trembling in time with my heart as she looked me in the eye again. "And you promise that things aren't weird now?"

I drew a cross over my chest with the tip of my finger. I don't think she believed me, though, so I said, "I had a similar reaction to reading *The Price of Salt*."

"Yeah?" she said, her eyes wide, and she looked so relieved it made my heart *ache*.

"So you like girls." She pointed at me, her cheeks red again. "Yeah."

Then she pointed at herself. "And I like girls."

"Yeah."

When I nodded, she nodded back. "That's very interesting."

"It certainly falls within the category of interesting."

She looked at me for a beat longer than was comfortable, the corners of her mouth twitching.

"Can I ask"—she leaned in—"how did you know that you, you know?"

"Prefer girls?" I laughed and I heard how silly it sounded. How nervous. "I didn't."

Nico frowned. "What do you mean?"

"I won't lie and say part of me always knew, but I did know I didn't feel what I was supposed to, you know? Then I read *The Price of Salt* and it articulated something I wasn't able to put into words yet. It made me feel what I was supposed to feel, but didn't, when I read the books and watched the films my friends loved."

Nico nodded.

"I don't know." I stopped to take a gulp of Fanta because I needed a second before I said, "I guess something changed after that. Something in me settled. Went quiet."

Nico nodded again.

"Michelle was the first to notice it, of course." I wiped a smear of lipstick from the lip of my glass with the pad of my thumb. "How every few months, I'd make a new friend and become *obsessed* with them. There was Jo Ferne in Year Eight, who I used to swap books with. We'd leave notes between the pages that said stuff like *Is this creepy or romantic?* and *Bella shouldn't be with either of them. She should be with Alice.*"

Nico almost choked on a chip. "Oh my God." She coughed, wiping her mouth with the back of her hand. "Is this when I confess to rereading the Twilight books I found hidden at the back of my wardrobe?"

The old Nico read Twilight? I was about to shriek.

Luckily, before I could, she said, "Bella should have *absolutely* been with Alice, not Edward."

I raised my glass to her as if to say, *Right?* and she laughed as I said, "Then there was Francesca Tate, who had *super*-shiny blonde hair and wore headbands and cute little pink cardigans, which isn't my thing at all, but I met her handing out flyers in Churchill Square and *made* Michelle and our parents go to her church."

Nico leaned back and stared at me. "Church?"

"I know," I said, still appalled with myself. "It lasted until Francesca told me that *Tipping the Velvet* was ungodly because it was about 'lesbians' and tried to get me to sign up for a ten-week Alpha Course."

Nico had to cover her mouth before she spat her Macho Peas on me.

"I'm sorry!" She shook her head when she'd recovered, but I could tell that she wasn't at all.

"Then there was Cat at Meowko. That was the summer I was addicted to bubble tea. Then there was Rachel Roland. She was the opposite of Francesca with her smudged eyeliner and cigarettes."

She kind of looked like you, I thought, but made myself take another sip of Fanta.

"And who was after Rachel Roland?" Nico asked eagerly.

You, I almost said as I felt myself melting under the heat of her gaze.

"No one," I lied. "I tried to stop doing it after Michelle pointed out that it was a pattern."

And it was. I'd meet someone, fall endlessly, senselessly in love with them, but do nothing about it and be heartbroken—and astonished—when nothing came of it. Then I'd mourn for weeks. Weep and wallow and lie on the floor listening to *Back to Black* by Amy Winehouse on repeat. Until I met someone else and did it all again.

Rinse.

Lather.

Repeat.

"What did Michelle say when she pointed it out?" Nico asked. "Did she ask you outright?"

"Sort of. It started with May, actually," I said, recalling that afternoon last Easter, a few months before I met Nico. "May had just got back from seeing her family in Greece and we all went to Five Guys."

"Which is how all special moments should be marked."

"Not Nando's?"

"It wasn't *that* special."

"True. It's not like one of us was getting married, or something."

"Laugh now, Malakar, but we're having our wedding reception here and I don't want to hear a word about it."

I was so flustered by the *our* that it felt like that trapdoor had opened and I was falling again.

But Nico didn't notice as she reached for another chip. "So you were at Five Guys?"

"Yeah." I nodded, then waited a second or two to catch my breath. "We were at Five Guys, and when we asked May how Greece was, she told us that she'd spent the entire time 'chilling' with someone called Amy. She just said it, *I guess I'm pan.* Then she sipped her milkshake and nicked one of my Cajun fries."

It was so easy.

So effortlessly, reassuringly easy.

"Were you surprised?" Nico asked.

"Yeah, but only because she'd never shown any interest in girls."

"Was anyone weird about it?"

"That was the only weird thing, how *not* weird it was. No one made a crude quip and Louise didn't ask May if she fancied her and, when we went to Beyond Retro afterward, May and Erin shared a dressing room, like they always did. It was like nothing had happened. Like May had told us her favorite color, or something."

"That's nice." Nico smiled to herself. "That's how it should be."

"That's what Michelle said. She said it was bullshit. She said if she didn't have to come out as straight, then you shouldn't have to come out as anything else. You should be allowed to just be." I chuckled to myself. "Trouble is, I thought she was using the royal *you*, but then she reached over and squeezed my arm and told me that it was OK, that I didn't need to do what May had just done if I didn't want to, and I almost fell off the bed."

"So Michelle knew before you did?"

"She knows *everything* before I do. She pointed out the friend-crush thing and that I didn't just think Zendaya was cool and I liked more than Billie Eilish's style. I mean, I hadn't liked a guy for two years."

"Who was it?" Nico asked with a wolfish smile.

"Timothée Chalamet," I admitted, but then I thought about it. "Although, with hindsight, I think that may have been more of a *Call Me by Your Name* thing rather than a Timothée Chalamet thing."

"I love that film." She sighed, then said, "So, that's when you knew you were into girls?"

"I guess." I shrugged. "But I had no idea that you could know something like that without it being, you know, *confirmed*. I'd never been with a girl, had I? But, as Michelle pointed out, she never needed to be with a boy to know she liked them and no one questioned that."

Nico thought about that, then peered at me from under her eyelashes. "Do your parents know?"

"It's spooky, because the following Saturday we were at my cousin Eshma's wedding. Mum and I were watching the first dance when my aunty Turvi passed our table, saying that would be me one day, and I must have looked as horrified as I felt, because Mum leaned in and told me that I didn't have to have that, if I didn't want it. She said that she'd fought the good fight for forty years so I could have whatever I wanted."

I blinked and shook my head. "But the strange thing was, *that's* what I was thinking about while I was watching Eshma and Aakash. Not that I *didn't* want that, but whether I *could* have it if I was into girls. The Sangeet. The Mehndi party. The saris. A spotlight as 'Moh Moh Ke Dhaage' played. Would anyone cry? Would anyone turn up? I don't even know if I want those things, but I at least want the option, you know?"

Nico nodded. "So what did you say to your mum?"

"I wanted to say something, but we were at a family wedding. Talk about time and place. I couldn't say anything with my aunties hovering and Dad heading back to our table with another plate of jalebi. So, I lost my nerve," I confessed with a defeated sigh. "I mean, I'd only just said it out loud to Michelle the weekend before, hadn't I? So I didn't know if I was ready to say it to my mother yet."

Nico nodded again.

"So, I brushed it off, said that I didn't know what I wanted.

But Mum said, *I think you know what you want and it's OK. You can have whatever you want with whomever you want."*

When I summoned the courage to look up again, Nico's eyes were *huge*. "She knew?"

"She knew."

"Did Michelle tell her?"

"No way. She would *never*."

"So how did she know, then?"

"I don't know." I shrugged. "She just *knew*."

"How did it feel?"

"Like I suddenly fit, you know? Like the universe shifted out of the way to make space for me."

Nico's chin shivered, her eyes wet. "I want to feel that."

"You will," I promised, and I didn't even think about it as I reached across the table for her hand.

It was the first time I'd touched her since we'd found each other again. Touched her on purpose, anyway. Our hips hadn't grazed while we walked. My cheek hadn't accidentally skimmed hers while we took that photo in front of the mural.

No, this time it was deliberate.

Intentional.

Expected and unexpected, all at once.

If this was a film, then that would have been the moment it all came back to her and she remembered.

But this isn't a film, so she just squeezed my hand and asked, "What if I never feel that?"

"You will."

When she smiled, I felt a *ping* in my chest, like a coiled spring, bounding forward.

"Thank you, Mara. I really needed to hear that."

I nodded, holding her hand a little tighter.

"I knew you'd understand. It's so weird. I've only known you for, like, three weeks, but I feel like I've known you a really long time." Her brow creased as she tilted her head. "Are you sure we've never met before?"

I didn't want to lie, but I had to, so I shook my head.

"Maybe in another life, then," she said with a smile so tender, it made my heart snap in two.

27

"I'm done," I announced the next morning, while we were sitting around our table at the library. "I can't do this anymore. I can't keep lying to Nico." I crossed my arms with a huff. "I can't."

There was a beat of silence, then Louise reached for her phone. "Who had three weeks?"

Erin thrust her hand up. "Me!"

"Nope." She shook her head as she peered at the screen. "Erin Alaba, you said *two* weeks."

She frowned. "Did I?"

"And I said two *months*." Louise seemed genuinely baffled by that. "What was I on that day?"

"You'd rewatched *The Notebook* the night before," Michelle reminded her.

"Oh yeah. So Erin and I are out. As is May. Sweet, sweet May Petrakis who said *Never*."

"Thanks, May." I nodded across the table at her and she nodded back.

"Which means," Louise announced, pausing for dramatic effect as Michelle and Erin did a drumroll with their hands on the edge of the table, "the winner with three weeks *exactly* is . . . Michelle Chen!"

"Thank you." She bowed with a smug smirk. "Thank you."

"So annoying," Erin muttered, inspecting her nails.

Louise threw her head back and whimpered. "This means you get to pick the next film we watch."

"You're gonna love this one, guys." Michelle grinned, holding her hands up. "It's a National Geographic documentary about these French scientists who fell in love while studying active volcanoes!"

There was a rumble of discontent around the table, which I interrupted with a scowl.

"Um. Excuse me. I can't believe you guys."

They stopped and looked at me like, *What?*

"You started a book on when I'd fold?"

Then they looked at me like, *Of course.*

"How is it any different from the one we started on when Chesca is going to Chesca again?" Erin asked.

"Hey!" May yelped.

"Which we *all* lost, by the way," Michelle said sourly as May mirrored me and slumped in her chair with her arms crossed. "Except this one"—she thumbed at me—"the hopeless romantic, who refused to take part."

May nodded across the table at me this time. "Thanks, Mara."

I nodded back. "I'm rooting for you, babe."

Michelle looked between us with a sneer. "I hate losing."

"You lost that one because you said *seven hours*," Louise told her as May yelped again.

Michelle looked unrepentant, though. "At least I won this one."

"Good for you!" I uncrossed my arms to clap at her. "You win. I'm a loser."

"Hey!" Michelle's face softened as she turned to me. "No one said you were a loser, Mara."

"Why do I feel like one, then?"

"You're not a loser. You can't do this because you're a horrible, *horrible* liar. You're terrible at it."

"And you couldn't have reminded me of that? You were *right there* when I was promising Nico's mum I'd lie!"

"Like you would have listened!"

That's true.

I refused to give her the satisfaction, though, so I closed my eyes and whined. "Guys, I feel awful." When I opened them again, they were looking at me with matching frowns. "Nico keeps confiding in me about stuff she doesn't think I know, but I do know, like her dad dying. Then, yesterday, she told me something *really* personal. One of the most personal things you can tell someone, and I just had to sit there, looking surprised."

May winced. "What else were you supposed to do?"

"I don't know." I crossed my arms and slumped in my chair again. "But I feel like shit. Nico told me that I was her only friend, and friends don't lie to each other, do they?"

There was a titter of laughter at that, which I interrupted again.

"Come on! Lying to Louise about liking her haircut is one thing, but—"

"Hey!" she interrupted with a gasp, bringing her hand up to touch her blonde curls.

Erin smiled sweetly at her. "It looks much better now it's grown out."

"But lying to Nico about being her . . ." I hesitated, then sighed. ". . . *whatever* we were, is quite another."

Erin raised her right shoulder, then let it drop again. "Yeah, but what's the alternative?"

"I tell her the truth."

May looked genuinely panicked. "But you can't! What if her head explodes?"

Michelle rolled her eyes. "Calm down, Sigmund Freud."

"Freud has a point, though." Erin tipped her chin up at May. "If this is what Nico's therapist has decided is best for her, you can't interfere, Mara. Nico's mum was honest with you from the get-go, and you agreed to it."

"I didn't know it would be this hard, though."

"What if you told her that you used to know her before, but you weren't, like, best mates," May suggested.

"I thought about that," I admitted with a sore sigh. "But I know what Nico's like. She'd just come at me with a whole new barrage of questions. How did we meet? Where? When? Do we have any friends in common? How often did we see each other? Where did we go? What did we talk about? *Ugh.*" I growled, putting my hands in my hair and fisting them. "I'll mess up and I can't mess up."

"Mara's right." Michelle nodded. "It's easier to say that she doesn't know Nico at all, rather than tell her that she sort of knew her. Because where's the line? How does she choose what she knows and what she doesn't?"

"Plus, it's been too long now," Erin agreed. "She can't just say, *Oh, by the way, we used to be friends.*"

I tugged on my hair again and groaned. "This is the worst."

"I know," Michelle said gently. "None of us thought it would take this long."

Louise nodded. "I for sure thought Nico would have remembered by now."

"It must be awful for her"—Michelle squeezed my arm when my gaze slid over to the encyclopedias and waited for me to look back again—"stuck in this weird limbo between the old Nico and the new Nico."

"Yeah. She's gone from one cliché to the next," Erin said with a brittle chuckle.

I turned to look at her. "What do you mean?"

"She's gone from the brooding, emotionally unavailable fuckgirl—"

"Jess Mariano in hot-pink lipstick," Michelle added.

"Exactly!" Erin pointed at her. "To the Manic Pixie Dream Girl who is everything you ever wanted."

Michelle shrugged. "But you don't know if she'll stay that way or go back to the old Nico."

"No wonder your head is wrecked," May said with a pout.

"I couldn't do it," Louise admitted, shaking her head. "It's like you're in limbo until she remembers."

"It's been *five months*, guys," I reminded them. "What if she never remembers?"

"Maybe she won't," Michelle said with a small shrug.

Six percent of the time, I reminded myself as I took my hands out of my hair.

"Maybe," she continued, "whatever happened that night is so bad that she has to keep it locked away."

That made my stomach turn inside out.

"Or maybe," she said, her tone a little brighter, "she'll remember everything but *that*."

"And she'll end up being someone in between the old Nico and the new Nico," Erin mused.

"Exactly." May gestured at her. "Nico hasn't found her final form yet."

"So what am I supposed to do until then?"

Erin looked around the table, then said, "Give her some time to work it out."

"Erin's right and you know I hate saying that." Michelle arched an eyebrow. "Give Nico some time to sort her head out. In the meantime, let her therapist do their thing. Like Nico's mum said, it might take months before she remembers, so you need to be patient. Trust the process."

Trust the process.

"But what do I do in the meantime? I can't keep lying to her, but I can't tell her the truth, either."

When they didn't say anything, just looked around the table at each other, I stuck both my thumbs up.

"Great. Thanks, guys. That's really helpful."

"Like Michelle said, give her some time to sort her head out," Louise offered. "If you took a step back now, she'd understand. She knows your GCSEs start next week."

"Exactly!" Michelle hissed, then jabbed at the table with her finger. "I want it noted for the record that the timing of all of this is horrendous. You need to focus, Mara. I'm not going to BHASVIC without you."

"Yes. Let's not lose sight of what's really important here." Louise gestured at her. "Michelle."

She held her hands up. "I'm just saying. This isn't worth Mara ruining her life for."

"Calm down, Miss Havisham," Erin told her. "Estella's not ruining her life."

"But I can't ghost her," I said, my brow tightening with panic. "Not after what she told me yesterday."

"No one's telling you to ghost her," Erin reassured me. "Just be her friend."

"Her friend," I repeated with a nod.

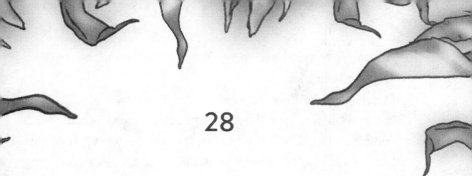

28

With that, Nico and I were back in the shallows. The future I'd felt roll out in front us that Sunday no longer a wide, ceaseless sea. Rather an eddy that I circled, stuck and exhausted, as I tried to be something I'd never been.

Her friend.

I was aching to see her, of course, but I didn't trust myself, suddenly grateful for the four and a half miles between her house and mine because I could blame study groups at school and being stuck in the library for not being able to see her.

Not that I needed to. She got sick after our afternoon at the Booth, and while I was worried that she didn't bounce back as quickly as she had before, she didn't seem concerned.

If anything she was furious that her mother was right.

She shouldn't be eating Nando's.

Nico being stuck in bed meant that we could only talk on the phone, which made the friend thing easier because we could keep the conversation light. Safe. I'd ask her which of her father's records she'd listened to the night before and she'd ask me what I was revising. I'd read to her from *Jane Eyre* and taught her the Periodic Table Song and told her about coastal erosion and the cracks in the cliff face at Beachy Head.

Anything to not have to say what I really wanted to say. That I missed her.

I thought I was doing a good job—that it was working—but after nearly a week of flimsy conversations and precise texts to confirm what time I could talk, Nico didn't check first, just called me on Friday afternoon while I sat on my bed, trying not to spill Cherry Coke on my laptop as I riffled through my notes.

I assumed it was Michelle, so I answered with a huff. "I hope you have Pocky for later because I just stress-eaten an entire box. Did I tell you that I hate Edward the Confessor?"

Nico didn't hesitate. "Well, he speaks very highly of you, Mara."

"Oh!" I almost did spill my Cherry Coke then. "Nico! Sorry! I thought it was Michelle."

"Is this a bad time?"

"Not at all," I muttered as I put the bottle of Cherry Coke on my bedside table. "I just . . ."

"Hate Edward the Confessor," she finished when I trailed off.

But I don't hate you, I almost said, but didn't, worried that was veering from friendly into flirty.

So I laughed, but it sounded fake.

Like I was laughing at a customer's joke at the café while I made their coffee.

Nico called me on it immediately. "I knew I'd made things weird."

When I heard her sigh, I felt wretched. "No. No. *No*, it's me, Nico. My head is all over the place."

Which wasn't a lie, in hindsight.

The inside of my head had felt like a full washing-up bowl since I'd last seen her.

"Are you sure?" she asked. "Last Sunday was *a lot*. It was supposed to be a fun afternoon at the Booth and now I'm thinking I shouldn't have told you all that stuff, not with your GCSEs starting on Monday."

"It's OK," I said as I waited for her to catch her breath. "I'm glad you told me, Nico."

"Yeah?"

"Yeah. I mean, that's what friends do, right? Tell each other things like that."

I'm not sure who I was trying to convince, though.

Me or her.

"Yeah. Friends," she said, and the word sounded strange— foreign—when she said it. Like one of the French verbs I'd been trying to memorize before I gave up in favor of Edward the Confessor.

Nous sommes amies.

Nous étions amies.

Nous serons amies.

"Did you get my card?" she asked then, and I felt even worse as I glanced across my room at it on my desk and remembered how my heart had leaped up in my chest when I opened it and realized it was from her.

She'd never given me a card before, and as I stared at it, there was something almost intimate about it as I imagined her biting her lip as she decided what to say, then the edge of her hand brushing along the inside before she picked it up and blew on the ink to secure the words in case they smudged.

"Don't read into it, Mara," Michelle told me when I showed her. "It doesn't mean anything."

But I still did, of course, letting the thought that it did settle in some secret place.

Where I kept all the other things about Nico that felt like more than a coincidence.

"I just opened it. I was going to call when I was done reading this chapter on Edward the Confessor."

"That's OK," Nico said brightly. "I'm just glad you got it in time. You know what Royal Mail is like."

When she went quiet, I realized that she was the one who was lying this time because it wasn't OK. She'd sent me a card to wish me luck with my GCSEs and I couldn't be bothered to call and thank her.

Friends don't do things like that.

But then she said, "I miss you, Mara."

And it was so sudden that she sounded as surprised that she'd said it as I was to hear it.

"I miss you, too," I told her before I could tell myself not to.

The words finally flying out of me like birds freed from the cage of my mouth.

Even through the phone, I could hear her relief. "You do?"

"Of course I do."

"I was thinking," she said, the relief gone now, replaced by a note of playfulness. "Tomorrow's Saturday, so you're at the library, right? Why don't you come here afterward? Just for an hour," she added, her voice higher when she thought I was going to object. "Your exams start on Monday, so I won't see you for, like, a month."

But she didn't need to because I wasn't going to object.

29

I'd never had cause to go to Rottingdean before. We'd driven through there once, on the way back from Saltdean two summers ago when my parents got it in their heads that we needed a bigger house. That was until they pulled up to a bungalow with UPVC windows and a family of gnomes in the front garden and turned the car around.

There was an accident on Marine Drive so we had to go through Rottingdean, and while we weren't there long enough to see much, the parade of trophy homes, with their high gates and sweeping driveways, was enough to confirm why my parents insisted that even if we won the lottery, we'd never live there. They were the sort of houses that footballers and plastic surgeons lived in, my mother said. People who weren't home enough to cook in the hand-built Italian kitchens or watch films in the home theaters.

So that's what I'd pictured when Nico first told me that she lived in Rottingdean. A big house with a big white sofa I'd be too scared to sit on and a big blue pool out back. But as I turned onto her road that Saturday afternoon, I was surprised to find that the houses were actually kind of modest. Don't get me wrong. If they were anywhere other than Rottingdean, they wouldn't be considered modest. Each one was detached and you could pretty much fit our three-up, two-down cottage in the garage. But like I said, you hear Rottingdean and you think high gates and sweeping driveways, not family houses with Volvos parked in the driveway.

Luckily for me—and my feet, given the new sandals I was wearing—Nico didn't live far from the bus stop, in a cul-de-sac set back from Marine Drive under the shadow of the windmill. I was surprised by that as well. I didn't think places like that existed in Brighton. It was so normal. So suburban with its neat lawns and sensible cars. The sort of road where I felt the net curtains twitching as I looked for her house.

Not like my road. Between the kids playing football in the street and our neighbor's dog, Chester, a scruffy miniature schnauzer who had something to say about everything, it was chaos in comparison. Then there was the couple who lived in the house on the corner who had just painted their front door to look like the TARDIS.

If someone did that here, they'd probably call the police.

"Mara!" Nico's mother sang when she opened the front door, then immediately pulled me into a hug so tight the soles of my sandals left the doormat.

"Hey, Mrs. Rudolph," I said when she let me go. "How are you?"

"Sweet, sweet girl," she sang, ushering me in. "How nice of you to come all this way just to see Nico!"

Rebecca clasped her hands together and I finally had a chance to look at her. Nico had never described her, so I didn't know what to expect. She was tall with skin as pale as the moths at the Booth, and huge blue eyes that settled on me as

I tried to meet her gaze but couldn't as I realized that she had Nico's hair.

Or Nico had her hair, I should say.

Thick and dark and *wild*.

"What's that, darling?" she asked, gesturing at the bag I was holding.

"Oh," I said, grateful for an excuse to look down. "I brought you guys some food. Carrot and coriander soup, dhal and parathas, and an apple and blackberry cake." When I saw the skin between her eyebrows pinch, I added, "Don't worry, it's all vegan, gluten-free, and sugar-free. Plus, my dad made it, so it's delicious, I promise."

Her face was still for a second—tight—and I remembered how it made the back of my neck burn because the way she was looking at me was as though she was looking for something, but couldn't find it.

Then it was like someone had hit a light switch.

"How lovely, darling! That's so kind! You must thank him for me!"

I tried not to stare, because I'd never met anyone like Rebecca before. She was like a Disney princess. Soft-spoken and light-footed as she took me by the elbow and literally *floated* to the kitchen in her long pink dress.

Actually, I had met someone like her before, I realized. She had the same energy as Nico—the new Nico—and the change in her suddenly made sense as I watched Rebecca waft around the kitchen. She was everywhere, all at once, as she took the glass dishes out of the bag and put them in the fridge, then filled the kettle and asked me question after question about my parents and the café and school and told me about the year she lived in Paris, then confessed that she was rusty but still offered to help me with my French verbs.

She even smelled the same as Nico.

That same sweet, pink perfume.

"Nico's meditating," Rebecca explained, and I bit down on a smart remark as she took two mugs out of a kitchen cabinet. "But that's good, because it gives you and me a moment alone, my dear."

She turned to me with a smile that made my heart hitch in my chest as she held up the mugs, then lowered her voice and said, "I wanted to thank you for not telling Nico about before. I know this must be hard for you."

"It's awful," I admitted with a miserable sigh that prompted her to tilt her head at me.

"But this is what you wanted, darling."

No, it's what you *wanted*, I almost said, but she suddenly looked so wounded that I swallowed it back.

"Mara, we discussed it, remember?"

She turned to put the mugs on the counter, and when she turned back, her smile was noticeably sharper. "We decided," she said, and there was that Head Teacher tone again, "that this was best for Nico, didn't we?"

"I know," I conceded, even though *we* hadn't decided anything. "But I hate lying to her."

A crease appeared between her eyebrows. "So, you think Nico's therapist and I are lying to her?"

No.

That's not what I said.

They were the same words but she'd rearranged them into something else entirely.

"Of course not," I said, suddenly short of breath as I watched her reach for a box of peppermint tea.

"So, what's the problem, then? I thought you agreed that this was best for Nico?"

I wouldn't say that I *agreed*, but then I didn't object either, did I?

"You agreed," she said over her shoulder, her back to me as she put a teabag in each mug, "that it was best for Nico to remember you in her own time. Although"—she turned to face me again, her eyebrow arched—"if she didn't recognize you as soon as she saw you, perhaps you didn't mean as much to her as you thought."

I don't know how I didn't yelp, my heart smarting from the blow of her saying what I'd always feared.

"But you know Nico," she said, her smile an interruption this time. "So restless. So fickle. I dread to think how many of you are scattered around Brighton right now, waiting for her to call."

Or London, my traitorous brain reminded me as I thought about Nya.

Then my traitorous brain reminded me of something else I'd been ignoring.

Mara, are you sure you want to do this again?

Rebecca laughed—a harsh, starched laugh that made the hair on the back of my neck bristle.

Then she turned away from me and sang to herself as she made the tea.

* * *

When Nico's mother was done, I offered to take the tray, desperate to get away from her and her satisfied smile as I stood there, still burning from what she'd said. But she wouldn't let me, my heartbeat quickening with each step until we reached the door to Nico's room. Rebecca went in first, and when she glided over to the desk to put down the tray, I finally saw Nico and my heart skidded into my ribs.

She looked *awful*.

As thin as a spider and hunched in bed under a heavy floral duvet, even though that day it was so warm I could feel the back of my dress sticking to me. Or maybe it was nothing to do with the weather. Maybe it was seeing Nico, frail and drowning in a pair of pink tartan pajamas that were several sizes too big for her.

Or they were then.

Maybe they fitted her once.

I couldn't move, fixed to the spot as Nico told her mother to stop fussing as Rebecca handed her one of the mugs of tea. But she didn't listen and straightened the duvet, smoothing it with her palms while Nico grumbled with disgust. But when she turned her cheek away to find me hovering in the doorway, her whole face changed.

"Mara!" Nico said, her heavy eyes immediately lighter. "When did you get here?"

I thumbed over my shoulder. "Just now."

"I'll leave you lovelies to catch up," Rebecca sang, sweeping toward me.

I managed to step out of the way as she headed out.

But then she stopped and arched an eyebrow at me. "Door open, please."

She said it so sharply that I took a step back, watching as she strode toward the stairs.

As soon as she left, Nico waved at me with a smile that I could tell took some effort. "Hey."

"Hey," I said back, the wave I returned equally awkward as I tried not to stare at her.

"Come in," she said, gesturing at me, then bringing her hand up to her hair, trying to tame her curls with her fingers. "God, I'm a mess," she said, and I probably should have told her that she wasn't, but the words wouldn't come as I watched her try to sit up without spilling her tea. "I was going to take a shower, I promise. I even had an outfit picked out, but I just can't get out of bed this morning."

"What's wrong?" I asked, panic licking my palms.

I knew she wasn't well, but it had only been a week since I'd last seen her and the change was *shocking*.

The skin under her eyes was so dark it looked like she had two black eyes, and the rest of her skin was so pale it exaggerated them even more to the point that the rest of her face almost looked translucent. As though she was disappearing right in front of me.

In a few minutes she'd just be a pile of pink tartan.

Nico waved her hand at me. "It's nothing."

I don't know if she was lying to herself or to me.

Either way, it obviously wasn't *nothing*.

"The Great Purge is kicking my ass," she grumbled, wrapping her fingers around the mug of tea.

"*This* is from detoxing?" I asked, finally closing the distance between us and standing by her bed.

She nodded.

I didn't know what to say.

So I made a joke.

"What the hell are you detoxing from, Nico? Heroin?"

That made her laugh, at least, some color back in her cheeks as she said, "Mum says I need to ride it out and, once I'm out the other side, I'll feel *so much* better."

I heard Rebecca's voice tinkling in my head.

Trust the process, darling. Trust the process.

But I ignored it and said, "Maybe you need to see a doctor."

"You know Mum doesn't trust any of that stuff."

"I know, but kale and reiki clearly aren't cutting it."

I didn't mean to be so blunt, but I was furious.

Or maybe I wasn't furious, maybe I was frightened. I remember how my heart hammered as I crossed my arms and looked down at her, her dark eyes wide as she raised her chin to look at me.

She just laughed it off, though.

"I'll be OK," she told me as she patted the bed and told me to sit down.

But I couldn't.

She looked so fragile I was scared that if I did, she'd fall apart. Collapse into a pile of bones and pink tartan. But I was so shocked at the sight of her that I couldn't trust my legs not to give way, so I had to sit down.

When I did, I glanced at the door, then lowered my voice. "You need to see a doctor, Nico."

She shook her head. "Mum won't let me."

"Why don't you call 111, or something?"

"I can't. Mum took my phone."

"Why did she take your phone?"

"I was asking too many questions."

"What do you mean?"

"Last night, I asked her about all the supplements I'm taking"—she gestured at them lined up neatly on the bedside table—"and I asked her why I'm not feeling better, I'm feeling worse."

"What did she say?"

"At first she was super evasive, but then she asked me why I was questioning her, and when she realized that I'd been researching it myself, she lost it and confiscated my laptop and phone."

So, that explains why she was so surprised to see me.

She didn't get my message to say that I was on my way.

Or the one I sent her when I got off the bus.

Nico let out a sluggish sigh. "She says I can have the laptop back, but she won't give me the Wi-Fi password, so it's pretty much useless. And she's getting me one of those phones that you can only call or text on."

I tried not to look horrified, but I must have because she added, "It's my own fault."

"No, it's not," I told her with a fierce frown. "It's your body. You deserve to know what's going on."

The corners of her mouth lifted slightly at that.

"Why don't you wait until she goes to bed tonight and call 111?"

"I can't. I don't have my phone, do I?"

"Do you have a landline?"

"Yeah." She perked up at that. "In the office."

"Perfect. She won't be able to hear from her room."

She nodded. "I'll call them tonight."

"I'm sure your mum's right and it's nothing, but it will put your mind at rest, at least."

I said *your*, but I meant *my*.

"I'll do it tonight, I promise."

I let go of a breath, then smirked. "Did the meditation help?"

"Please," Nico said with a sour chuckle. "I told Mum I was meditating so she'd leave me alone." She sat a little straighter and adjusted the duvet. "The only thing that helps is listening to Dad's albums."

"Yeah?"

"That and talking to you."

I felt my cheeks flush as I asked, "What was last night's album?"

"*Blue* by Joni Mitchell."

I grinned. "That's our Sunday morning album."

"It is?"

"I've woken up to pancakes and Joni Mitchell every Sunday morning for as long as I can remember."

"I wonder if I have any traditions like that?" she asked, fiddling with the string on the teabag.

"You must do. Ask your mum. In the meantime, you have a new one, at least."

"Dad has *loads* of albums," she said, her eyes suddenly big and bright again. "There's a whole room of them downstairs, but Mum says that's only half of them. There are tons more up in the attic."

The pride in her voice made my heart double in size.

But then it deflated again as I asked myself where her records were.

I couldn't see any of them in her room.

Maybe the ones in the attic aren't all her father's, I realized as I watched her sip her peppermint tea.

We sat in silence for a while, Nico sipping her peppermint tea while I watched her sipping her peppermint tea and reminded myself of what my mother had told me the night before.

"It won't be like this forever," I told Nico. "The sun will come around again."

As soon as I said it, I saw a spark—somewhere deep behind her eyes that I would have missed if I had been able to look at anything other than her—and I swear that she began to take shape again. The curve of her face and sweep of her jaw, each of her thick black eyelashes curving toward me, one by one, framing her dark eyes.

Then, finally, her mouth, pink and full as she smiled.

And it looked like less of an effort this time.

"So, what have you been up to while I've been stuck in bed? Let me live vicariously through you, Mara."

"Nothing." I shrugged. "Just revising."

I stuck my tongue out and made a show of rolling my eyes, but she wasn't having it. "Oh, come on. There must be *something*. What about May and Chesca? How's that going? She hasn't, you know, Chesca-ed, has she?"

"Not yet. They're even planning a trip to Tuscany in the summer. Chesca's parents have a house there."

"Thank God! I'm rooting for those two."

"Me too," I admitted with a silly smile.

"What else?"

"Speaking of trips, Michelle's pissed with Lewis because he's going to Butlin's with '*the lads*,'" I said, using air quotes. "But I don't know what she's more appalled at, the lads thing or the Butlin's thing."

"But don't you guys have your Super Sixteen camping trip coming up?"

"Yeah, but that's different, apparently."

"How?"

"I think she's just upset that she's seeing someone who refers to their friends as *the lads*."

Nico giggled at that and it was nice.

Light.

Free.

"How's Erin?"

"She's started talking to someone on Instagram, who seems really sweet. But he's a Tottenham supporter, and before Erin moved to Brighton when she was three, they lived in Highbury, so her dad supports Arsenal."

Nico pretended to swoon. "It's like Romeo and Juliet!"

"Exactly." I sniggered. "And Louise just binged *RuPaul's Drag Race*, so on Thursday, instead of studying tectonic landscapes and hazards, we had an hour-long debate about what our drag names would be."

"What's yours? Something bookish, I bet."

I pulled a face as if to say, *Of course*. "Eliza Doo-me."

She nodded. "Nice."

"How about you?" I asked, even though we'd already discussed what our drag names would be when I was trying to persuade her to go to the Christmas drag brunch at Proud Cabaret.

So I was suddenly sick with guilt when she said, "Camp Crystal Lake."

That's what she said the last time, but I tried to hide it with a smile that I struggled to maintain as I heard her mother crashing around in the kitchen, slamming doors. Then she opened a drawer with such force, the cutlery inside clattered and the sound of it—this awful, nerve-plucking scrape of metal against metal—made me jump. I jumped again when I heard her voice calling up to us. "Nico? Mara? Do you girls need anything?"

"Mum, we're fine," Nico called back, then rolled her eyes at me.

I told myself to keep smiling as she sat a little straighter, then raised her mug.

"See? I've missed loads of stuff."

"Not *that* much."

"Well, given I've been stuck here for a week, that's loads. Trust me."

When she waved her other hand at the room, it suddenly struck me that in the shock of seeing her looking so rough, the thrill of finally being in her bedroom hadn't registered. I'd never been there, but I'd seen glimpses of it in the mirror selfies she used to take, so I saw enough to know that she was as messy as May.

Today it was immaculate, though.

There was nothing in there but her bed, a desk and chair, and a chest of drawers.

"You're very neat," I told her as I looked around.

Plus, the smell was striking.

Almost astringent, like an unnaturally white Hospital Clean Yankee candle.

"Mum is." Nico sighed. "I still managed to lose my journal somewhere, though."

"How?" I asked, looking around at the near-empty room.

There wasn't even anything on her desk apart from the tray with my mug of tea on it.

Where was all her *stuff*? Granted, my room was so small that if I stood in the middle and held my arms out, the tips of my fingers would brush the walls, so I didn't need to do much to make it look cluttered. Still, you knew it was mine. There were books everywhere and there was a patchwork of photographs and neon-colored Post-it notes on the noticeboard with the affirmations left over from the manifestation phase Michelle and I went through a couple of years ago that didn't result in her marrying Jimin from BTS, sadly.

There was nothing in Nico's room, though. Just a row of crystals on the windowsill and the supplements on her bedside table. I tried to read the labels and had to swallow a laugh when I saw that one of the brown glass bottles was turmeric and asked myself what my grandparents would say about that.

But that was it.

Crystals and supplements.

Where were her books?

Her records?

Her guitar?

Nico never went anywhere without her guitar.

"You'd better drink your tea," she told me, nodding over at the desk, "or Mum will tell you off."

"Oh yeah," I muttered as I got up and walked over to where it was still steaming on the tray.

As I did, I chanced a look through the open door in the corner and gasped.

I turned back to her and pointed at it. "You have a walk-in wardrobe?"

"*Walk-in wardrobe* is a stretch. It used to be a linen closet."

"Still. That's the dream! Michelle would die. She's always wanted one like Cher Horowitz's."

Nico turned her finger in a circle. "The revolving one?"

"Yes!" I pointed at her, then thumbed at it. "Do you mind?"

"Go ahead. There's nothing interesting in there, though."

There wasn't much room between the neat rows of clothes, so I had to stand sideways, but it was still preferable to my tiny wardrobe with the rail that kept collapsing under the weight of too many coat hangers. But when I turned on the light, I frowned as I blinked at the carefully curated sections. Sweaters all in the same place, then shirts, then T-shirts, then dresses and finally skirts and jeans, her shoes in a neat row on the floor beneath them, like in a department store.

But as obsessively organized as it was—which *had* to be her mother's doing—that wasn't what threw me. I didn't recognize *anything*. Not one thing. Every rail an uninterrupted line of cotton and cashmere and lace in the same sickly-sweet pastel colors. It should have been black—black, black, black—with the odd deviation. Where were her band T-shirts? Her vintage Purple Rain T-shirt that she'd found on Depop and was so proud of. And the Camp Crystal Lake one she bought at Beyond Retro. And where was her red-and-black-striped sweater? The one with the hole in the sleeve that she would stick her thumb through while she was talking.

There was one exception, though.

A shock of navy blue at the end of one of the rails, like a full stop, that made me suck in a breath.

I didn't need to reach for the coat hanger, because I already knew.

A Brighton College uniform.

A curling pink ticket pinned to the label inside the blazer from the last time it was dry-cleaned.

"I'm so mad at Mum," she called out, and I almost dropped it as I hooked it back on the rail.

"Why?" I asked, hoping I sounded more curious than stunned as I walked back into her bedroom.

"She ruined my kaftan." Nico pouted as I headed over to the desk to retrieve my peppermint tea.

My hand shook as I reached for it.

Luckily, she didn't notice as her face tightened into a scowl. "It was dry clean only and she washed it."

"Oh no."

"She had to throw it out. She said she'll get me another one, but I loved that one."

I did too, I thought as I took a sip of tea.

"How do you drink this stuff?" I winced, holding up the mug. "It tastes like hot chewing gum."

Nico laughed at that, so hard that she almost spilled her own tea.

"That's nice," her mother said, suddenly in the doorway. "I haven't heard you laugh like that for months."

My chest warmed at the thought that it might be because of me as I waited for her mother to keep going, to her bedroom or the bathroom or wherever she was headed.

But she didn't move.

She just stared at me.

"I should go," I said, putting the mug back down on the tray.

"I think that's best," Rebecca said. "Nico's very tired."

"But you only just got here," Nico whined, then glared at her mother.

She was adamant, though. "You need to rest, darling. Mara can visit again when her exams are over."

When her mother left, Nico looked as forlorn as I felt at the thought of not seeing her for a month.

"I'll call you later, yeah?" I said brightly. But when that did nothing to smooth her frown, I added, "Maybe we can listen to *Blue* before we go to bed? It'll help me get Edward the Confessor out of my head."

That worked; Nico beaming at me as she said, "I'd love that."

"Or maybe something new?"

"Something that's just ours?"

"Something that's just ours," I promised, my heart shivering at the thought.

I figured it would be rude to leave without saying goodbye to Rebecca, but I couldn't see her. Downstairs was as neat as Nico's room, but it at least looked like someone lived there. Car keys and a small bottle of hand sanitizer on the table in the hall. A black leather handbag hanging from the banister at the bottom of the stairs. A sagging sea-blue sofa in the living room and a pile of photo albums on the coffee table.

Rebecca must have just been sitting there because the mug on the side table next to the armchair was still steaming and there was an open purple leather notebook on the seat. *Maybe she's upstairs*, I thought as I looked around the hallway to find that, much like at my house, there were framed photographs everywhere. Her parents' wedding. The day Nico was born, her mother in a hospital bed, her and Nico's dad smiling with a mixture of exhaustion and wonder. Nico's first birthday. Her first Christmas. But then my heart curled in on itself when Henry disappeared.

Then the photographs were just of Nico and her mother.

Holidays and birthdays and Christmases.

All just the two of them.

I suddenly felt terrible as I thought about what Rebecca had lost when her husband died. I'd only ever thought about how it affected Nico, but Rebecca lost everything, didn't she? Not just the love of her life, but her future.

Nico was all she had left of that future, so I couldn't blame Rebecca for being overprotective as I watched Nico get slightly taller—slightly bolder—in each photograph until they stopped as well. Or the ones in the hallway did, anyway. The last one I could find was one of Nico looking about thirteen in front of what looked like the Christmas tree at the Rockefeller Center. Nico all in black, her arms crossed as she scowled at the camera, her mother, holding her tight as she smiled just as tightly.

Then I saw it. A sunny room between the living room and kitchen and stopped in the doorway. There they were. One wall covered from floor to ceiling with rows and rows of her father's records. There was a turntable on a sideboard below the window next to a battered black Eames lounge chair and stool. I imagined Nico sitting in it every night, and as I asked myself if *Blue* was still on the turntable, I was glad she had that, at least.

A room of her own.

I was still smiling at the thought when I walked past the kitchen to find her mother cleaning the floor. She wasn't just cleaning it, she was *scrubbing* it, her curls flying with the effort. I remember how the frantic *squeaksqueaksqueak* of the mop on the tile put my teeth on edge, the smell of bleach so over-whelming that my head swam. That's when she noticed me, the mop stilling as she peered at me through her dark tangle of hair.

"Hey, Mrs. Rudolph," I said with a small wave. "I just wanted to say goodbye."

She straightened and stared at me. "There's something rotten in here. Can't you smell it, Mara?"

I shook my head because I couldn't smell anything.

Just bleach.

"Well, there is, and try as I might, I can't seem to get rid of it," she told me with a tight smile.

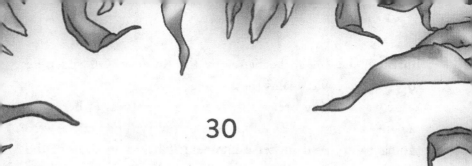

30

Things were strange after that.

Strange, but easier, somehow.

Even though I still had no idea what Nico and I were, just that we weren't friends.

We spoke every day, but her mother was always there, always in the background, laughing lightly or chiming in with an anecdote, which made it hard to talk. The only time we got to ourselves was when Rebecca had gone to sleep. Then Nico would sneak downstairs and call me, whichever of her father's albums we were listening to that night keeping our breathless, sleepy secrets as we finally had a chance to speak without interruption.

Even then we didn't *talk*. We did, but we talked about everything and nothing, but not about her. I asked, of course. Asked how she was feeling and if she'd called 111, but whenever I did, she'd just say that she was fine and ask how my revision was going. So I let it go, because she did sound fine. She told me that she'd given in and was finally doing as she was told. No more coffee. No more Nando's. No more questioning the battery of supplements Rebecca insisted she take. So she was drinking green juice and going for long walks with her mother on the Downs to get some vitamin D because, she insisted, she *had* to be better by the time my GCSEs were over so we could spend the summer together.

It was working because there was a brightness to her voice again—a lightness—as we spoke about everything that we were going to do. And in her excitement, I heard an echo of the old Nico as she talked and talked and talked, interrupting herself as she thought of something else she wanted us to do, then circling back to what we were planning before she did. But unlike before, I could keep up this time because she wanted to do all of it with me.

She'd even started a countdown until my last exam. (Maths, of course. Talk about saving the worst for last.) *Twenty-three days to go*, she'd say when she answered the phone. Then she'd help me revise, which her mother *loved* because she said that Nico needed to keep her brain active. I'd see her hovering while we were on Zoom and she'd congratulate me when I got something right or correct me when I didn't.

That's how the month passed, a blur of revision and exams punctuated by those swift, sweet moments with Nico. She sent me flowers on my sixteenth birthday. They were the highlight of the day, given that I'd decided to postpone celebrating thanks to my history exam. They were delivered just before I left for school. Pale, papery pink peonies that I put in a vase on top of my chest of drawers so Nico could see them the next time Rebecca let her go on Zoom to help me revise.

They stayed there until they began to wilt, then Rebecca pointed at them one afternoon and told me to throw them away.

Then it was over.

Not just the flowers, but everything.

Revision.

GCSEs.

School.

Summer was finally here.

All I wanted to do when I walked out of my last exam was see Nico, but after a month of brimming with energy and excitement as she counted down to that day, she was suddenly sick again. So, her mother had taken her to see a specialist in London. I was relieved, of course, grateful that Rebecca had agreed to let Nico see an actual doctor, but if she'd just waited *one more day*, I could have seen Nico before our Super Sixteen camping trip.

It's two days, I told myself as Michelle and I sat on the bus to Peacehaven. *It's worth it if she gets better.*

Maybe thinking about something other than Nico and exams will do me some good.

Thanks to my need to be on time for everything, Michelle and I arrived at the campsite at precisely four thirty, just in time for check-in. The owners, Barry and his wife, Jen, were waiting for us, and when they walked over, I saw that Louise, Erin, and May were with them and I almost dropped everything I was holding.

"How did you guys beat us here?" I said. They laughed and told us they thought check-in was at four.

Michelle arched an eyebrow. "So you just got here, then?"

"Ten minutes ago," Barry confirmed as he pulled me into a hug so tight, you'd think I'd just returned from war. When he let go and I took a step back, I saw that he looked *exactly* the same as he did last summer. He was even wearing the same yellow-and-blue Hackett polo shirt and there was something so comforting about it because Michelle and I loved Barry. We loved Jen, but we *loved* Barry. We only saw him once a year, but each time we did, we wished that we could see him all the time, even though we couldn't imagine him anywhere other than the campsite. He had a big smile and a bigger heart and told the worst jokes that would make us murderous if our fathers told them, but when Barry did, we always laughed. He helped us carry our water bottles and taught us how to build a fire and to wait before we ate the marshmallows we toasted on it. (Not that we ever did.)

He was like our favorite uncle.

Jen ran over to hug me then and she looked the same as well. She even smelled the same, of Elnett hairspray and something else.

Something I'd only ever smelled at the campsite.

"Your friends are lovely," Jen told me when she stopped to hug Michelle as well.

"We've given them the tour." Barry took our bags, then pointed to the seating area overlooking the sea. "And showed them where you guys took your first steps."

Jen slung her arm around me. "And they've claimed their yurts."

"And your favorite one is ready," Barry told us as he somehow managed to carry all our bags at once.

"Yay!" Michelle and I clapped, jumping up and down as the five of us followed him and Jen.

Then we clapped again when we saw that our yurt was as adorable as we remembered.

The bunting.

The red-and-white-painted door.

The wooden loungers on the grass out front.

"Have fun, girls!" Barry told us when he dropped our stuff inside.

"See you around the firepit later!" Jen waved as they walked off.

We borrowed bicycles from Barry and Jen, and as soon as we left the campsite, I felt the shift as we rode aimlessly along the narrow country roads around Peacehaven, shrieking and overtaking one another in a way that my mother would absolutely not approve of. At one point, Erin lost a flip-flop and we had to stop as she dropped her bicycle and ran back to get it. Then Louise challenged us to a race, which Michelle won, of course.

We rode until we were tired, then we sat in a field and talked while we ate wedges of the first birthday cake of the day. Mine. Chocolate and cherry, which my father had stayed up until midnight making.

I can't remember the last time we'd talked like that. Not bickered about which film to watch or what to have for lunch, but really *talked*. May told us that she and Chesca were taking a year off to go traveling before they went to uni. Then I confessed that I was thinking of applying to the University of Sussex because I wanted to stay at home and Louise grabbed my arm and told me that she wanted to stay at home as well.

That gave Michelle the courage to confess that she'd been researching the astrophysics program at Yale, which would have made me vomit up my birthday cake if I didn't already know. Then Erin told us that she spoke to her grandparents the night before and they called her Erin and we wept because we thought they'd never refer to her as anything other than her deadname.

When we were done, May—sweet, sweet, sentimental May—insisted we take a photo so we'd remember the moment, but when Erin went to post it on Instagram, she realized that we had reception there—which we didn't have back at the campsite—and, with that, everyone was distracted by their phones again.

It was a shame, but it meant that no one noticed when May gave me a look.

"Hey, Mara," she said, trying to sound casual, "can you take a Snap of me climbing that tree?"

"Haven't you learned your lesson after what happened to Robin last summer?" Michelle asked without looking up from her phone as May and I got to our feet and brushed the grass from the backs of our legs.

"That's the point," May smirked at her, even though she wasn't looking. "I want to wind her up."

"Be careful," she, Louise, and Erin said at once as May took my hand and we ran over to the tree.

As soon as we got to it, she looked back at them. "Take it from this side, with the sun behind me."

She said it a little too loudly, so I knew it was for their benefit not mine.

Not that she needed to. Even if they weren't absorbed with their phones, we were far enough away that we couldn't hear them, so they couldn't hear us, either. Still, May pulled me around the wide trunk to the other side of the tree, where they wouldn't be able to see us from where they were sitting.

As soon as she did, she lowered her voice, her eyes wide as she asked, "Have you checked Insta?"

"Not since I posted that photo of us."

May's eyes got even bigger. "Nya liked it."

I opened Instagram and sure enough, there among the string of new notifications, was one from Nya.

And a message.

"She DMed me again," I said with a groan.

"What did she say?" May asked, coming to stand beside me and peering over my shoulder to read it.

Have you given Nico my number?

I groaned again, more theatrically this time. "Why won't she leave me alone?"

May stepped back and thought about it for a second, then said, "I think you should call her."

"*What?*"

She shushed me, her hands flapping as she peered around the tree trunk. I did the same to find the others still sitting cross-legged on the grass, the bicycles discarded around them, as though they were dozing in the sun.

When she looked back at me, I whispered it this time. "What?"

"You said it yourself, Mara. Until Nico sent that text on New Year's Eve, she'd never talked about any friends. Now here's one who's desperate to get hold of her. Aren't you even a tiny bit curious why?"

Of course I was.

But if Nya was Nico's ex—and liking my photos and pestering me to pass on her number was doing nothing to convince me otherwise, was it?—then that was a can of worms I wanted to leave the lid on.

Still, it didn't look like Nya was going to let this go. And while I suspected—or perhaps recognized—that was out of broken-hearted persistence, there was another part of me that asked, *But what if it isn't?*

I clicked on Nya's profile to find that it wasn't private anymore.

"What?" May asked when I gasped.

"Nya must have followed me," I told her, showing her the grid of photos.

"Scroll down."

I did until I saw a photograph of Nico I'd never seen, dated April last year.

It was definitely her, but she looked younger.

Brighter.

Happier.

Not like in her moody mirror selfies.

And she was surrounded by a group of people in matching school uniforms.

The same uniform Nya was wearing on TikTok.

I felt the prick of something then.

Something that made my heart beat very, very slowly as I scrolled to find dozens of photos just like it.

Nico and Nya sharing a chocolate milkshake in one of those old-fashioned glasses, somewhere sunny.

Nico and Nya cackling and holding hands, wearing matching black denim dungarees.

Nico, Nya, and their friends outside the O2 in front of a poster of Beyoncé.

Nico, Nya, and their friends dancing in floor-length prom dresses, their arms in the air.

Photo after photo, not unlike the ones on my Instagram.

My heart sped up then.

So fast that I could feel it ticking in my ears.

Nya wasn't Nico's ex.

She was her Michelle.

"Keep a lookout," I told May as I called Nya.

"Why?" she asked, peering around the tree again.

"In case one of them comes over."

I said *one of them*, but I meant Michelle.

May looked slightly panicked. "What do I do if someone does?"

"Create a distraction."

She considered that for a second, then nodded solemnly. "I'll strip."

But before I could tell her that she didn't need to take her clothes off, Nya answered.

"Yeah?"

"Yes. Hi. Hey. Hello. This is Mara. Mara Malakar."

There was a sharp stretch of silence, then I heard her suck in a breath. "Mara! Thank God! Thank you so much for calling me. I've been going out of my mind since I heard what happened to Nico."

She was so relieved that I couldn't help but soften.

"Is she OK?" Nya asked, and she sounded like she'd just run up a flight of stairs.

I started to tell her that she was, but I stopped myself.

After all, just because they used to be friends, that didn't mean they still were.

"How do you know Nico?" I asked with such nonchalance, I startled myself.

But, to my surprise, she mirrored me. "How do *you* know Nico?"

There was another long silence and Nya must have realized that one of us had to back down.

"She's my best friend," she sighed, confirming I was right. She paused, then sighed again, more tenderly this time. "Or she was. I haven't heard from her since she moved to Brighton."

"We met the first day of school," Nya explained with a warm chuckle. "She marched up to Tom Larson, who'd just tried to pull up my skirt, and pushed him over, then complimented my Hello Kitty backpack."

I could hear the affection in her voice and I suddenly felt terrible for leaving her hanging all this time.

"Nico and I were inseparable. But then . . ."

When Nya trailed off, I held my breath while I waited for her to find the words.

But when she didn't, I realized that it wasn't that she couldn't find them.

It was that she didn't know what to say because, like me, she didn't want to betray Nico.

"Listen, Nya," I said softly. "I know Nico. I know how hard it is to be her friend sometimes."

I heard a shriek of laughter then and looked over to see Louise with her hand stuck in a can of Pringles.

I caught myself smiling, but then Nya said, "It wasn't hard to be her friend, though." That made the corners of my mouth tighten again as she went quiet for a moment too long, then asked, "Have you met her mum?"

"Yeah," I said, and I hoped she didn't know that I was rolling my eyes.

"Is she still a psycho?"

When that stunned me into silence for a second, I wondered if she regretted saying it. I don't know what it was like at her school, but at Stringer, if you called someone's mother a psycho, it wouldn't end well for you.

I waited for her to apologize, but when she didn't, I realized that she'd gone from relieved to angry so quickly, it took me by surprise. I could hear it—and the pain—in her voice and it turned my stomach inside out.

"I mean, I get it," Nya said sharply. "Nico was *so young* when her dad died, so it was just them against the world. They were more like sisters than mother and daughter. I used to envy it, to be honest, how close they were. How Nico could tell her anything. They hung out all the time and shared clothes and had all these private jokes."

I thought about Nico's new pretty pink clothes.

And pretty pink purse.

And pretty pink perfume.

"But then," Nya went on, and I could hear it was a struggle, "when Nico turned thirteen, she started to hang out with me and her other friends more, and her mum got *really* weird about it. I don't know why. It's not like we were smoking weed and chugging cheap beer in Stratford Park. We were just hanging out at Westfield.

"But it was like Nico's mum was jealous, or something. She'd say stuff like *Why don't you want to be with me anymore? You only want to be with your friends.* It would really upset Nico, so she wouldn't go out as much. Then, when she did, her mum would get pissy and ignore her. So, Nico wouldn't see us for a few weeks and her mum would go back to normal. But as soon as Nico told her she was meeting us, it'd start again."

When Nya cleared her throat, I did the same in an effort to dislodge the pearl of pain suddenly stuck there. "It was a nightmare. Her mum would call constantly while she was with us, demanding she come home."

Then the pearl grew a little bigger, making it harder to breathe as I thought about before.

About how Nico's phone would buzz every time we were together.

Then the look on her face when she checked it.

"There was always an emergency," Nya said with a sniff. "Her mum forgot her door key. Something that meant Nico had to go home. Then the reasons started getting bigger. Like once, she was mugged at the bus stop. Then, another time, she fell down the stairs and Nico had to rush to A&E."

"That's awful," I said.

But Nya just snorted, then said, "Nico got tired of it. She had enough of being made to feel bad for wanting to see her friends, so she stopped telling her mum that she was meeting us. Then, when that didn't work, she'd sneak out."

That sounds like Nico, I remember thinking, recalling our plan on New Year's Eve.

"But then her mum started getting sick."

"Sick?" I asked, my fingers tightening around my phone.

"It started with these mad headaches, so she thought she had a brain tumor. Then it was cancer. Then it was an autoimmune thing. Nico missed loads of school because she was always at the hospital while her mum had tests. And when she did come to school, she had to stop at the chemist on the way home to pick up a prescription. Every week it was something else. Another load of pills that didn't work."

No wonder she doesn't trust Western medicine, I remember thinking.

"It went on for *months*, Mara, but no one could find out what was wrong with her. She just got sicker and sicker. She lost weight. Her hair fell out. Then she couldn't walk. So when Nico's grandmother died, her mum announced that they were moving to Brighton because there's less pollution there. Something about negative ions. Plus, she's one of those people who believes that you can cure cancer with ginger shots and good vibes."

Nya laughed at that, loud and bitter. "But as soon as Nico left London, she blocked me on everything and I never heard from her again. Not until I saw that photo of her on the news."

"Nya, I'm sorry," I said, and I hope she believed me. "I can't imagine losing my best friend like that."

I think she did because her voice was even thinner when she said, "Thanks, Mara."

Then she went quiet for so long that I thought that was it.

But after a minute or so she said, "Is she OK?"

"Nico's mum? Yeah, she seems fine."

And she did.

She was the picture of health.

Moving to Brighton had obviously worked.

"Not her mum," Nya said softly. "Nico."

I hesitated then, unsure if she would want me to tell her.

But Nya was her Michelle, and if it was me, I'd want Michelle to know.

"She doesn't remember."

"What do you mean?"

"She's lost her memory."

"What? Completely?"

"Yeah. She doesn't remember a thing from before they rescued her from the sea."

"Did she hit her head, or something?"

"No, she's fine physically, but she's got amnesia."

Nya cursed under her breath, then said, "I know it sounds awful, but I'm kind of glad."

I didn't know what to say to that.

But after a moment, she added, "When I didn't hear from you, I thought Nico was mad at me."

"Why would she be mad at you?" I asked, then held my breath.

"Because I thought her mum was lying."

"Lying about what?"

"About being sick."

31

I didn't tell May what Nya had said. I couldn't have, even if I wanted to, because it felt like it did after I saw Nico's photo on the news. My brain like a snow globe. Everything scattering for a moment, then falling.

Falling and falling.

Except, I could feel it falling into place this time.

"What were you two doing behind that tree?" Michelle asked when we returned.

"I needed to wee," May said, putting an end to any further questions.

Luckily, the others didn't object when she and I grabbed our bicycles and suggested we head back.

"Race you," Michelle said with a cackle as soon as she grabbed hers.

And I played along. I groaned when she won—of course—and cheered when May finished last with a wheelie. Then, when we got back, we sat around one of the picnic tables and ate the food my father had packed for us.

It was nice, there in the dark, familiar embrace of the campsite, everyone talking and laughing like everything was OK, the smell of sea salt and burning burgers in the air. But I couldn't stop thinking about what Nya had told me, as I stabbed at my father's potato salad with a wooden fork.

"OK." Michelle clapped happily. "Time for *my* birthday cake. Aka the best one."

We'd agreed to have May's the next morning, on her actual birthday.

Colin the Caterpillar.

She'd already claimed his head.

"Wait," Erin said. "We haven't done candles and sung 'Happy Birthday' yet."

"Don't worry," Michelle said as she cut into the cake. "We did all of that on our actual birthdays."

"Yeah, but we can have a toast, right?" May said, waggling her eyebrows.

Then she leaned down and pulled a two-liter plastic bottle from her tote bag with a wicked smile.

"With Sprite?" Michelle frowned, licking vanilla frosting from her finger.

May's smile sharpened to a smirk and Louise cheered.

"Did you bring cups?" Erin asked. "I have some in my yurt if we need some."

Louise snatched her plate of cake and jumped to her feet. "Let's go to the firepit!"

To my surprise, Michelle resisted and I almost kissed her. The firepit was already cluttered with people, so when I heard "Moves Like Jagger" playing, I actually shuddered. I could think of nothing less I wanted to do in that moment than hang out with a load of drunk strangers.

"We're going to head back to our yurt," Michelle said, taking our plates and handing me one.

I braced myself, sure they were going to object and plead

with us to go with them, but they just grabbed their stuff, then hugged Michelle and me and headed off toward the building laughter around the firepit.

"Go easy, OK?" Michelle warned with such urgency, it was enough to make them stop and turn back to look at us. "If anyone gets wasted and puts the fire out by puking on it, Barry and Jen will tell our parents."

They looked at one another, then May's eyes widened. "Mads will kill us."

"Dead," she confirmed, drawing a line across her neck with her finger.

"We'll be good," Erin promised as they turned and carried on toward the glow of the fire.

"Let's eat this inside," Michelle said when we got back to our yurt. "Less bugs."

So we sat cross-legged on the bed and ate her birthday cake.

"Are we being antisocial?" I asked, licking the frosting from my wooden fork.

She didn't look up from her plate. "Aren't we always?"

"Maybe we should join them," I said.

It was the last thing I wanted to do, but I was worried that we were missing a montage-worthy moment. After all, isn't that what nights like that were for? Laughing and singing with your friends, then falling asleep with the smell of bonfire smoke in your hair and the taste of cheap vodka on your tongue.

"Mara, do you really want to drink whatever's in that Sprite bottle and dance to Maroon 5?"

"Absolutely not."

My montage did not include Maroon 5.

"Exactly," Michelle said around a mouthful of cake. "Besides, we need to talk, don't we?"

"We do?" I asked, avoiding her gaze.

"Come on, Mara. What's going on?" she pushed, and I considered lying.

Not because I didn't want to tell her, but because I didn't know *what* to tell her.

All of it was still a flurry of tiny white flakes in the snow globe of my head.

But it was Michelle.

I had to tell her.

"OK." I stabbed my cake with the fork and left it there. "To be honest, I'm still trying to process everything, so you're going to have to give me a second while I do."

She didn't, of course.

"Is this about Nico?" she asked, even though she knew it was.

Wasn't it always about Nico?

"I didn't tell you this," I started to say, then trailed off when she raised her eyebrows.

"Tell me *what?*"

"Remember that day you went to Eastbourne for năinai's birthday?"

"Yeah?"

"Someone called Nya DMed me on Instagram. She's one of Nico's friends from London."

"OK," Michelle said warily as she slid another forkful of cake into her mouth.

"She asked me to give Nico her number, but I didn't."

"Because you thought she was Nico's ex."

I ignored that. "Then earlier, while we were in the field, she sent me another DM, and I saw all of these pictures of her and Nico, you know, *before*, so I called her."

Michelle pointed her fork at me. "So *that's* what you and May were doing behind that tree."

"I just wanted to know why she was so desperate to speak to Nico."

"Because she's her ex," Michelle said again.

"Actually, she's not. She's Nico's *you*."

That made Michelle's smirk slip.

"They've known each other since they were kids."

"So, what did you tell her?"

"It wasn't so much what I told her, rather what she told me." Michelle's gaze narrowed as I told her what Nya had said.

"Then . . ." I stopped, not ready to say it out loud yet. I tugged the fork out of my slice of cake, then plunged it back in as I took a breath and said, "Then she said something weird."

"Weird?" I heard Michelle say as I rubbed my hands together. They were sticky with frosting and I wished the toilet block wasn't so far away so I could wash them.

"Yeah," I muttered, still avoiding her gaze. "Nya said that she thought Nico's mum was lying."

Michelle didn't miss a beat. "About being sick?"

I looked up at her then, my heart lunging.

But Michelle was perfectly—almost pathologically—composed. "Nya thinks she has Munchausen's."

I raised an eyebrow at her. "What do you know about Munchausen's?"

She raised one back. "What do *you* know about Munchausen's?"

"I read a novel about it." I shook my head. "Actually, it was about Munchausen's syndrome by proxy. Still, I know enough about it to know that Nico's mum can't have it."

Michelle put down her fork.

"OK. Let's break this down. Nya is Nico's me, right?"

"Right."

"And everything was good between Nico and her mum until she turned, what, thirteen?"

"That's what Nya said," I told her as I recalled the framed photos in Nico's hallway.

How they stopped suddenly.

"Then her mum got all weird and possessive?"

I nodded.

"But then Nico's mum gets sick, like, *really* sick, but she doesn't know what's wrong. So Nico stops seeing her friends and misses school because she's at the hospital all the time or at home, caring for her mum."

I nodded again.

"But they never found out what's wrong with her and now her mum's magically OK?"

I didn't nod this time because I knew what Michelle was going to say next.

"That sounds like Munchausen's to me, Mara."

And it did, I realized, as a shiver of dread scuttled across my scalp.

"But now Nico's the one who's sick."

314

It took me a moment to realize what she was saying.

But then everything began tunneling toward a single, inescapable point.

"You think Nico's mum is making her sick?"

When she didn't flinch, I forced out a laugh.

"Michelle, that's ridiculous!"

"Mara, think about it."

But I wouldn't. "In that book, the mum did it because she liked the attention from other people. She went on television to raise awareness for whatever weird disease she said her kid had. She started a charity and conned people out of loads of money. Plus, she loved being at the hospital. She made her daughter have loads of painful procedures she didn't need, but Rebecca doesn't do that, does she? She won't let Nico *near* a doctor."

"That's not the only reason people do it, though, Mara."

"What other reason is there?"

"Control." Michelle shrugged. "To keep Nico close. Keep Nico reliant on her."

"No way." I shook my head.

"Mara, listen."

But I didn't want to, my head in my hands as I listened to everyone laughing outside. I could hear "Shake It Off" playing and I knew Louise, Erin, and May were dancing to it. I swear I could hear them shrieking and imagined them twirling each other as they sang along, and I suddenly wanted to be out there with them.

Not in here with this.

Michelle wouldn't let it go, though. "That's what people like Nico's mum do. They isolate you. Think about it. Nico's mum has no contact with any of her family, right? Because they didn't approve of Nico's dad?"

I made myself sit up and look at her. "That's what Nico said."

"What about her dad's family?"

"They're in Korea."

"OK. But do they talk?"

"I don't know, but her mum said she'd take her to see them when she's better."

"And all the photos you saw in her house were just of Nico and her mum, right? No one else?"

"Her dad was in some of them. Before he died."

"OK. But don't you think that's weird, Mara?"

"Maybe there are more photos upstairs, or something? Or in the living room?"

"Yeah, but she only ever talks about her mum, right? No one else?"

I nodded.

"And she's never mentioned Nya before?"

I shook my head.

"So Nico never sees her family, then moves to Brighton and loses contact with all her friends."

"I guess." I shrugged.

But I could see what she was pointing me toward.

Shoving me toward, actually.

"But then she meets you and Nico goes back to her old ways, sneaking out and going to gigs and stuff."

I pulled a face.

What did I have to do with it?

Nico wasn't sneaking out to go to gigs with me, was she?

I hardly saw her.

"Then whatever happened on New Year's Eve happens. Nico falls in the sea and emerges a blank slate. I mean, what a gift? Just as their relationship is falling apart again, Rebecca gets her daughter back and she can tell her *anything*. Re-create Nico in her own image. The perfect daughter who wears pink and eats kale and always comes home on time. But *you*." Michelle wagged her finger at me. "You're the fly in her ointment, Mara."

Or the rotten smell she can't get rid of, I thought as I remembered the frantic *squeaksqueaksqueak* of the mop on the kitchen floor as Rebecca scrubbed it, the memory of it putting my teeth on edge again.

"You called the police to report her missing," Michelle reminded me. "Then you bump into her again, which could potentially undo whatever she's told Nico about her being the perfect daughter who wears pink and eats kale and always comes home on time *and*"—Michelle wagged her finger again—"goes to Brighton College."

"The Brighton College thing *definitely* doesn't add up," I was forced to concede.

I told her about the flowers and the Ms./Mr. Fisher confusion and the unworn Brighton College uniform in Nico's closet and she looked stunned.

She thought about it, then said, "OK. Here's what I think, Mara. I think Rebecca wanted her daughter back so badly that she lied about how perfect everything was before Nico fell in the sea. How perfect *she* was. A self-fulfilling prophecy sort of thing. Like if she told Nico she was the perfect daughter, she would be.

"But then Nico started asking questions, like why she'd not heard from any of her friends, and Rebecca panicked. She had to tell her something, right? She couldn't tell her the truth, though, because what if it triggered something and the old Nico came back?"

"OK." I nodded, eyeing her warily.

But I could feel something shifting.

Slotting into place.

"So she picks a school at random, somewhere Nico has no connection to so it won't trigger anything. Then she tells Nico that she's missed too much and has to retake the year."

Before I could tell her to slow down, she pushed on.

"But you." She jabbed her finger in my direction again. "You almost messed everything up, Mara."

"*How?*"

"You knew her before."

"I didn't know what school she went to, though."

"Yeah, but her mum didn't know that. That's why you couldn't tell her that you knew her before."

"I guess," I murmured as I tried to follow the red string that she was connecting between each thing.

"When was the last time Nico spoke to her therapist?"

"I don't know." She hadn't mentioned her for a while. "But she hasn't been well, has she?"

"True. But do you see what I mean, Mara? Nico's mother has isolated her from *everyone*. It's as though she's actively trying to stop Nico remembering."

"But why?"

"So they don't go back to before."

I shook my head again, but then I remembered what Nico had said on New Year's Eve.

She went fucking mental about LIPA.

"Or so she doesn't leave home to go to uni," I heard myself say.

Michelle's eyes widened, but she knew not to say anything.

To let it register.

Let it settle.

Then she gave me one last nudge over the line.

"Mara, think about it: Nico is only sick after she's seen you."

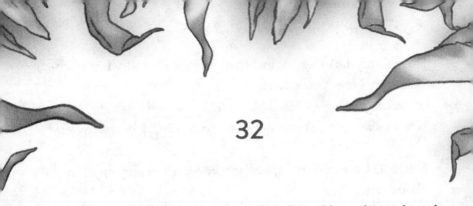

32

I looked up at Michelle, but before I could catch my breath, there was a knock on the door and I jumped.

Then I jumped again when Michelle barked, "Not now!"

But the door opened anyway and we looked over to see Nico hovering in the doorway.

I looked back at Michelle, sure I was seeing things, but she looked as shaken as I felt.

Shaken and clearly horrified at how awful Nico looked.

I was as well.

I thought she was getting better, but she looked even worse than the last time I saw her.

"Nico!" Michelle gasped. "What are you doing here?"

"Sorry to show up like this," she said, and when I glanced back at her she looked like a little kid as she shuffled nervously. "But I really need to speak to Mara. I've been calling, but it keeps going to voicemail."

"There's no reception here," I explained, then frowned. "How did you even find me?"

"This is the only campsite in Peacehaven."

"I'll leave you two to it," Michelle muttered.

Then shot me a panicked look, which did nothing to calm me down as she hurried out of the yurt.

Nico and I watched her go, then she turned to me, her cheeks flushed.

"I'm sorry to show up unannounced, but I really need to talk to you, Mara."

"What's wrong?" I asked.

But all I could think was *She knows.*

She knows.

She knows.

She knows.

"Mum says I can't trust you. She says that you've been lying to me."

And there it was.

Rebecca's final attempt to rid the ointment of the fly.

I held my hands up. "Nico, I can explain."

But she took a step back. "So, it's true? You have been lying to me?"

When I nodded, she stared at me, her forehead corrugated with confusion. "Lied to me about *what*?"

Just say it, Mara.

Say it.

Say it.

Say it.

"I knew you before," I blurted out, and Nico's eyes widened. "Before?"

"Yeah. You were supposed to see me that night."

"What night?"

"New Year's Eve."

Nico barked out a laugh, but when I didn't laugh back, she stiffened.

"What do you mean, I was supposed to see you?"

I couldn't catch my breath quickly enough, the words just beyond my grasp.

In the end, I didn't have to say it as her whole face hardened. "We were together."

I nodded, which wasn't enough, I know, but it was all I could manage as my heart *thundered*.

So loudly I don't know how she couldn't hear it.

"That's what Mum told me," Nico told me, then shook her head. "But I didn't believe her."

She turned away from me and started pacing.

There wasn't much room in the tiny yurt, but she managed it, her hands balled into fists at her sides as she muttered to herself. And I should have left her alone, I know. Given her a minute to think. To put the pieces together. But she was quiet for so long that I panicked and started babbling.

"I'm sorry, Nico," I said with a heave and a sob. "I should have told you."

She finally stopped pacing and turned to face me again. "I get why the first time. We only saw each other for, like, a minute. But the second time? When we met outside that café. Why didn't you tell me then, Mara?"

"I should have," I told her, pressing my palm to my forehead. "I should have. But I was thrown because you were, like, a completely different person."

"What do you mean?"

"The Nico I knew wanted to be Joan Jett." I took my hand away from my forehead to shrug. "She was all smudged eyeliner and black nail polish. I mean, she had this red-and-black-striped sweater that she wore so much there was a hole in one of the cuffs and this vintage Purple Rain T-shirt she'd found on Depop that she loved because it was super rare, or something. So, when I saw you in that pink coat, I didn't recognize you."

I swear I saw it then.

A flicker.

But then Nico resumed pacing and I resumed shuddering with panic.

"I was going to tell you when you came to the café the next day," I persisted, pointing at the door. "Ask Michelle. I was going to tell you as soon as I saw you. But your mum called and—"

"My mum called you?" Nico said, stopping mid-step, then turned to face me again.

"Yeah," I mumbled, fiddling with the bottom button on my shirt.

"How did she even get your number, Mara?"

"From you, I thought."

"Why would I give my mum your number?"

"I don't know."

"What did she say?" she spat, suddenly furious. "When she called you? What did she say?"

I'd never seen her like that, so it took a second or two to recover. "That she'd discussed it with your therapist and they'd decided it was better for you to remember in your own time. She told me not to tell you I knew you before because it might trigger something and they didn't know if you could cope."

"*They* were worried," Nico hissed. "Or *she* was worried? Which one, Mara?"

"They. She definitely said *they* discussed it. She said it could overwhelm you and I didn't want that."

"So, let me get this straight." There was a chill in her voice so sudden, I thought the door to the yurt had blown open. "My mother called you and told you to lie to me about knowing me before?"

I nodded.

"And you did because my mother told you that's what my therapist recommended?"

"She said you were fragile." I pressed my hands to my chest. "Helpless."

"*Helpless?*" She snorted. "And whose fault is that, Mara?"

I sat back on my legs and looked up at her as she pinched the bridge of her nose.

"Sorry. This isn't your fault, Mara. It's hers. But I guess it explains *this*."

Nico threw something on the bed in front of me.

I was so taken aback at seeing her that I hadn't noticed she was holding anything.

"What's that?" I asked, looking down at it.

Nico sat on the edge of the mattress, a black leather duffel between us, then took an unsteady breath and said, "Remember when I said that Mum told me that there were loads more of Dad's records in the attic?"

I nodded.

"Last night, after I spoke to you, I couldn't sleep. So I went up to look for them and I found this."

We both looked down at the duffel again, then up at each other.

"Nico, what is it?"

I saw her hands shaking as she unzipped it, and when I saw what was inside, mine did as well.

Her red-and-black-striped sweater.

She pulled it out, then pulled everything else out as well, throwing each thing on the bed between us. Her vintage Purple Rain T-shirt. A bottle of black nail polish. A battered Moleskine covered with stickers.

She didn't say anything, just unzipped a pocket inside the duffel, reached in, and held up a phone.

Her phone.

Her old one.

She stood up and turned to face me, her hands on her hips. "Mara, I need you to tell me everything."

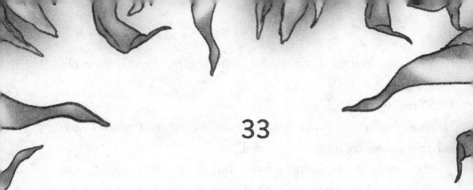

33

"We met last summer."

"*Last summer?*" Nico frowned, her knees bumping into the bed as she took a step toward me.

"You were busking—"

"Busking?" she interrupted again as she looked at me like she didn't recognize the word.

"You're a singer," I told her, and she looked so astonished that I remember thinking that it was such a strange thing to know something about someone that they don't know about themselves.

"A really good one," I added, the words coming a little easier now.

"I mean . . ." She blinked at me. "I like singing in the shower."

"And you play the guitar. You were playing the guitar the morning we met."

"I don't even have a guitar."

"You do. I don't know where it is now, but you do. You used to take it everywhere."

"There's a broken one in the attic," she said to herself. "But I thought it was Dad's."

I let her process that for a second, then said, "And you play the piano and the violin."

Nico seemed even more startled by that. "What was I? Some sort of savant?"

"Not quite," I chuckled lightly. "But you're very talented."

I almost used the past tense as well, but managed to correct myself before I did.

"That explains the Moleskine. They must be my lyrics, not other people's." She reached down and picked it up, flicking through it as she asked, "Where was I busking when we met?"

"Outside Brighton station."

Nico went quiet again and I could tell that she was trying to remember, so I held my breath as I waited.

But nothing came.

"What happened?" she asked.

"When you were done, we chatted and you gave me a sticker with your Instagram."

"I have an Instagram?"

I nodded, achingly aware of how confused Nico looked.

How lost and found, all at once.

But it was *right there*.

I could see it in her face.

It will be the next thing I tell her.

The next thing.

"I followed you," I said carefully, like a lighthouse guiding her back to shore, "and we started talking."

"Then what happened?"

"We met for a coffee a couple of weeks later. But then we ... um ..." I lost momentum, unsure what to say.

Nico turned her cheek to look at me. "Mum said we were together."

I shrugged awkwardly. "I mean, I guess."

"You *guess?*"

"It was nothing serious. Just casual."

"*How* casual?"

"We didn't go on dates or anything. We'd meet up, get a coffee, and walk around."

Like we do now, I almost added, but I managed to swallow back the words before I did.

"We'd see each other, but then we wouldn't for a few weeks. Then we would again. Like I said, casual."

"Casual," she repeated with a slow nod.

But that obviously didn't trigger anything, either, as she shook her head.

"What happened on New Year's Eve? You said that I was *supposed* to see you? Why didn't I?"

"You didn't show up."

I saw something flutter across her face then, and I was sure that was it as she tilted her head and looked at me, her forehead pinching. "I didn't show up?"

"You sent me a text," I said sheepishly, the tops of my ears burning at the memory.

"What did it say?"

"That you'd bumped into friends." I forced myself to take a breath and said, "Then you dumped me."

She looked horrified. "Dumped you?"

Nico parted her lips to say something, but nothing came out as she shook her head and started pacing again. I could hear her muttering to herself and she did it for so long I was sure that was it, she was going to grab the duffel and leave, but then she stopped and looked down at the pile of her stuff on the bed between us.

"I did what you said, you know?" she told me, her gaze settling on the red-and-black-striped sweater.

"What did I say?"

"You told me to call 111, remember?"

I remembered.

I'd asked her if she'd called the next day and she said it was fine, didn't she?

She said she was fine.

What if she's not fine?

"I called them that night, but I didn't want to tell you until I was sure."

I had to suck in a breath before I could ask, "Sure about what?"

I tried to brace myself, sure that she was about to tell me that she had cancer, or something.

But how do you brace yourself for something like that?

"I'm fine," she said, and I stared at her until she said it again. "I'm fine, Mara."

"Fine?"

"Yeah. They said that I'm fifteen. I'm young and on an obsessively healthy diet, so there was no need for me to detox. They told me to stop taking the supplements to see if it made a difference."

"OK," I said to myself, the inside of my head a snowstorm again. "That makes sense."

"But I knew Mum would never let me stop taking them. So I'd wait, then flush them down the toilet."

"And what happened?"

"Nothing."

"Nothing?"

"Absolutely nothing. Within three days, I felt better than I have since the morning they pulled me out of the sea. But I didn't say anything because I was terrified that whatever it was would come back. Then it did."

"Yesterday?" I asked, but I already knew.

Nico nodded.

"When you were supposed to see me."

She cleared her throat, her voice a note weaker than it had been a moment before as she said, "So, when I got sick again yesterday, I *freaked* and told Mum that I needed to see a doctor. She promised to take me to see a specialist. The *specialist* being a biomagnetic therapist called Soren who reeked of patchouli."

She laughed, but it quickly turned into a sob as she sat on the edge of the bed with her head in her hands.

"Mara, what's going on?" she asked, her shoulders shaking as she wept.

But she knew.

We both did.

"It's OK, Nico. It's going to be OK," I told her.

Even though I had no idea if it would be because how do you recover from something like that?

From knowing that your own mother is making you sick so you won't leave her?

"It's OK," I said again, desperate to reach for her.

I could see her coming apart at the seams in front of me, but I was terrified that if I touched her, she'd unravel completely.

I couldn't just let her cry, though, so I inched my fingers forward and let them curl around her shoulder. As soon as I did, Nico breathed my name, turning into me as she looked up at me with those dark, dark eyes. I caught her in my arms before she folded and held her as tightly as I could.

We stayed like that—her sobbing and me with the tip of my nose in her hair, telling her it would be OK over and over, like a prayer I was tucking between her curls—until she stopped crying. When she did, she nodded and I let go, wiping her cheeks with the cuff of my denim shirt as she tried to catch her breath.

"Thank you, Mara," she said as I waited for her to stop shaking.

After a few minutes I pressed a kiss to the top of her head. "It'll be OK," I whispered into her curls again. "Stay here tonight. Get some rest and we'll deal with this in the morning, OK?"

"OK," she said with a sniff as I caught a fresh tear with the pad of my thumb and swept it away.

I saw that Michelle's phone was still on the bed then and I reached for it.

"Where are you going?" she asked as I clambered off the bed.

I smiled when I got to the door. "To ask Erin if she doesn't mind bunking with Michelle tonight."

When I got back into the yurt, Nico looked so pleased to see me that I mirrored her loose smile.

She was sitting up in the bed, waiting for me, her shoes discarded by the door.

My mother would be apoplectic if she knew I was getting into bed with outside clothes on, but I was too exhausted to care as I kicked off my slides and crawled into the bed next to her as though I'd done it dozens of times before. I thought I would at least tense when I lay next to her, but the sheets were cold and Nico was warm, her curls spilling onto my pillow as she snuggled into me and immediately fell into a deep, easy sleep.

I must have done the same, because I woke up suddenly. It was still dark. After four, according to my phone. I realized then how cold I was, and when I went to tug the duvet over me, I realized that Nico was gone. I sat up, my heart throbbing as I told myself that she was fine, that she'd just gone to the toilet, which is probably what woke me up. So I put on my slides and grabbed my phone and the flashlight my father had insisted I pack and went to look for her.

As soon as I opened the door, the air stuck to my cheeks. The June dryness had passed, the smell of the firepit shooed away by another kind of smokiness as a thick mist dulled the stars and smothered everything ahead of me, forcing me to walk a little slower in spite of my swelling panic.

I could feel a charge in the air, the spark of something that seemed to be getting closer, making it harder to keep up with my breath as I checked the communal toilets to find them empty. Still, I checked each stall as I tried to call Nico's phone, but when it wouldn't connect, I remembered that there was no reception at the campsite.

So, I hurried over to the seating area to find the fire was out and the chairs were empty, a pair of white leather sandals forgotten next to an empty bottle of wine. My heart began to beat even faster as I asked myself where Nico could be. Then I *really* began to panic as I shot a look over to the cliff edge.

That's when I saw her, her back to me and her hair wild.

She was standing so close to the edge that I wanted to run over and yank her back. But I realized that she could have been sleepwalking and told myself not to run—to be careful—because I read in a book once that you're not supposed to wake someone when they're sleepwalking because the shock could kill them.

But when I stood beside her, Nico shivered and said, "There's a storm coming."

The way she said it made me shiver as well as I looked out at the sea. The moon was hidden by the mist, which blurred the line of cliffs on either side of us. But the sea was loud, the waves gathering pace, and when the wind howled, it sounded like all the doomed souls lost beneath it were crying out at once.

"There's a storm coming," she said again as I carefully slung my arm around her waist.

She was right, I knew, as the gulls shrieked, almost drowned out by the sea hissing back and forth—back and forth, back and forth—over the pebbles and rushing up the rocks to touch the big black sky.

"Let's get out of here," I told her.

Nico let me lead her away as the heavens opened, the rain so sharp it felt like the stars were falling as we ran back to our yurt.

As soon as I got inside, I wished there was a lock, and pushed my backpack up against the door.

She was already in bed when I slid in next to her, her breathing slower.

Steadier.

"Promise me," she said, her breath hot on my cheek as I heard a rumble of thunder followed by a crack of lightning so bright, it drew a white line around the door. "Promise me that whatever happens, I'll always be your pearl." She found my hand beneath the duvet and threaded her fingers through mine. "Your pearl of a girl."

I squeezed her hand. "I promise, Nico."

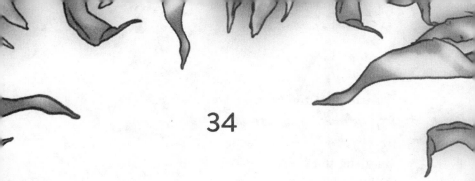

34

I woke the next morning to find Nico curled into me like a comma, her head on my pillow. I could feel her breath on the back of my neck, and when I rolled over to face her, the first thing she said was my name.

"It's going to be OK," I told her as she reached for my hand under the duvet. "I know what to do."

And I did.

I knew exactly what to do.

I had to call my mother.

I used Barry and Jen's landline. All I said was that I needed her to come get me, and half an hour later our car pulled into the campsite, my mother's face tight with concern when she saw Nico and me waiting for her.

"What's going on?" she asked as soon as she pulled away.

But before either of us could answer, Nico and I looked down as our phones lit up in our hands.

Message after message from Nico's mother on mine.

Dozens and dozens of them.

More than I could—or wanted—to read.

I've just been into Nico's room and she's gone.

Where is she?

I know she's with you.

This is all your fault.

I'm calling the police.

You're an evil, rotten girl, Mara Malakar.

Stop turning her against me.

Give me back my daughter.

Then she started calling.

Calling and calling.

When I turned to look at Nico, I saw her face get tighter and tighter as she stared at her phone.

"It's OK," I told her, reaching over to take it from her. "It's going to be OK. Just ignore her."

"What's going on?" my mother asked as she watched me turn it off, then put mine on silent.

When we didn't say anything—just looked at one another, Nico pale and panicked and me trying to smile as I reached for her hand—my mother said, "Tell me everything."

"I don't know everything," Nico finally admitted.

But she told her what she did know.

And my mother nodded, her eyes on the road and her fingers curled tightly around the steering wheel.

She waited until Nico was done, then nodded and said, "Thank you for telling me."

She stopped the car, and when I realized that we were outside the police station, I slid closer to Nico on the back seat as she slid closer to me, our hips touching as she squeezed my hand.

"Wait here while I park the car," my mother said, then looked at us in the rearview mirror, her eyebrow arched. "Don't go in until I get back, OK? I'll be back in a minute, I promise."

We did as we were told, our hands clasped as we stood on

the pavement, Nico shivering beside me, even though the sun was already high and bright in the sky, as though it was watching over us until she returned.

Sure enough, a few minutes later, my mother strode around the corner. She looked exhausted, her arms crossed and her face tight with concern again. But then she looked up to find us watching her and caught herself, uncrossing her arms and lifting her chin to flash us a sure, steady smile.

And I don't know which of us it was for.

Nico or me.

I held Nico's hand tighter as my mother led us inside and told us to sit on one of the gray plastic chairs while she went to the counter. I couldn't hear what she said to the officer standing behind it, but I could see a fold appearing in the pale skin between their eyebrows that got more and more pronounced as they nodded solemnly, then reached for the phone.

When they did, my mother came and sat beside Nico.

"Right," she said, in that way only she does when she somehow sounds perfectly calm yet unbearably tender, all at once. "Someone is going to come out and speak to us about what you told me, Nico."

As soon as she said it, I felt Nico tense beside me and I slid my arm around her.

"I can't." She shook her head. "What if I'm wrong?"

A tear skidded down her cheek and I caught it with my fingers as my mother said, "You're not wrong."

But she shook her head again. "I can't, Mads. I can't."

"You can. You won't be alone," my mother reassured her. "I'll be with you the whole time, I promise."

Nico turned her cheek to peek at her from under her wet eyelashes. "You will?"

"You're under seventeen, so you need an appropriate adult and I pass for one, apparently."

That made the corners of Nico's mouth lift slightly.

Just for a second before they fell as she shook her head again.

"I can't," she said, her chin quivering as she whispered, "It's my mum."

That made my mother's chin quiver as well.

But she recovered quickly. "She needs help, Nico."

When another tear slipped down her cheek, I swiped it away with the pad of my thumb, then took her face in my hands. "You're doing this for her, Nico."

A door next to the counter opened then and someone in a creased gray suit walked out. They scanned the reception area, then strode over to where we were sitting and crouched down in front of us.

"Hey, Nico. Remember me?"

"DS Delgado." She nodded as I let go of her face and slid my arm around her again.

Detective Delgado nodded back. "You wanna tell me what's going on?"

Nico looked panicked as she turned to my mother, who just smiled smoothly and held out her hand.

Nico looked down at it for a moment, then back up at her, and when she nodded, Nico took it.

* * *

338

My mother suggested I go home, but of course I didn't. I stayed there until Michelle and the others rushed in with hot chocolate and hugs. They didn't ask a single question, just sat with me, taking turns holding my hand until my mother finally emerged through the door next to the counter and we all ran toward her at once.

"Nico's going to be OK," she told us, her eyes on me.

And I didn't know who was holding my hand or who had their arm around my waist.

Just that they were there.

The only thing keeping me upright as my mother said it again. "Nico's going to be OK. She's given a statement and now we're going to the hospital—"

"The hospital?" I gasped.

"Nico's fine." My mother nodded. "It's just a precaution."

"That makes sense," I heard Michelle say, and I felt a little steadier.

But then I heard Louise say, "They're probably going to do blood tests to see what her mum gave her."

"Nico's fine," my mother repeated. "But you should go home, because—"

"No way." I shook my head fiercely. "I'm coming."

"Mara, you can't," my mother said, then waited for me to meet her gaze. "You won't be able to come with us, so you'll just be in the A&E waiting room with all the drunks and screaming babies."

"Your mum's right," May said, pulling me closer, and I realized it was her arm around my waist. "Trust me, if it's anything like it was on New Year's Eve, it will be like a scene from *Resident Evil.*"

I had no idea what that meant, but I believed her.

"I don't want Nico to be alone," I whimpered.

"She's not alone." My mother pressed a kiss to my forehead. "She's got me."

So, I went home, because what else could I do?

I went home and sat cross-legged on my bed, Michelle beside me and the others dotted around my room. A solemn, stunned silence settled as they looked helplessly at one another, then at Michelle, who looked back helplessly at them, before turning to me.

I waited for her to reach for my hand and tell me that it was going to be OK.

But she just let out a miserable sigh. "Mara, I'm so sorry."

"It's OK." I nodded, trying to cough away the lump in my throat. "Nico's going to be OK."

"No." Michelle shook her head. "I'm sorry for getting it wrong."

I was so startled that I laughed. "Wrong?"

"About Nico." Her eyelashes dipped for a moment before she raised them to meet my gaze again. "For dismissing her behavior as bullshit and swagger when it was *so* much more than that."

The others agreed, their foreheads creased and their eyes wide as they gathered around my bed.

"It's OK," I told them with a sniff as they apologized, all at once.

And it was.

They were just looking out for me, weren't they?

"How could any of us have known what Nico's mum was doing?"

They shook their heads, and when they started talking among themselves, I sat there like I did the night they showed Nico's photo on the news, my brain a snow globe again as they batted questions back and forth and traded furious, breathless theories about why Nico's mother did it while the day died around us.

Then, just after ten o'clock, I heard the front door and literally *flew* down the stairs to find my mother.

And Nico.

"Oh my God!" I said with a heave and a sob, then launched myself at her from the bottom step with such force that she fell back and almost knocked a framed photo of my grandparents off the wall.

Nico hugged me back and through the tunnel of it all—the relief, the uncertainty, the fear—I could hear my friends asking her the questions that were currently warring in my head.

Are you OK?

What happened at the hospital?

What did the police say?

Are they going to arrest your mum?

You can't go home by yourself! Where are you going to stay?

You can stay at mine.

Or mine. We have a spare room.

Eventually, my mother held her hand up and said, "OK. Take a breath, girls!"

When they did, I finally let go of Nico and stepped back to find my mother smiling sweetly at Erin, May, and Louise.

"Nico needs some space. Why don't you guys go home and you can talk tomorrow?"

She sent them upstairs to get their stuff, and when they returned, in a whir of kisses and hugs and demands to be kept in the loop, she ushered them out the front door.

When they were gone and the house was still again, she let go of a breath and nodded up the stairs.

"Nico, why don't you take a shower?" Then she tipped her chin up at Michelle. "Can you get Nico a towel and something to wear, please? You know where everything is, right?"

"On it!" Michelle said, clearly relieved at having something to do.

"Hey, baby girl." My mother pressed a quick kiss to my cheek as they disappeared upstairs, then put her arm around me and led me down the hall into the kitchen. "I don't know about you, but I need a cup of tea."

My father had his back to us as he stirred something on the stove.

"Mads!" he said when he heard us walk in and spun around holding a wooden spoon. "How's Nico?"

"Hungry, probably," she said, her eyes wide, "but I see you've got that sorted."

"I didn't know what to do, so I've been stress cooking." He shrugged, then said, "Tea?"

But he didn't wait for a response as he put the wooden spoon down, then grabbed the ladle from one of the steaming saucepans and began decanting some chai into a smoked glass mug.

"How do you always know, Vas?" my mother said with a sigh, rubbing his back with her hand.

She kissed him as he handed her the mug, then sat at the table with a wearier sigh.

"Mum, what's going on?" I asked, sitting opposite her.

She rubbed her face with her hands. When she took them away and opened her eyes, I saw how red they were and I remember holding my breath as I waited for her to tell me.

But before she could, I heard Michelle.

"Wait for me!" she yelled as she thundered down the stairs. As soon as she skidded into the kitchen, my father handed her a mug of chai, which she almost spilled in her haste to join us. "What'd I miss?" she asked, out of breath, the chair scraping loudly on the tile as she pulled it out and sat down.

If you didn't know Michelle, when you saw her run into the kitchen like that, her cheeks flushed and her eyes wide, you'd have assumed it was because she didn't want to miss a single, juicy detail. But I hope you know Michelle a bit better now, so you'll believe me when I say that it wasn't that at all.

She was worried about Nico.

"What happened?" she asked, still out of breath as my father sat with us. "Is Nico OK?"

"She's fine," my mother said, then stopped to sip her tea. "I mean, she's not *fine* given the circumstances, but they were very thorough at the hospital and the doctor I spoke with was happy to discharge her."

"She got her blood test results back that quickly?" my father asked before I could.

My mother shook her head. "Some of them. The rest will be another day or so. But they examined her and checked everything, her temperature, pulse, blood pressure, oxygen levels, and they're all normal, so that's good."

That made something in me settle, but Michelle frowned. "So we don't know what her mother gave her?"

My mother shook her head again.

"But Nico hasn't taken any supplements for a month," I said, and I was the one who sounded out of breath this time as panic pinched at me. "What if there's nothing in her blood and they think she's lying?"

My mother reached across the table for my hand and squeezed it. "They know she's not lying, Mara."

"Plus"—Michelle reached for my other hand—"she must have given Nico something yesterday to make her sick so she couldn't see you. The chances are, there are still traces of it in her blood."

"Besides," my father added, "I'm sure the police will test the supplements."

"So, what happens now?" I asked, looking between the three of them.

My mother lowered her voice, even though I could hear water running in the bathroom upstairs. "Nico's very concerned. She's anxious that the police are going to go to her house, kick the door in, and drag her mum out."

"They should," Michelle said under her breath.

After everything that had happened, I should have agreed, but there was something about the way my mother was looking at me as she held my hand a little tighter that reminded me that it hadn't always been that way between Nico and her mother. They must have had moments like that. Quiet, tender moments when Nico thought her mother would protect her from anything. So I got why she wouldn't want the police to do that.

"Do you remember the detective you met at the station?" my mother asked. "Detective Delgado?"

Michelle and I nodded in unison.

"He promised Nico that they would be discreet. That they won't humiliate Rebecca."

"They should!" Michelle said out loud this time, her face flushed again. "She tried to kill her!"

"She wasn't trying to *kill* Nico," I told her when she let go of my hand to sit back and cross her arms. "She was trying to keep her close. Stop her from leaving because she was terrified of losing her."

"Same thing."

"No, it's not, Michelle."

I stared at her, but I shouldn't have been surprised that immovably logical Michelle couldn't see that.

That's the trouble with being immovably logical, it often only presents you with two options.

Right or wrong.

So she couldn't see that there was a murky midpoint between the two.

"Whatever Rebecca did, she's still Nico's mum, Michelle."

"Plus, she's the only parent Nico has ever known," my mother reminded her.

That made Michelle soften, her shoulders lowering.

"Are they going to arrest Rebecca?" my father asked with a frown.

"Nico's asked the police to speak to her first," my mother

said with a small shrug. "She's convinced that if they're not confrontational, Rebecca's less likely to get defensive and deny everything."

He thought about it for a moment, then nodded.

Michelle obviously didn't agree with that tactic, though. "As soon as the police show up unannounced, she'll know Nico has said something, and she'll charm them into thinking it's all in her head."

I remembered that first phone call.

All of those *darling*s and *sweet girl*s.

How Rebecca made me believe that it was a good idea not to tell Nico that we knew each other before.

How she convinced me it was for the best.

And the panic full-on winded me as I turned to look at my mother.

But she squeezed my hand again. "She can't charm her way out of this, Mara."

"She knows it's over," my father agreed with a sad sigh. "She's known for a while."

"She knows she can't keep doing this to Nico forever. She has to let her go."

My mother's gaze dipped for a second, and when she looked up again, I asked, "So, what now?"

"We wait for the police to do their thing."

"What happens to Nico in the meantime? She can't go home, can she?"

"Where's she going to live?" Michelle asked.

"They were talking about finding her a temporary group home—"

"No way," my father interrupted, shaking his head. "She's not going into care."

"Care?" I gasped, but my mother held her hand up again.

"I told the police she could stay with us, Vas."

He nodded. "Of course."

"It won't be for long. Detective Delgado told me that Nico has an aunt and uncle who live half a mile up the road from her in Rottingdean."

"What?" Michelle and I said at once.

"Her mum's sister and her husband, apparently. They got in touch with the police when they read what happened in *The Argus* and asked them to pass on their details to Rebecca, but she never got in touch. Nico had no idea they were there."

"So, Nico's going to live with them?" my father asked as he finished his tea.

"The police will check them out first, but Detective Delgado says family is the preferred option, so . . ." She crossed her fingers and held them up.

But I was stunned. "I can't believe Nico had an aunt and uncle half a mile away this whole time. She could have walked past them in the street or been behind them in the queue at the Co-Op and didn't know."

My mother closed her eyes and shook her head. "I'm guessing there's a lot more that Nico doesn't know."

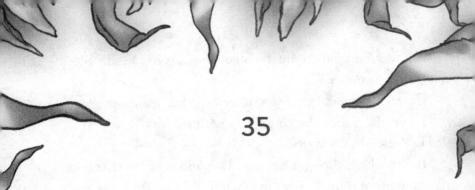

35

It all happened so quickly that I didn't get a chance to fantasize about what it would be like to live with Nico.

All of those long, late-night conversations when everyone had gone to bed. The pair of us lying in my garden like a couple of cats, dozing in the sunshine and reading to each other from whatever books we'd chosen to while away the afternoon with. Brushing our teeth together, side by side in my tiny bathroom, still managing to continue our conversation, even with mouthfuls of foam. Passing bowls back and forth as we sat around the kitchen table, trying to decide what film to watch after dinner. Nico in my *I WOKE UP LIKE THIS* T-shirt, the one with the cockroach that only she understood, smelling like my shampoo and my soap and my laundry detergent.

Smelling like me.

None of that happened, though.

I was on the sofa while she rarely came out of her—or should I say *my*—room.

She slept a lot, ate a little, and said nothing.

The few times I did see her, usually during dinner while she picked at her food and Michelle tried to fill the silence by telling us about a podcast she'd listened to about the Deep Space Network, or something she'd read about how most people fall asleep in seven minutes, which can't be true. Or it wasn't in my case. But I appreciated her efforts while I stared across the table at Nico and Nico stared down at her plate.

It should have made me panic, because it was so achingly familiar. Nico, moody and brooding, the skin under her eyes bruised with some unspoken agony she didn't want to talk about.

But it didn't, because this time I knew exactly why she didn't want to talk about it.

Then it was in *The Argus*—GIRL FROM THE SEA'S MOTHER ARRESTED—above the photograph of Nico they used on the ten o'clock news. And when Nico saw it, she went up to my room and didn't come out.

The others didn't dare mention the article when we met for lunch. But that afternoon while Michelle and I were in her garden, me tense and quiet and her on the blanket beside me with a copy of *To All the Boys I've Loved Before* open on her chest as she dozed, I gazed up at my bedroom window and finally gave in to it.

I wept, Michelle's book slipping to the grass between us as she curled into me.

And when I was done, I was ready to talk about it.

About everything I'd missed.

All those things I thought were red flags but I now knew were huge, flashing neon signs.

"I should have known something was wrong," I said with a pathetic sigh, guilt pinning me to the blanket as I looked up at my window and imagined Nico on my bed, doing exactly the same thing.

Trying to sew each thread together.

But the fucked-up thing is, I did know something was wrong, didn't I?

I just presumed it was me.

"How could you have known?" Michelle said, but there was an edge to it—a sharpness—that I felt like a paper cut across my heart as I realized that she wasn't just mad at the situation.

She was mad at herself for not knowing.

For dismissing Nico's behavior as bullshit and swagger.

"You were looking out for me," I told her.

"I'm not sorry for that," she said, shaking her head.

It went on like that for days.

Then, one Wednesday afternoon, as June was about to give way to July, I was in my kitchen eating cold cubes of watermelon straight from the fridge when I closed the door and there she was.

"Sorry!" Nico held her hands up when I jumped back. "I didn't mean to scare you, Mara."

But that's not why I jumped.

I jumped because the old Nico was suddenly in front of me in her red-and-black-striped sweater and black jeans, her dark eyes darker and her wild curls wilder than I'd seen them for *months*.

"Do you fancy a walk?" she asked.

And when she began to chew on her bottom lip, I saw the new Nico.

Awkward and unsure, as though I might say no.

"Sure," I said and, again, I wish I'd said something more meaningful.

Something worth committing to paper.

But when Nico let go of a breath and smiled at me—slow and easy—that's all I needed to say.

It's funny because that day had started off slowly, warm but gray and groggy, as though Brighton was struggling to keep its eyes open. But then Nico was back and it was as though someone had turned a light on, the sun suddenly *blooming* as we left my house and walked to Queens Park.

When we reached the café by the entrance, we were greeted by an apricot cockapoo who jumped up, excited and wiggling.

"Hey, pup! Hey! Hey!" Nico giggled, crouching down to cuddle the dog as it nuzzled her ear.

Hang on.

I don't know why I'm telling you about the dog.

But then, why am I telling you any of this?

What's my role here?

Am I simply a commentator or the protagonist in a love story you've been patiently waiting to play out?

I don't know, but I'm suddenly painfully aware of my responsibility here. Of what is mine and isn't mine to tell. I guess I can only tell you my own story and how Nico changed the trajectory of it. And that while I watched Nico playing with that dog, I recalled what Michelle had said after they'd rescued her from the sea.

About how she would probably want a fresh start and that might not involve me.

That, one day, Nico would remember.

Then she'd want to forget.

Usually that would have sent me into a tailspin, but I remember being uncharacteristically calm as I told myself that it would be OK.

That whatever she was finally ready to say, it would be OK.

Even though I didn't want OK.

I wanted one of those perfect endings I'd only ever read in books.

But as I said, things don't have to be perfect, they just have to be true.

So, she got a coffee and I got a hot chocolate and we walked.

I didn't think that we were walking anywhere in particular, until she led me to the pond.

To *our* bench.

"So, how long did you wait for me on New Year's Eve?" she asked, looking down at it.

"Not long."

She turned her cheek to raise her eyebrows at me.

So I chuckled and said, "Two hours."

She sat down with a groan, and when I sat next to her, she turned to look at me again. The sunlight caught on the curve of her eyelashes when she did, dazzling me for a second. "I didn't send that text, you know?"

"Which text?"

"The last one I sent you," she said, and I saw her jaw click. "Mum sent it."

I stared at her. "How do you know?"

"The police managed to get into my old phone." She nodded. "I've seen it all."

All I could manage was, "Oh."

Which was hardly helpful, but my chest suddenly hurt too much to speak as I thought about Nico opening her phone to find her entire life laid out in front of her.

I can't even imagine what that must have been like.

In a single moment she went from knowing nothing to knowing everything.

"And it was Mum who deleted my social media." Nico raised her paper cup to her mouth, but before she took a sip, she said, "Luckily, she couldn't get into my phone, so I still have all my photos and messages."

"That's good," I said, even though all I could think about was how much she knew about me.

About us.

"I was awful to you, Mara."

"No, you weren't," I said, too quickly for it to be convincing.

"Yes, I was, Mara. I've read the texts."

It took me a second or two to recover before I could shrug again. "It's OK."

"No, it's not. But you get why now, right?"

I made myself look at her.

Then I made myself nod.

When I did, she said, "When I told you I wasn't feeling great, I really wasn't."

I nodded again, although it wasn't as easy this time.

"I didn't know what Mum was doing, just that something wasn't right, you know?"

I nodded again and she raised her chin and peered at me from under her eyelashes. "I know you spoke to Nya."

"You do?"

"When I got into my phone, I saw that she'd sent me, like, two hundred and twenty-seven messages. I called her and she told me that you spoke. *God*," she said through her teeth. "I was so mad at her when she told me that she thought Mum was lying about being sick. So when we moved here, *I* was the one who deleted my social media. I swore I'd never speak to her again. I just wanted a fresh start, you know?"

A fresh start, I thought, my heart clenching.

"And it worked. As soon as we moved here, Mum changed. Just like that." Nico snapped her fingers. "She was so happy. So excited about her Bikram yoga class and the health food shop she'd found on the high street. Within a month, she'd gained weight and her hair started growing back and she was how she was before. So, I wanted to call Nya and tell her she was wrong. Tell her Mum just needed to get out of London."

Nico sank deep into her thoughts for a second, then said, "I should have known something wasn't right, though. Her mother had just died, so why was Mum so happy? But grief is complicated, isn't it? Besides, they hadn't spoken in, like, twenty years, so I figured Mum had already mourned her, you know? She lost her a long time ago."

"Anyway." Nico closed her eyes and shook her head. "Like I said, as soon as we moved here, Mum changed. She didn't ask me where I was going every time I went out or tell me off for being on my phone. But then I met you"—her gaze flicked up to meet mine—"and I didn't tell her because she was just *so happy* and I didn't want to risk triggering the old Mum, you know?"

She stopped to lick her lips, then said, "But she knew. She kept saying I'd changed, that I was the old me again. Then she was weird when I asked her what school I'd be going to. I told her I wanted to go to Stringer, because that's where you go," she admitted with a smile that made my chest warm. "She said she'd look into it. But then, in August, she told me that we'd left it too late. Everywhere was full. So I was on the waiting list."

"So you were waiting for someone to move or get excluded, or something?"

"Yeah. In the meantime, she homeschooled me, which . . ." She trailed off with a tender sigh. "God, it was *awful*, Mara. We were together *all the time*. Which she loved, but I couldn't breathe." She slipped her index finger under the collar of her sweater and tugged. "She'd tell me off for reading something that wasn't one of the English literature texts or for listening to music when I should have been perfecting my French pronunciation.

"And then she was right," she said, leaning forward and resting her arms on her knees. "The old Nico returned. I started answering her back and sulking in my room. Then, one day, she took away my bedroom door."

I blinked at her. "She did *what*?"

"She took my bedroom door. Took it off its hinges and hid it."

"How do you hide a door?" I asked, which wasn't the point at all.

Still, it made Nico laugh. "I know. She was out of control. But then I was as well. I started sneaking out and not coming home until, like, two in the morning, because I couldn't take being in that house with her." She stopped to rub the bridge of her nose, then said, "That's when she asked me who Mara was."

My heart hurled itself at my ribs.

"She must've gone through my phone." Nico thought about it for a second, then frowned. "I guess that's how she got your number."

My heart shuddered as I pictured Rebecca scrolling through Nico's phone. Not just reading our messages but looking at her photos and the notes Nico had made of lyrics and lines in books.

Secret things.

Things we all have on our phones that we shouldn't have to explain.

"So she knew." Nico stopped to sniff. "*She knew* how close we were getting."

I went to reach for her hand, but then she sat back and said, "That's when I started getting sick."

My hand curled into a fist. "Sick?"

"It was September. I remember because I was supposed to go with you to Erin's sixteenth."

So it wasn't an excuse.

She really was sick.

"Mum was vomiting as well, so she said I must have picked up norovirus when I was out with you."

Something nudged at me as I remembered the conversation

we had the morning after we bumped into each other as I was leaving the library, when she called to tell me that she couldn't meet me because she was sick.

She reckons I have a virus that I passed on to her.

But I didn't want to interrupt, so I let her go on. "Then it happened again. And again. And again. Every time I was supposed to see you, I got sick." She closed her eyes and shook her head. "But I didn't put two and two together. I just thought she was right, that I had a weird virus, or something."

She cursed herself under her breath, then said, "It became an excuse for her to monitor *everything* I was eating, which is why I'd rebel with Nando's." She sniggered to herself. "But then I'd get sick again and think it was my fault. That if I just did as I was told and ate the mung beans and drank the ginger shots, I'd feel better. But then she'd say something to piss me off and I'd storm out to meet you, eat a load of extra-hot peri-peri chicken, and get sick again.

"It was like this cycle." She turned her finger in a circle. "Mum was *so angry* all the time. And I was *so angry* all the time. Everything she did set me off. Everything I did set her off. Then, on New Year's Eve, we had that row about LIPA after I saw you at the café and, I don't know." She stopped to pick a piece of fluff from her jeans. "When I saw how *normal* your parents were, I knew Mum wasn't. So, when I went home, we had another row. Which is why I packed a bag and left to meet you. I knew I'd be safe with your parents."

"You are," I reminded her.

"I know," she said, but she didn't look at me, her eyes on the pond. Mine were as well, the pair of us sitting side by side in silence as we watched a moorhen skim across it, its head high and proud.

Finally, she said, "I hate her, but I don't, because none of this is Mum's fault. She's got some mental health issues."

She didn't say anything for a while, just continued to look out at the pond, as I looked at her.

"Her mum used to do the same thing to her, you know? Make her sick." She stopped to poke her thumb through the hole in the cuff of her sweater and looked down at it. "Her father had this whole other secret family. He was about to leave, but then Mum got whooping cough. He didn't leave her side and I guess my grandmother thought, *I know what I can do to make him stay.*"

Nico shrugged. Then she cleared her throat and said, "Mum learned that being sick was a way to make someone stay. So, when I got older and started making friends and wanted to see the world, she panicked because after Dad died, I was all she had left. I mean, her own mother almost killed her for a man who didn't even stay in the end."

"Nico, I'm so sorry. That's awful." She just nodded, and after a beat, I asked, "When did your mum tell you all of this?"

"Yesterday."

"*Yesterday?*"

"I went to see her," Nico said, drumming on the lid of her cup with her fingers.

"You didn't say," I said, trying not to sound wounded.

"I know, but I was supposed to see her last week, but it didn't happen. And the week before that. And the week before that." She tugged on her earlobe. "But then I finally got to see her yesterday and I was hoping for some closure, you know?" When she turned her cheek to look at me, I nodded, but she shook her head. "But it wasn't quite the tearful apology I was hoping for."

"What did she say?"

"Everything and nothing. They're still trying to balance her medication, so she was there, but she wasn't. She didn't cry when she saw me or hug me, or anything. She just sat there, her shoulders back and her chin up. So prim and proper, like someone from a Jane Austen novel, or something."

She rolled her eyes, but I could see the tears gathering. "It was all about her. How hard this has been for her. How hard her childhood was. How hard it was to lose her husband. How hard it was to raise me by herself. You know"—she blinked—"she never once referred to my dad as my dad, only *my husband*."

Nico turned her head to look back out at the pond. "Detective Delgado said that's common. It's her way of disassociating herself from what she did. And I know I should hate her, but I can't because I get it, you know?

"I just hope that she hasn't fucked me up like her mum fucked her up."

I didn't even think, just reached for her hand, and she grabbed it. "She hasn't fucked you up, Nico."

She leaned in and whispered, "What if she has?"

"Remember what we promised each other? You don't have to be anyone other than *exactly* who you are right now."

Of all the things to come back to her, I hoped that had.

"And if you don't like who you are right now, Nico, then you don't have to stay that way. You can be whoever you want to be."

She nodded.

"It's going to be OK," I said gently.

She nodded again.

More firmly this time.

"You're going to live with your aunt and uncle, right?"

"I'm meeting them tomorrow. Detective Delgado says they're nice. Cathy's a nurse and Chris works for the council." She looked down at our clasped hands. "I don't know what Mum will make of that, but it's either I live with them or end up in care. Besides, I like the idea of having family, you know? It's always been me and Mum, so it's kind of nice. I've even been talking to my family in Jeonju-si. They haven't seen me since Dad's funeral. *Fucking Mum*," she muttered, looking back down at her thumb poking through the cuff of her sweater. "Apparently, they even hired a private detective to find us, which is why we moved to Brighton."

"No *way*," I said, trying—and probably failing—not to sound like Louise if she'd heard that.

"That's why she didn't want me to have any social media."

I didn't know what to say to that, so I just closed my eyes and shook my head.

When I opened them again, I saw her chin quiver. "I don't want her to go to prison, though, Mara. I just want her to get better."

"Of course you do," I told her when she tried to blink away the tears. "And she will."

"I mean, it's not her fault. She didn't stand a chance in that house, did she?"

"I guess not."

"Neither did I, I suppose."

When her shoulders slumped, I squeezed her hand until she looked up at me.

"Do you even know how strong you are, Nico?"

"I didn't think I was. There were days I thought I'd never make it out of bed."

"You're OK," I reminded her. "You're still here."

"Yeah. Thanks to *you*. I would never have gotten through any of this without you. Look what you've done for me. Look what your parents have done for me. You literally *saved* me, Mara. I was an absolute asshole to you. I wouldn't let you in, tried to keep away, keep you at a distance because I didn't know what was wrong with Mum, just that she kept saying that it was me and I believed her. But you're the only person who has ever seen me, really *seen* me, and didn't tell me to change. You wouldn't give up on me and I have no idea why."

I told myself to breathe, but it required more effort than it did before she said that. "What do you mean?"

"Look how I treated you, Mara. And you're still helping me."

"Nico, it's fine."

I shrugged it off again, but she turned to look at me, her eyes huge.

"Please, Mara. I need to acknowledge how I treated you so I can never be that person again."

"OK," I consented with a small nod because she obviously needed to say it.

Or maybe I just needed to hear it.

"I was so worried about finding out that I was someone I wouldn't be proud of, and it turns out I was." She wiped her cheek with the sleeve of her sweater and said, "That's what Mum told me on New Year's Eve. *Screamed*, actually. She told me how ungrateful I was. How selfish. That I was an awful daughter. That she was ashamed of me. She even broke my guitar."

"She broke your guitar? You loved that guitar."

"I know. So, I packed a bag and told her I was going to see you and she *lost* it. I couldn't understand what she was saying, she was so hysterical. She wouldn't let me leave, blaming you for me being so disobedient. Saying it was your fault. She even threatened to lock me in my room, but she couldn't because she'd taken my door."

She let out a low, empty laugh that made me shiver as I asked, "What happened then?"

"I got on the bus and texted you. But Mum must have given me something." Her eyelashes fluttered slowly. "I guess she must have put it in my water bottle. Anyway, not long after I Snapped you, I started feeling woozy. The last thing I remember is getting off the bus at Black Rock, because I needed to puke, then nothing until I woke up on a boat."

"The fishing boat that rescued you?"

"No, one of those old-fashioned narrow boats. I don't even know whose it was, just that I was in this tiny room with a bed and the door was locked. I don't know how long I was unconscious, but it must have been a while, because then I heard Mum talking to me through the door, babbling about how we were going to start again. Somewhere no one knew us."

She stopped to suck in a breath. "That's why I couldn't let you get close to me, Mara, because I *knew* it would happen again. I didn't know what Mum was doing to me, but I could see everything unraveling like before we left London and I knew it'd always be like that. Mum and me arguing all the time, then leaving everything and everyone to move somewhere else. And I couldn't do it to you."

She started shaking, so I brought our clasped hands up and held them to my chest.

"So when I heard the engine of the boat start, I knew I had to get out of there. I managed to get the window open, crawled out, and started swimming. I thought that if I could just make it to the shore, I'd be OK, you know? But it was so dark and I was so cold and so tired. Then the sun came up. It looked like the sky was on fire, and I swear, I thought that was it. I was dead."

Your mother probably did too.

That's why she didn't report Nico missing, isn't it?

God knows how far she got before she went to check on her and realized Nico was gone.

Nico's face was still for a moment, then she smiled suddenly. "But, from nowhere, I saw this boat and I remember laughing as I grabbed the nets and held on. Held on until they found me. I swore ..." She stopped to shake her head. "I swore that I would never tell *anyone* who I was because I was terrified Mum would find me. So I just let it go. Let it sink down into the water, and when they hauled me on to the boat, it was all gone."

"Nico," I breathed, bringing our hands up to my mouth and pressing a kiss to her knuckles.

"Then you," she said, lifting her eyelashes to look at me. "You found my journal, Mara. I think about that all the time. Do you ever think about that? About how if I hadn't left it behind or if you'd gone to that café three minutes later, we would have missed each other. Do you ever think about that?"

All the time.

"I don't know why any of this happened to me, Mara, but I know that has to mean something. Because someone, somewhere, wanted us to find each other again. For me to have a second chance so I could do everything I should have done the first time and be exactly who I am, and for you to let me be exactly who I am, even though you knew who I used to be, but you still let me and I have no idea why. Just that I'm so grateful you did because I like the me when I'm with you. I want to be that me all the time."

Even if I could have caught my breath to speak, I don't think I could have.

"Maybe that's what all of this is about." She pulled our clasped hands away from my chest and held them to her own. "About wanting to be the best person you can be for someone, and them letting you and not punishing you when you fall short. Maybe I'm too young to know that, but I do. I can't unknow that. And I can't unbe the person I was before. I can only be exactly who I am now because you're right, there's nothing wrong with who I am now as long as I keep trying. And I promise to keep trying if you promise to let me."

"I promise," I told her when she finally stopped to take a breath, and she was so startled, she laughed.

"Sorry. I don't know where that came from. I was just supposed to ask you if you wanted to go for a coffee sometime. I rehearsed it, like, *seventeen* times last night, while I was lying on your bedroom floor listening to 'The Blower's Daughter' on repeat."

Our song, I thought, biting down on a smile.

"That's our song, you know," she said, not biting down on hers. "Am I allowed to call it *our song* if you don't know it's our song? It's what I was singing the morning we met. Do you remember?"

"I remember," I told her, the corners of my mouth twitching.

She nodded, her pupils swelling. "So how do you feel about the coffee thing?"

"We just had one." I nodded at the paper cup in her hand. "So why don't we cut to the end of the date?"

She frowned. "The *end* of the date?"

"Yeah, you know the bit when I kiss you or you kiss me and we, you know? Kiss."

Nico's eyelids lowered slightly. "That's usually how dates end, isn't it?"

"I think so," I said, leaning in as she did.

But what do I know?

I'm just a girl who's read too many stories.

The girl who told you this one.

The one about the girl who met a girl, then lost her and got her back again.

And while I don't know how this one ends yet, I do know one thing for sure.

Nico will always be my pearl of a girl.

Acknowledgments

If you've read the acknowledgments of my last novel, *Afterlove*, you'll know that before it was published, I stopped writing for a while. It seems that in the intervening years the landscape of publishing has changed. The most notable of these changes being social media and the artery it now provides between myself and the people who read my books.

I must admit, I found this startling at first: the inboxes of my various accounts slowly filling with messages from people who had discovered *Afterlove* and could get in touch in a way that they weren't able to with my previous books. Whether that was a few urgent lines on Instagram to let me know how keenly they felt something or tagging me in a video on TikTok of them wallowing in bed, asking where their Poppy is.

Each message lingered for days, but the ones that have remained with me were the ones from readers who were desperate to read *Afterlove*, but couldn't because of the cover.

It hadn't even occurred to me that the cover would be an issue. I remember how I gasped when I first saw it, then the tears that followed because after nine years of fighting for a cover like that, there it was ... two girls kissing and one of them is brown. It felt like more than a triumph, it felt like something was finally shifting, a fierce flare in the sky to signal a change was coming.

But then the messages began trickling in. Messages that were gushing and tender at first—how pretty *Afterlove* was, how desperate they were to read it—but the joy swiftly faltered as they asked if there would be an alternative cover that wasn't so shamelessly sapphic.

It made me unreachably sad, but it took a while to realize why . . . because fifteen-year-old Tanya wouldn't have been able to read a novel with a cover like that either, and I felt for those readers in a way I am still not able to appropriately articulate.

I'm forty-seven and given the increasingly hysterical rhetoric about the LGBTQ+ community that has led to books like *Afterlove* being banned, it would be forgivable to say nothing has changed since I was a teenager and to fold beneath the weight of that. I almost did myself, but then those readers began to get in touch to say that they'd found a way to read *Afterlove*. They'd had it delivered to a friend's house or their school librarian had kept it so they could read it during lunch. One person even read a chapter every day at their local book-shop after school.

Perhaps nothing has changed, but that's definitely one thing that never will: the resilience and resourcefulness of teenagers. So, to those readers, please know that I see you and I appreciate you and I promise to always be honest with you and that I will do my very best to not waste your time and try to write stories that are worth the effort you've made to read them.

And to echo my dedication, I want any teachers, librarians,

or booksellers reading this right now to know how grateful I am that you make sure books like these end up in the hands of those that need them the most. I don't know how I even begin to thank you for something like that, but for now, these few sentences will have to suffice.

Thanks also to the libraries and bookshops like the Queery in Brighton, Gay's the Word in London, and Queer Lit in Manchester that not only champion books like this, but provide warm, welcoming spaces for readers to discover them.

While I'm shouting out bookshops, I must extend my eternal gratitude to my favorites in Brighton ... much love and thanks to Sam and the team at Waterstones, Ruth at the Feminist Bookshop, Julie and Vanessa at the Book Nook, and Rem at Kemptown Bookshop, who have all been *hugely* supportive and not only hand sold *Afterlove*, but put it on tables and in windows and made it a Staff Pick.

Without those people, *Afterlove* wouldn't have reached so many readers and I am forever grateful.

And without these people, you wouldn't be reading this book right now ...

First and foremost, my long-suffering agent, Claire Wilson, who puts up with *so much* yet never waivers in her conviction that I can do this. My wonderful and equally patient editor, Lizzie Clifford, and the rest of the team at Hachette Children's Group who have worked so hard and been so passionate about the story I was trying to tell and made sure that you got to read it. To the sensitivity readers who were so honest and generous with their feedback despite the difficult subject matter, I am so touched by your kind words and encouragement.

To the astonishingly talented Sarah Maxwell, who illustrated the cover of *Afterlove*. I was blessed to have Sarah illustrate this one as well, which is even more beautiful, if that's possible.

To my brother, Hannah and the boys, and my friends Hannah, Suzi, Tracy, Angela, and Maya, who put up with me saying, "I can't! I'm on deadline!" and are still there when I'm not. To Holly and Sara, who talk me off a ledge at least once a week and always remind me that the misery of writing is worth it because when it works, it's magic.

To everyone who has taken the time to read, review, and recommend my books and to those of you who have sent me messages and made TikTok videos, done artwork, made friendship bracelets, and curated playlists, please know that it's you that I write for and I hope you continue to enjoy the stories that I tell.

Finally, I want to thank the person who got in touch with me after they read *Afterlove* to say, "This is the love I deserve and I will accept nothing less." To you and anyone else who needs to hear it . . . yes, you do, darling, and don't let anyone tell you otherwise.